UNKEPT PROMISES

JUDE KNIGHT

TITCHFIELD PRESS

ISBN: 978-0995-1101-68

✻ Created with Vellum

This book is dedicated to my Golden Redepenning readers. Many of you have been with me since Farewell to Kindness was published in April 2015. Others have joined the journey in the years since, and I often get asked what is going to happen to Mia. Here it is, folks. Mia's story. Of course, it is the story of Jules, too, and of his children.

And those of you who berated me for Hannah's loss at the end of the first book? Be happy. In this book, she finds someone, even though she isn't looking.

I'm dedicating this book to you because this book owes everything to your enthusiasm, your support, and your requests for more. I could easily have wandered off to another series, but you asked for this one and here it is. Fingers crossed that it's everything you hoped for.

UNKEPT PROMISES

Naval captain Jules Redepenning has spent his adult life away from England, and at war. He rarely thinks of the bride he married for her own protection, and if he does, he remembers the child he left after their wedding seven years ago. He doesn't expect to find her in his Cape Town home, a woman grown and a lovely one, too.

Mia Redepenning sails to Cape Town to nurse her husband's dying mistress and adopt his children. She hopes to negotiate a comfortable married life with the man while she's there. Falling in love is not on her to-do list.

Before they can do more than glimpse a possible future together, their duties force them apart. At home in England, Mia must fight for the safety of Jules's children. Imprisoned in France, Jules must battle for his self-respect and his life.

Only by vanquishing their foes can they start to make their dreams come true.

1

North Kent coast, 1805

At first, Jules thought the blow on the head had robbed him of his sight. As he surfaced from the weight of the enormous headache that pinned him to the stone floor, he decided darkness was a more likely explanation. He moved cautiously, with protests from the bruises and aches left by the various kicks and blows the slime ball smugglers had landed.

His sword was gone, and his purse. But they'd left the bun and cheese he'd shoved in his pocket for later, and they'd missed the tiny knife in the sheath built into the sole of one boot. It didn't take long to grope his way around the small uneven rock cave in which they'd placed him. It was featureless but for a sturdy wooden door and he was alone.

Time crawled by as he waited for something to happen; time enough for hunger and thirst to gnaw away at his usual blithe disregard for his own mortality. The bun weighed heavy in his pocket, but eating it would increase his thirst. He'd wait, and see if they brought him something to drink.

He was sitting with his back against the wall, contemplating the mistakes that had brought him here, when he heard other humans, so close they were almost in the room with him.

A groan. Then a girl's voice, light and high. "Are you awake, Papa?"

The light came as a surprise, shining like a beacon from the other side of a barred opening set high up in one wall. Standing, Jules managed to reach the bars and pull himself up. Beyond was another cell very like his own. A man lay still, curled on a mess of rags and clothing. His eyes were shut, and he had not responded to the girl who crouched beside him. She was a skinny child, still boyish in shape, but Jules did not suppose that would discourage the smugglers from making use of her body or selling her to someone for that purpose. He made an instant vow to save her, whatever the cost.

The girl held a candle so it cast its light without dripping its wax, and used her other hand to brush back the hair that fell over the man's forehead. "Oh, Papa," she said, her voice trembling.

"Miss," Jules hissed. The girl startled back from her father. Her face, already white, turned whiter as she faced the door, putting her body between herself and the unconscious man.

"I'm a prisoner," Jules reassured her. "In the next cell."

The girl lifted the candle high as she stood and peered towards the sound of his voice. He kept talking to guide her. "Lieutenant Julius Redepenning of His Majesty's Royal Navy, at your service, Miss. I am going to get out of here, and I'm going to take you and your father with me."

The face turned up to him was just leaving childhood behind, but the eyes shone with intelligence and her response indicated more maturity than he expected. "I hope you can, Lieutenant, but if your cell is as sturdy as mine, I beg leave to reserve judgement." She sighed. "I am sorry for your predicament, but I will not deny I am glad to have company."

"May I borrow the candle?" Jules asked. Her eyes widened in alarm and he rushed to add, "Just for long enough to check my cell. They left me without light." Without food or drink, either, but he would not tell her that. Perhaps the smugglers intended to supply him, and if they didn't, he would not take the supply she needed for herself and her father.

She passed the candle up, her worry palpable, and he hoisted himself higher with one hand so he could stretch the other through the bars. "I will be careful, Miss, I promise."

"Euronyme Stirling," she said, "and my father is William Stirling. Please, call me Mia. Formality seems out of place, here."

He returned her smile. She was a brave little girl; he had to find a way out for her. "Call me Jules," he offered, "as my friends do."

He rested the candle—a stubby bit of wax with a rope wick—on the sill between the bars and he dropped, shaking the ache out of the shoulder that had taken most of his weight. When he reached the candle down, a sound followed it through the bars and into his cell: an involuntary whimper at the loss of light.

"I have it safe," he soothed. "You shall have it back in a minute."

"I do without it most of the time," she replied. "It's just—I have always known I could light it again."

Most of the time? "How long have you been here?" Jules asked, keeping his voice light and casual against the lump in his throat at her gallantry.

She answered the question with one of her own. "What is today? Tuesday? Or later?"

"Tuesday, probably. It was late Monday evening when I came across the smugglers. They knocked me out, but surely not for long."

"The tenth of June? It was the seventh when Papa and I…" she trailed off, a small gulp the only sign of her distress.

Three days. Perhaps four. "How long has your Papa…?" Surely, she had not been nursing a sick man all this time?

"They hit him when they attacked us, but I think—I wonder if he has had an apoplexy, Lieut–Jules." She took a deep shuddering breath and spoke again, her voice once more under her control. "He has not woken since that day. I have managed to get some water into him, but…"

"Nothing to eat," he guessed.

"They have given us nothing to eat."

Bastards. They'd left her mostly in the dark, with no food, little water, and a dying father. He had been exploring his cell while they talked, and found no comfort in it. The door was firmly set, its hinges on the outside where he couldn't reach them, though he ran his knife through the gap between the wood of the door and the stone of the walls, and guessed the hinges were iron by the sound they made. The door had a small hole, just big enough for someone outside to peer in, or for food or a small mug to be passed through. He pushed the shutter that blocked the hole from the other side, but it didn't shift.

The only other gap in the stone was the high barred window between his cell and Mia's. He put the candle up on the sill, and then added the bun, still wrapped in his handkerchief. That meant pulling himself up by the bars at the other end of the window, and the one closest to the edge shifted slightly as he put his weight on it.

"I think I've found a weakness," he said cautiously, then picked up the wrapped bun and held it out through the bars. "Here, Mia. Something to eat."

She took the package eagerly and unwrapped it. "I will save you some," she offered.

"It's for you, Mia, but make it last. We don't know how long it will take to get out." He dropped back down on his own side and stretched his arms, flexing his muscles before lifting himself up again.

Yes. The loose bar wobbled when he pulled at it, and a closer examination by candlelight showed that it and the next one had wider sockets than the others, the edges crumbled as if someone had patiently chipped them away. An earlier prisoner? Hoping for what? This would get Jules access to Mia's cell, but they would still be trapped.

Still, the smugglers would be expecting her to be unprotected and vulnerable. He might be able to take advantage of that.

He wriggled the bars again, but they weren't loose enough to slip out.

A rattle at Mia's door had him handing the candle down to Mia and dropping back on his own side, listening hard.

"Water, girlie." Jules could have stayed. From the sound, the water carrier had not entered the cell, but was using a hole like the one in Jules's cell door.

"My father is very sick. He needs a doctor," Mia begged.

The only answer was the rattle of the shutter sliding back into place, blocking the hole in her door.

Jules waited, but apparently watering the naval officer was not on the list of tasks for the day.

He pulled himself back up on the bars, to find Mia waiting for him, lifting up the candle so he could reach it.

"I have been thinking, Jules," she said. "How did they get the bars in?"

He frowned at them. She was right. How did they get them fixed top and bottom when the bars were longer than the gap? He could see no cement.

Mia was still a step ahead of him. "Try lifting the bar," she suggested.

Of course. He gripped the loosest bar and lifted it, and it worked! It slipped up into the socket above, giving him just enough clearance to slide the bar out of the bottom hole. He passed it down to Mia. It would make a hefty weapon.

The next one took a stouter tug, the bottom hole being less chipped, but he managed it. The third wouldn't shift. Perhaps if he had not been dangling from one arm while lifting and tugging with the other… but two bars might leave him enough space to wriggle into the next cell.

It took some contortions, and he didn't make it without adding further scrapes and bruises to his collection, but at last he dropped down beside Mia, who threw herself into his arms and kissed his cheek, then drew back flustered.

"I beg your pardon. I do not know what came over me."

Jules reassured her. "We're celebrating our win, Mia, and quite right, too. Have we not already decided we shan't stand on ceremony?"

He knelt down beside the man on the floor. Up close, he could confirm what his ears had already told him. Stirling was not long for this world, his breathing shallow and irregular, his skin pallid and cold. Jules shrugged out of his great coat and placed it over the poor man, tucking it around him. It wouldn't help, but it might make Mia feel better.

"He is dying, isn't he?" Mia said, a catch in the last words betraying the matter-of-fact tone she attempted.

He honoured her courage with the truth. "I'm sorry, Mia. I believe he is."

She bit at her lip, then said, "We should blow out the candle to save what is left."

She settled next to Jules, holding her father's limp hand, and suited action to words.

In the sudden darkness, Jules reached for her free hand and she tucked it confidingly into his larger one.

"Tell me about yourself, Mia. Do you live near here?"

Bit by bit, they shared stories. Mia and her father rented rooms in a village the other side of Margate, but were seldom in residence, since Dr Stirling was an archivist, making his living—a meagre one, Jules guessed—by applying his knowledge of books and the classics to the book collections of the great houses of South East England.

It must be a lonely life for a girl; three months in one house, four in another, two in a third; not part of the family nor one of the servants. She was used to it, she said, and sometimes the people were nice.

Jules talked about what he was doing in England instead of on the other side of the world, where he had been posted for the past eight years with the Far East Fleet. His trip home as Master and Commander of one ship in a fleet of captured vessels, had let him catch up with his father and sister, but he was anxious to get back to Madras, where his mistress waited.

"Kirana was with child when I left, and will have given birth before I arrive home," he fretted, and then apologised, remembering too late that he shouldn't be discussing his informal relationships with a female of his own class, and a child at that.

But Mia brushed off the apology. "We are friends, are we not?" she reminded him. "Kirana—is that a Hindi name?"

"Batavian," he explained, and he found himself telling her about rescuing the daughter of a Dutch official and his Batavian mistress when the Dutch pulled out of Ceylon, leaving the English to take over.

"And you…" Mia paused, searching for words. "You made a home with her."

He smiled in the dark at her delicate tact, but corrected her assumption. "She was little more than a child. My captain of the time said he'd make sure she got back to her family." A bereaved little girl, who had watched her mother and her twin sister die in a vicious attack. Very like Mia, whose father was dying as they sat here beside him. He silently repeated his vow to rescue this child, and see her safe—safer than Kirana had been after he abandoned her to the non-existent mercies of his captain.

"Then how did she come to be in your keeping?" Mia wondered. "I know. You never forgot her, and when she was old enough, you went to find her."

Not quite, but he couldn't tell the whole story. Mia didn't need the ghosts that haunted him crowding into this darkness. "I met her years later when I was sent back to Ceylon during the war with the Kandian Empire. By then, she was on her own again."

They were both silent for a while. Jules was thinking of all he'd left out—a heap of painful detail that had ended in him facing disciplinary action for punching the man who had once been his senior officer. He'd do it again, too, under the same circumstances, but maybe not in front of a flotilla of fleet captains. His righteous indignation at the man's despicable behaviour towards Kirana and her babies had not impressed his superior officers, though the fact that Hackett was no longer in the navy helped. So did Jules's connections into the highest levels of the Admiralty, the Horse Guard and the aristocracy. His punishment was commuted from dishonourable discharge to demotion and a posting to a packet ship sailing the tedious mail route around the Indian subcontinent.

He'd installed Kirana and her surviving child in Madras, and come home to her between voyages. Since then her warmth and support had bolstered his determination to rebuild his career until the incident two years ago was nearly forgotten.

Mia hadn't spoken for some time. Had he shocked her, speaking of his sweet Kirana? Most of his class regarded kept women with contempt, even those men who were more than happy to take advantage of the comfort they offered. "She had no choice, you know," he told her, his voice stiff. "She is a gentle, loyal person, and a good woman."

But this unusual girl surprised him again. "I was just thinking how close I am to sharing her fate, and hoping that I fall into the hands of a kind man like you."

Jules wasn't sure if the lump in his throat was admiration at her courage or pain at his memories of the suffering he had seen—and not just Kirana's. War was hard on unprotected women. Hell. *Life* was hard on unprotected women.

He put his arm around Mia and squeezed her shoulder. "I will get you out of this," he promised.

"Thank you. I trust you to try, Jules, but you must not blame yourself if you fail. Papa and I were just in the wrong place at the wrong time."

They had been fossil hunting, she explained. "Papa has frequently managed to sell some of the curiosities we have found in the cliffs and on the shore." She sighed. "It has been several months since Papa's last commission, and the rent must be paid regardless."

They had found a whole skeleton of a large toothed creature, and stayed late to dig it out. Too late, as it transpired, because when they'd completed their digging, they were surrounded. "Why did they not just leave us alone?" Mia asked Jules. "If they had stayed out of sight, we would have gone home none the wiser."

"I think they must have something important planned," Jules told her. He'd wondered the same about his own capture—he'd stayed too long in Essex visiting friends, and thought to cut the travel time in half by borrowing a sailing skiff to skim around the coast to the mouth of the Thames. Had the vessel that cut him off just continued past, he'd not have given it another thought. "If so, they'll be waiting for a dark night."

"A smugglers' moon," Mia commented.

"Which is to say, no moon at all," he agreed. "Soon, in fact. If it is Tuesday, the moon will be a mere sliver and won't rise till after midnight, and if it's Wednesday, tonight will be perfect for them." If it was Wednesday, he would be in trouble for failing to report for duty. But he couldn't worry about that now.

Mia yawned. The poor girl had probably slept little, if at all, in days. "Put your head down and sleep, Mia," Jules invited. "You'll need your strength for our escape."

She obeyed, curling into a ball and using his thigh as a pillow. "I have my toes tucked under your coat," she confided, and yawned again. "Good night, Jules. I am so glad you are here."

With no way to mark time in the darkness, he could not have said whether minutes or hours crawled by as he listened to Stirling's irregular breathing, and felt the girl shifting softly in her sleep. He sat and let his mind wander where it would. Kirana. The ship he had sailed to England and the one he would be taking back to Madras. The friends he had seen in Essex. His father, sister, and brothers, who would be upset if he disappeared without a trace.

Catching a gang of smugglers would help mitigate his failure to re-join the fleet in time. They were west of Margate, Mia had said. His godmother had a residence somewhere near, which might be helpful if they could get free.

He began to turn over plans, none of which had the least chance of working if he couldn't get that door open.

Deep in thought, it took him a while to notice the change. Stirling had stopped breathing. He fumbled for the man's hand, which Mia had been holding when she fell asleep. Yes. There it was. Sure enough, he could not feel a pulse.

"Jules?" He had disturbed Mia. The weight of her head lifted from his thigh. "Jules, what is happening? Is it Papa?"

"I'm sorry, Mia. I think he is gone."

Her hand—the one that held Stirling's—shifted, groping for the man's cold wrist. He waited silently while she searched unsuccessfully for the pulse he'd already failed to find. She moved again, fumbling to strike a spark to light the candle. There. The flame lit her face, tears running disregarded down her cheeks.

She ignored Jules and leaned over her father, placing a thread teased from the seam of her coat across his open lips. It lay still, unmoving. "Oh, Papa." It was almost a wail, and she turned into Jules's waiting arms, buried her head on his shoulder, and let the tears flow.

She cried almost silently, her shoulders shuddering with her grief, and he held her, patting her back but saying nothing. What words could he offer, locked with her in the flickering light of single candle, not knowing what tomorrow would bring? Even so, he would not deny her any comfort she took from his touch.

After a while, she cried herself to sleep, and she wasn't disturbed as Jules set about making them both more comfortable. He managed, without letting her go, to blow out the candle, retrieve his great coat from the dead father to keep the living daughter warm, and wriggle a foot or so backwards until he could lean against the wall. At last he relaxed, and slept himself.

They woke and talked, slept some more, and woke again. "What chance do we have?" Mia asked.

"Our best opportunity will be when they come to get you out," Jules said. "I'm hoping they'll come for you first, and won't be expecting me. We have weapons—the bars and my knife. They won't expect that, either."

He and Mia would have the advantage of surprise. Whether that would tip the balance in their favour would depend on the number of men sent to fetch Mia. Once again, Mia showed she was following the same train of thought. "Perhaps most of them will leave with the shipment. After all, how much fight will they expect from a sick old man and a little girl?"

"We'll show them, won't we, Mia?" Jules said.

She managed a chuckle.

"And then what?" he asked. "You have someone to look after you, do you not? An aunt or an uncle?"

She was silent for a long time, and when she spoke, her voice shook. "I am sure I shall be perfectly fine. Perhaps Mrs Wilson, in my village, might take me on as a junior schoolmistress. I have helped before, and she says I am very good with the little ones."

It sounded like a gruesome fate. Perhaps Jules's father could find something better for the brave child. The duchess! Surely, he would have time to talk to his godmother before he reported for duty?

Mia correctly reported his lack of response. "You must not worry about me. Why, I expect my father's personal collection of fossils might fetch as much as thirty pounds! I shall be fine."

"I am confident you will." Jules would make sure of it.

"What of you?" she asked. "Where will you go when you are free? Back to Madras?"

"That's the plan," Jules agreed, accepting the change of subject. "Back to the Far East fleet."

"And to your family there." Mia's hair brushed his cheek as she nodded. "Kirana will have had her baby, you said. When was it due?"

"Sometime this month." It was his turn to sigh. "I wish I was with her. I left money, and I made arrangements for her to get more if anything happened to me, but I should have told my father about her. He might not approve of me keeping a native mistress, but if I was gone, he would make sure she was looked after, she and the children." Mia had made such a valiant effort to choose a cheerful subject, and he'd turned the mood gloomy again. "Don't mind me, Mia. We'll get out of here."

"We must," Mia agreed. "You need to go home and look after Kirana."

Brave girl. Jules hoped she had people who would look after her.

"Where will you go when you are free?" he asked. "Do you have family?"

"Do not worry about me, Jules. I will think of something."

That would be a no, then. He changed the subject. "What would you do if you could do anything in the world?"

"Travel," she declared, without hesitation. "I would love to see the places I have only read about in books. Greece, and Rome.

Egypt and the pyramids. Persia, where Alexander went with his armies. India! Jules, tell me about India!"

He was in the middle of a story about hunting tigers from an elephant's back when the now familiar rattle came from the door, and the grating voice. "Water, girlie. Come and get it."

Mia stood and made her voice tremulous. "Please. Won't you help? My father… he is very sick. He needs food, and blankets."

Clever girl. If her plea worked… Jules slipped his knife from his boot before taking station beside the door, hefting one of the bars in his other hand.

"Won't be long, girlie," their jailor replied. "We'll have you out of there in the morning—you and your Pa."

"Even just a blanket," Mia pleaded. "I'll do anything."

Muttering from beyond the door. Two of them, arguing in low tones a few paces away. Jules heard a word, a phrase, another word. "Cap'n said…" "won't know" "virgin price". Then the original speaker, just outside the door again. "We won't spoil the little skirt. Just have a bit of fun. Are you in?"

Jules offered a quick prayer Mia had no idea what these sea-scum had in mind, though without much hope. Her ungoverned reading through the classics and her own sharp intelligence gave her more knowledge than his mother would have considered suitable for a young lady.

"Girlie? We'll give you a blanket if you're nice to me and my mate."

Mia's voice cracked when she tried to reply, and she gave a hard gulp before asking. "Just the two of you?"

"Aye," the jailor agreed. "Just the two of us."

If he told the truth, Mia and Jules were luckier than Jules expected.

"Blanket first," Mia bargained. "If I'm not worrying about my father, I can…" she trailed off.

"Fetch a blanket," the jailor instructed his mate. "Fetch two. We can leave one with the little skirt after."

Moments later, the scraping of metal on metal spoke of bolts being drawn back. Jules stood ready. He'd have to let them both pass, and attack fast enough that no sound escaped to alert others in the cave system.

Light flooded into the cell ahead of the two smugglers—a lamp, bright after the extended darkness. A quick glance in Mia's direction showed her standing just beyond her father, her hands clenched at her sides, half hidden in her skirts. Jules's greatcoat was nowhere in sight, and his admiration of the girl's quick thinking went up another notch.

"See, now, girlie," the jailor's voice was wheedling. "A blanket for your Da. There's a good sweeting."

"What…?" Mia's voice cracked again. "What do you want me to do?"

"Got more'n one 'ole, ent she?" the other man suggested coarsely. "Pull up yer skirt, lovey, and bend over."

Mia blanched and swallowed, then began to gather her skirts as the two men crowded into the cell, the rear one putting down the lamp without taking his gaze from the girl. Anger fuelled the sweep of Jules's dagger across the coarse man's throat. The leading man swung around at the escaping gurgle, throwing himself at Jules while Jules was still entangled with the coarse man's body.

Jules swung the bar, but his foe shrugged off the glancing blow and grabbed Jules by the neck. A moment later, the smuggler crumpled. Mia stood over him, the bar she held in both hands matted with hair and blood.

Jules leant over the collapsed smuggler. "Not dead," he said, resisting the urge to complete the task she'd started. He wasn't a cold-blooded killer who would slit a man's throat when he was already unconscious, whatever the man had done. Instead, he picked up the smugglers' lamp while Mia touched a kiss to her father's forehead before leading the way out of the cell. Jules bolted the door, and for good measure turned the heavy key in the lock, withdrew it, and put it in his pocket.

Hand in hand, they crept through the tunnels, following the hint of light to a large cavern that showed signs of recent occupation: a cooking fire, boxes for seats, crates and barrels in stacks around the edges, but no other people.

A rivulet ran from a pool on one side of the cavern and out through another tunnel, where it bordered a well-worn track.

"Let me go first," Jules said, and he handed her the lamp so he could lead the way with his bar in one hand and his knife in the other.

They encountered no one as they crept down the slope from the cavern, finally turning a corner to come out through a tall slit opening onto a small sandy area with sky above, and rock ahead.

The path skirted the rock, and brought them out to the beach. Mia doused the lamp before Jules had time to suggest it. Somewhere ahead of them in the darkness, the low hum of voices competed with the soft sound of waves brushing the shore. Here and there, a light glowed for a moment and went out. A crash followed by an oath, quickly shushed, told the story of something dropped.

As their eyes adjusted, they could see the dark shapes of the smugglers at the water's edge and in a cordon across the beach to the right. Not that way, then. Wordlessly, he took Mia's hand and led her to the left. They hurried as fast as they could, keeping in the shadows of the cliffs, careful to make no noise, until Mia stopped and pulled at his hand. He bent to let her whisper in his ear.

"I think I know where we are. I used to play on this beach with my friend Kitty when my father was cataloguing the Duke of Haverford's library. That's Haverford Castle up there!"

She pointed up to the bluff that rose above other cliffs and curves, and the dark geometric shape that crowned it, dominating the coastline for miles in both directions. He knew it well. The lady of the castle was a close friend of his father's and his own godmother.

"If we get separated, go there and seek help," he ordered. She squeezed his hand, but nodded. "The path should be just up here," she said, leading the way.

"Oy!" The shout came from ahead, and in moments Jules was fighting a burly man with a club—one, furthermore, who was shouting for help. Absorbed in the fight, he still spared a moment to pray Mia had got past, that she would obey him and keep going to the Castle, that someone there would listen to her and keep her safe.

As footsteps thudded behind him, and blows began to rain on his shoulders and head, his last thought was to hope he had bought enough time for Mia to get away.

2

Jules surfaced to pain. Someone was beating his head with a mallet from the inside, his shoulders and hips throbbed with dozens of bruises, and so did his torso. He'd have guessed that several ribs were broken even without the tightly-bound bandages. He cautiously cracked open one eye. The room was dim, and he opened the other. He was in a clean bed, and he knew the man seated beside it reading by the light of a lamp that was considerately shielded so Jules did not look into the direct flame. If the Marquis of Aldridge was here, he must be in Haverford Castle, for the Merry Marquis was the Duke of Haverford's heir. Which meant that Mia had succeeded.

"Mia?" he asked. Croaked, rather, his dry throat adding a burning sensation to the catalogue of his other ills.

Aldridge looked up from his paper work. "Miss Stirling is in bed. Asleep, I hope. She has had a trying time." A trying time! That was a typical Aldridge understatement.

"The smugglers?"

Aldridge put his papers to one side and crossed to the bed. "A drink? The doctor left laudanum to help you sleep, but I thought you might prefer brandy. Your choice."

Turning his head, Jules could see a glass, a bottle, and a decanter waiting on the table beside the bed. "Brandy," he confirmed. "The smugglers, Aldridge?"

Aldridge poured a generous serve of brandy into the glass. "We captured most, and their cargo. I've men out searching for the rest."

Jules voiced his suspicion. "French spies?"

"As you say. I've sent messages to the Admiralty and the Horse Guard." He helped Jules to sit up against the pillows, and offered the glass, then rescued it when Jules's grip faltered. "I have the smugglers and their passengers locked up in the Haverford Castle dungeons, though I had to gently remind the Preventives of the social and political order here in our lands."

Jules sipped from the glass held to his lips. He wished he had witnessed what had probably been a fiery confrontation. The Preventives could be prickly about their authority, but they'd be no match for this duke-in-waiting claiming the ancient rights that had lost none of their power for being no longer official; the rights that had made the Haverford ancestors all but kings in this corner of England.

"So, all is well," Aldridge assured him. "Relax. Sleep. You have nothing further to do tonight. Your Miss Stirling is safe, your villains are captured, and the threat to the Realm has been neutralised."

As he spoke, the Marquis helped Jules to drain the glass, and moments later the darkness claimed Jules again.

Next time he woke, the room was flooded with daylight. His bladder woke him, screaming to be drained, a pain clamouring more insistently than a dozen others. Jules tried to swing his legs out of the bed, and sucked in a deep breath when the pain ramped up a notch.

His near whimper brought Aldridge's attention from the meal he was eating at a table by the window, to protest, "What are you up to, Lieutenant? Ah. You need the convenience?" He collected a gourd-shaped china receptacle from the cupboard of the room's wash stand, and brought it over to the bed, handing it to Jules. "Can you manage? I will hold it for you if you wish."

"No need," Jules insisted, and was pleased to find it was true.

"How is Mia— Miss Stirling?" he asked once Aldridge had removed the full receptacle and dealt with it by the simple method of replacing it in the cupboard.

"Still asleep. I shall be informed when she leaves her bedchamber. Do you know, both times you have awoken, your first thoughts have been for her?" Aldridge sat back at the table by the window, but kept his attention on Jules. "I don't blame you, mind. She is a revelation, that child. Smart as a whip, and will be a beauty in a year or two. Brave, too. Her only fault appears to be her belief that you walk on water and pull swords from stones."

Jules dismissed that piece of exaggeration with a shake of his head. "She had as much to do with my rescue as I did with hers. Did she tell you she lured our guards into our cell, and she knocked out the man who was trying to strangle me?"

"And you locked him in with two dead bodies, where we found him. Mr Stirling is laid out in the family chapel, by the way, and we will hold his funeral tomorrow. No, she didn't tell us the part she played in your escape."

Jules smiled, remembering her courage. "She fled when I told her to run, and came to get you. Lucky for us you were here, by the way. I thought she might have trouble convincing anyone at the castle to take action."

"Hmmm." Aldridge picked up his fork and then put it down again. "Lucky for you, certainly. I could have wished she had not arrived in the middle of a—er—a garden party, shall we say?"

Jules could make no sense of that through the throbbing of his head. "A garden party? In the middle of the night?"

Aldridge raised an elegant eyebrow, his lips curving in a saturnine smile. "It was not the usual kind of garden party. Indeed, Miss Stirling's common sense first impressed itself upon me when she refused to be distracted by the—er—activities taking place around her, and insisted on gaining my unfocused attention to her need."

Oh. That kind of a garden party. The kind that got the Merry Marquis his reputation. "Her father was a classics scholar," Jules explained. "She is rather more widely read than most fourteen-year-olds."

"That may explain it," Aldridge agreed. "It is unfortunate, Jules.

I wish I could be confident that neither the servants nor the guests would speak of her arrival, but…" he waved one hand. "You know what people are."

Jules frowned, but before he could comment, there was a knock on the door, followed by the entrance of a maid, who curtseyed to the Marquis and said, "The little Miss is awake, my lord. She is asking after Lieutenant Redepenning."

"Of course she is," Aldridge agreed. "Tell her the Lieutenant is awake, and is about to have breakfast. You would like breakfast, would you not, Jules?"

Would he? He wasn't sure, but perhaps the hollowness in his middle was hunger rather than incipient nausea. Jules nodded as the servant scurried off, and Aldridge went to the door to give orders to someone outside.

Aldridge helped Jules don an ornate brocade dressing robe over the bandages that wrapped his naked torso from chest to hips. "For I can't have you offending the sensibilities of my mother's maids," the Marquis explained, every bit as if he had not been holding an orgy in the garden just the previous evening.

"Where are your 'garden party' guests?" Jules demanded. He would not have Mia subject to insult.

Aldridge grinned. "Protective of our little lady, aren't we?" he mocked. "It's all right, Sir Galahad. I sent them into Margate. Miss Stirling is quite safe."

A succession of servants interrupted before Jules could respond, bringing in enough food for a small army. Aldridge had them set it on the table, and was beginning to serve Jules a plateful when Mia arrived, the maid who had been watching over her fluttering in her wake.

With a huge smile for Jules, Mia curtseyed to the Marquis. "My lord," she said, "Polly here said you and Lieutenant Redepenning were having breakfast, and that I have to eat too. So here I am, ready to have breakfast with you."

Aldridge cast his eyes up to the ceiling. "It is probably too late to make a difference," he observed, then fixed Polly with a stern look. "Polly, you will stay with Miss Stirling at all times."

In just a few bites, Jules decided that eating had been a bad idea, and lay back on the pillows, his stomach lurching as his head reeled. Mia noticed first, and instructed him to go back to sleep, abandoning her own breakfast to come and take his plate. "You need a lot of rest when you are healing," she said. She placed a hand on his forehead and he closed his eyes, revelling in the cold touch of her palm. "He is burning up, Lord Aldridge," she said.

Jules felt another hand brushing his cheek and then Aldridge spoke. "Send for the doctor, Alfred. The lieutenant is unwell."

The voices came and went, now at a great distance and then loud in Jules's ears. "I could stay here and watch over him." That was Mia, once again holding his hand.

"I do wish you would not require me to preach propriety," Aldridge complained. "I am quite unsuited to the job. No, Miss Stirling. You may not stay in a gentleman's bedroom. Do not fret for your lieutenant, however. He will have someone with him at all times."

"I do not see the sense in you keeping me out," Mia objected. "We were alone together for a day or more in the smugglers' caves."

She should not have said that in front of the servants, Jules thought, but he could not remember why. His thoughts scattered, and the voices, the bedroom, even the pain faded away.

He swam in and out of consciousness, not always sure what was a fever dream and what was really true. Kirana could not be here in this cold English castle. Mia could, holding his hand and anchoring him to the world. Aldridge, too, joking with a man who examined Jules with swift competent hands. Fleming, one of the captains assigned to the fleet he ought to be sailing with, must be halfway to the Canaries by now, not at Haverford Castle. Nor would his father or his sister be here. What would they be doing in Kent, all the way east nearly to Margate?

But when his head cleared at last, he recognised the voices of his family, before he opened his eyes a slit to see Aldridge, Father, and Susan, his sister, talking quietly by his window.

"Mia sees that marriage is her only chance of surviving the rumours and restoring her reputation, but still refuses." That was

Susan. Jules frowned, trying to make sense of it. Mia was to be married? But to whom?

"What is her objection?" Father sounded bemused. "She clearly adores the boy. Thinks the sun rises and sets in him."

"That is why," Aldridge suggested.

None of this made sense, and nor did Jules's surge of protective jealousy. What boy did Mia adore? *Whoever it is, he had better be worthy of her.*

"Aldridge is correct, Papa. She thinks marrying would spoil Jules's life. She told me all about his mistress and children in India, and wants him to be free to return to them."

Jules squeezed his eyes shut, thinking about that. He was the one Mia adored? As a result of which she wouldn't marry him? Wait. She was ruined without marriage?

Father was replying to Susan. "She cannot think he plans to marry his mistress? A native woman at that? Perhaps he could carry it off without the black marks already against him, but as it is? It would be the end of his career."

Jules hadn't thought of marrying Kirana. He hadn't thought of marrying anyone. He liked his life as it was! Besides, Father was right. Twenty years ago and more, many Englishmen in India took local wives, and still remained part of Society. But increasingly, they and their children were isolated and ignored. Worse, he would have to go wherever the navy sent him. Could he bring Kirana to England as his wife? He didn't doubt his father would accept her for his sake, however he might disapprove. But the rest of his social class? Never.

Nor did Kirana think of marriage. Her history—wouldn't that give the gossips a field day if it came to light? That foul sewer-swimmer who'd debauched her was alive to tell the tale, so it would come to life. Her history had made her, in her own mind at least, unfit for a life more respectable than the one he tried to give her.

But then what of Mia? The twisted mess made his head pound again.

"Nothing can be decided until your son returns to the land of the living, Uncle Henry," Aldridge said. "We have a bride, a license, a chaplain, and a chapel. It is for Jules to decide whether we have a groom."

"Tell me about the rumours," Jules commanded.

The three gathered around his bed. Susan fussed over helping him to sit then left the room so the men could see to his comfort. She returned to say she had sent for breakfast. "Just a coddled egg and some thinly cut slices of bread, Jules. Nothing to inflame your fever again."

"Tell me," Jules repeated.

"Eat first," Father suggested, "and get a little of your strength back."

From what he'd heard, Jules would need it.

The egg and bread came with a few mushrooms, some bacon, and a cup of warmed milk flavoured with honey and spices. Jules rejected the drink and demanded some of the coffee that had been fetched for the other three. "Now tell me what they are saying about Mia," he demanded. "Surely people realise the circumstances? She was trapped with me, yes, but her father was there too, and she is, after all, just a girl."

"Gossip," Aldridge said. "Rumour paints her as your lover, of course, but worse is being said." He held up a hand. "Not my servants. They know how to be discrete. It seems a mix of village small-mindedness and a couple of females who should never have been invited to one of my parties. I am sorry. They shall be, too, but not soon enough to undo the damage."

Jules turned to Susan. "How bad is it? She hoped to be able to return to her home."

"She insisted on going," Susan said. "It was not a happy experience. Apparently, the rumours had arrived first. Thank goodness I persuaded her to allow me to go with her. Her landlord has evicted her, and even the woman who runs the local dame school…"

"She believed the gossip?" Mia had spoken so highly of the woman.

Susan shook her head. "Not at all. But she depends on the money she receives from the parish and the wealthier parents." She shrugged.

"It is the other two roles ascribed to her that have done the damage," Aldridge explained. "Mutually conflicting, but when was the mob ever rational?"

One story said she was a member of the smugglers' gang (and whore to one or more of those ruffians). "She fell in love with your pretty blue eyes and killed several of the smugglers, including her lover, to free you," Aldridge explained. "The number of people she killed in order to get you out of your cell grows with each repetition of the story. The latest round has her father cast as the smugglers' secret leader, and accuses her of parricide."

Jules and his sister snorted in disgust, and the marquis quirked one corner of his mouth in a twisted smile. "People are idiots," he agreed.

"The other story has her providing entertainment at Aldridge's party," Susan added. "Some have to invent a whole new messenger to tell Aldridge about the smugglers, and some knit the two stories together to say she sold herself to Aldridge in return for help to rescue you. Either way, she purportedly accompanied the Marquis to the rescue, on his horse, semi-clad."

"Partly true," Aldridge conceded. "Not the semi-clad bit, obviously, but she did come on my horse." At identical glares from Lord Henry and Jules, he held up defensive hands. "She would not take no for an answer, and I certainly couldn't leave her at the castle until my guests had departed. Not those guests."

"Jules," Father said gravely, leaving the point, "her father appears to have been her only family. She has been left near destitute and with her reputation in ruins. But she refuses the remedy that would save her."

"I heard," Jules said. "Marriage to me. Because of Kirana." He met his father's gaze, his own solemn. "Kirana and I have two children, Father, if all went well with her lying in. I cannot desert them. My life is in Madras. I am posted to the Far East fleet, and should have been on my way back days ago. In addition, Mia is a child— just fourteen. Her peculiar upbringing has made her mature in many ways. Even so, she is not ready for marriage."

"Mia is…" Susan began, but Father waved her to silence, leaving Jules to finish his own arguments for and against.

He was thinking about what his life might look like with Mia as his wife. He could think of worse fates. As Aldridge had implied, she would be a magnificent woman when she grew up. "Can I leave her with you? If I marry her… Would you take her in as a daughter and look after her until I come home?" Which could be years from now, and anything could happen. He was going back into the war. He might die. Any of them might.

Yes. He would marry Mia and let the future look after itself.

It happened quickly after that. Mia argued when he proposed, but he assured her he was not being coerced. She studied him gravely as he explained his proposed arrangements for leaving her in England, and agreed. "That would be best, I expect. Kirana would not wish you to arrive home with a wife."

Would Kirana be upset? He worried about that for a moment, then put the thought aside. He was doing the best he could for everyone, and they would just have to cope with it.

Fleming, who turned out to be here in person and not just in his dreams, claimed the right to stand up as his best man. "My ship is anchored off Margate, Redepenning. The Admiralty will give you your wedding night, and then we'll up anchor and follow the rest of the fleet."

"We'll go straight after the wedding, Fleming," Jules declared. "My wife is fourteen. A wedding night would be premature."

"Mia is fifteen," Susan corrected. "Yesterday was her birthday."

A birthday. Jules had to send a footman to Margate chasing after Aldridge, whom Jules had commissioned to buy Mia a wedding present, with instructions to buy a birthday present as well. Aldridge returned triumphant with a pretty wedding ring, a locket, and a carved dressing table box.

By early afternoon, Jules was standing in the chapel, with Fleming and Father ready to catch him if he collapsed.

Mia didn't keep him waiting. She walked down the aisle with Susan as her attendant, her expression stoic. She put her hand into Aldridge's, and he smiled down at her. Jules soothed the possessive desire to punch the rake with the assurance that Aldridge's smile was fatherly.

In a grown-up gown hastily altered to fit Mia's slender form, she looked younger than fifteen, a little sprite playing dress up in silver lace over gold silk, with a diaphanous shawl across her shoulders. She wore the locket he had sent up to her ten minutes ago, and touched it with her other hand as she gave Jules a tremulous smile.

Aldridge declared himself the person who was giving the bride to be Jules's wife, and passed the little cold hand into Jules's keeping.

A stray sunbeam shone through the windows down the side of the church, striking Mia's hair and touching the brown with shades of auburn and gold. Jules looked into her eyes as they repeated the vows that would bind them together for life. He had promised to keep her safe. Now he made more promises, wondering how on earth he was going to keep them. Later. He would be a good husband to her later. When she was grown.

The Haverford chaplain pronounced them man and wife. It was done. Jules pressed a kiss to Mia's forehead, then turned to accept the congratulations of his friends and family, blinking to hear Aldridge and Fleming address Mia as Mrs Redepenning.

He and Fleming left shortly after. Mia stood at the top of the steps with Father on one side and Susan on the other. "Will you send me a painting of you to keep in the locket?" she asked.

"I will," Jules agreed, "and you send me one of you. You will write and let me know how you go on?"

"And you will write back and tell me more stories of the wonderful places you are seeing." Mia managed a beaming smile, though tears stood in her eyes. She had buried her father not three days earlier, lost everything she knew, and been handed over to strangers, and still she smiled. His heart full, Jules promised to write and gave her a hug. Another hug for his sister. He shook hands with Father and Aldridge.

"Coming, Redepenning?" Fleming shouted from the carriage.

Jules gave Mia one more kiss, stooping to plant this one on her cheek.

"Look after her," he charged his father, and hurried down the steps as fast as his healing ribs would allow. He stopped at the carriage door and turned back to wave. "I'll be back, Mrs Redepenning," he promised.

As the horses drew them down the carriageway, he repeated the words in his own head, a solemn vow to add to the others he'd made on this day. "I'll be back."

3

C*ape Town, South Africa, 1812*
    "Soonest done, best begun, Mrs J.," her servant Hannah Cottle said. "Time to go in." Hannah's voice startled Euronyme Redepenning from her reverie. Had she really been standing in this dusty Cape Town street long enough for Hannah and the hire carriage driver to stack their trunks on the platform by the front door?

The *stoep*. That's what Kirana called it in her letter telling her about the house. Even as she let her mind drift to vocabulary Mia knew it was yet another excuse to hesitate. It was all very well for her husband's mistress to be friendly by letter, but would Kirana really welcome Mia into the home she had made for Mia's husband?

Enough of this prevarication. Mia nodded to Hannah, who stood with her hand on the knocker, waiting patiently. Hannah rapped the knocker several times, a sharp sound that breached the silence of this residential street. Mia skirted the luggage that contained their immediate needs: two trunks, two duffel bags, a hat box, the bag with her folding desk.

Captain Jason Thrushmore, a friend to her brother-in-law Rick

Redepenning and a courteous host on the trip from England, had assured her the rest would be delivered. Did he discern her doubts about her welcome?

Moments later, the door opened, but only enough for the opener to fill the gap with his body, one hand on the door jamb, and the other wrapped around the door. Mia had expected the Tamil butler described in Kirana's letters, but this man was surely not he. Skin such a dark brown that the white teeth he showed in a flash of a grin seemed larger than mouth sized in his narrow face. Black hair in dark curls forming a close cap on his head. Only a little taller than Mia who was under five feet, whereas Kirana had said the Tamil was taller than Jules, who was over six feet. Perhaps the butler was on his day off.

"Yes'm?" The servant's voice lifted in a question.

"I am here to visit Kirana Redepenning," Mia said. Seven years of apprenticeship with Susan Cunningham and her other sisters-in-law ensured that none of Mia's doubts expressed themselves in her posture or voice. She took a step closer to the door, and the servant flinched but stood his ground, his face twisted in a worried frown.

"She not receiving. Miz Kirana, she sick." He made to shut the door, but Hannah put her shoulder against it and pushed, and Mia put her foot over the door step.

"You do not understand." She waved towards the luggage, and the servant's eyes widened. "I am Mrs Julius Redepenning, and I have come to stay."

Wordless, the servant backed out of her way. Mia entered the relative coolness of the hall, Hannah following close on her heels.

At a glance, Mia could see why the large entrance hall was used as entertainment space. It was of excellent proportions, taking up more than half the width of the house. Double doors to the right, according to Kirana's description, opened to a more private parlour, while matching doors to the left led to the master's bedchamber. Kirana's room adjoined it, so Mia led the way through the wide doors opposite the entry, into another space of equivalent size to the front room. This one let out onto a small outside courtyard through a wall of doors.

Mia turned left, but the servant darted in front of her, his arms wide. "Missus can't go in there," he said. "Missus go away. Come back another day. Captain wouldn't like it."

She raised her brows and glared. "The Captain is my husband, which makes this my house. Out of my way. Now."

The glare, copied from her more formidable sisters-in-law, did the trick. He faded sideways.

"And you can make yerself useful," Hannah said, "by bringing in Mrs Redepenning's luggage before every street scamp in the town takes off with it."

Mia had her hand on the door handle before the servant mustered another protest, and had turned it by the time he finished. "Miz Kirana, she not there."

One glance in the room made that clear. The door to what must be Jules's room stood open. A European girl lolled on the bed of this one, spooning fruit and cream into her mouth from a bowl—Scots or Irish by her pale skin and flaming red hair. She was much of an age with Mia, at a guess, whereas Kirana was Eurasian, and in her early thirties, only a few years younger than Mia's husband.

The girl confirmed her origins when she opened her mouth, her Irish accent plain. "Who're ye, bustin' into me bedchamber? Japheth, you half-wit, who is this gobermouch? And why did ye let 'er in?"

"I am Mrs Julius Redepenning," Mia said in her driest tones, "and you, I take it, are my husband's most recent bed partner." She ignored her sinking heart. It had been easy to overlook Jules's attachment to Kirana, who had been his mistress for two years before Mia met him. This was more challenging. Were her hopes of making a real marriage to founder before she had a chance to even see him again?

A harrumph from Hannah. Her low opinion of men made her dubious about that part of Mia's mission, but Mia would not give up. Not yet.

She scanned the room, untidily strewn with clothing and jewellery. The woman had clearly been trying on garments in front of the large mirror before dropping onto the bed.

"Tidy up in here before you leave the room," Mia instructed. "Do not think to take a thing that is not your own. My husband no longer requires your intimate services."

She turned her glare on Japheth. "Take me to Kirana."

A widening of his eyes and a flinch warned her to duck before the bowl sailed past, breaking against the door jamb and splattering fruit and cream across the floor and walls. Mia lifted the hem of her dress and examined the stain there before looking at the thrower. The red head crouched on the bed, her face drained of colour, the whites showing around her pale blue irises.

Mia dropped her voice to little more than a whisper. "Clean that mess up, too. I want this room ready for Mrs Kirana's occupation by the time I return." Then the bullwhip of a near shout. "Now!"

It worked. The woman leapt from the bed and began picking up the nearest discarded pile of silk on the floor. Silk pantaloons of some kind. Kirana's surely? Or did Jules require all of his mistresses to wear eastern garb?

Japheth led the way across the house, corralling another servant on the way to send him to bring the luggage into the entrance hall. On the pattern of the first level, the second had two adjoining reception areas, one overlooking the courtyard and one the street. Japheth took them to a hall running down the side of one wing, lined with windows onto the courtyard on one side and doors on the other.

He opened the second door, and stood to one side. "Miz Kirana, she's very sick," he mumbled.

The room was small, the tiny single window shrouded in heavy drapes that kept out air and light. Even in late winter, the room was oppressively hot. It contained a narrow bed and a single bedside table, on which sat an empty jug and glass. The bed's occupant had been tossing so the sheet that covered her was tangled around her legs. When they entered, she tried to sit up, and the movement set her coughing. She bent in half with the strength of the spasms, and the cloth she held to cover her mouth sprouted new splodges of red blood.

"Hannah, get those curtains down and the window open.

Japheth, fetch something for Mrs Kirana to drink. I will also need a bucket of hot washing water, soap, a flannel, clean night clothes… Hannah, you know. Go with Japheth. Kirana, it is Mia. I have come to look after you."

⁂

*J*apheth watched the diminutive English woman out of the corner of his eye as he led her to the kitchen. The other lady—the Captain's lady—was in charge, beyond a doubt, but he'd not needed more than a few words from the one she called 'Hannah' to know she was a force to reckon with. At last! He and Pranisha had feared they'd have to wait for the Captain to get home and deal with Maureen and her lover, Dench, and Miz Kirana might not have that long. She failed day by day.

"Get Miz Hannah what she ask for," he told the maids, "and do what she tell you." He squatted down on his haunches to look past Pranisha, the cook, who stood guard before the door to the store room. "Missy Ada? Missy Marsha? Miz Captain come to look after your Mami," he told the girls hiding inside. "Everything going to be fine now."

Pranisha did not loosen her grip on her largest soup ladle. "Is this Missus Captain?" She squinted suspiciously at Hannah. "Our captain's missus?"

Japheth was unsure how to explain Hannah, but the woman herself arrived at his elbow, having sent Maria and Rosa scurrying to fetch what she needed. Perhaps she saw part of a dark head and the flash of an eye as Miss Ada, always the bolder of the two girls, peaked out from behind a sack of flour to see what was going on. Perhaps she just took her cue from his words. In a softened voice, she spoke, keeping her eye on the interior of the storeroom as she held out a hand to the cook.

"I am Hannah Cottle. I came with Mrs Julius Redepenning to help look after Mrs Kirana and the children. I am their new nanny."

Pranisha introduced herself, still suspicious but warming.

Hannah smiled. "Mrs Redepenning wants us to help make your lady comfortable, and move her to a clean room, but after that, I would like to come and meet my new children. Would they like that, do you think?"

She did not wait for an answer, but turned back to the maids, and asked Rosa to find clean night clothes for Miz Kirana. Ada peeked after her.

"What of that Maureen?" Pranisha asked Japheth in a hushed whisper.

Japheth met Ada's eyes as he told the cook, "Miz Captain tell her to get out," he said, not bothering to hide his pleasure.

ithin a couple of hours, Kirana was settled. She insisted on Mia taking the room Maureen had vacated, and chose for herself a sunnier, more airy room on the upper floor at the far end of the other wing. Hannah had led a team of servants to scrub it top to bottom, removing drapes, the rug, and most of the furniture to leave a clean bare room. Mia had commandeered a large and comfortable bed from a guest room and had it made up with fresh linen and a stack of pillows. The room smelled of soap and the flowers that Hannah had found somewhere and arranged on a wooden table in easy line of sight from the bed.

Mia had bathed Kirana and changed her soiled night gown for a fresh one that an eager maid fetched. Maureen, the redhead, had apparently commandeered all of Kirana's possessions when she had ordered the sick woman removed from the room adjoining that of the master of the house.

Hannah retrieved Kirana's daughters from the kitchen, where Maureen had sent them after ousting their mother. They had been well enough treated, and had been creeping in to sleep with Kirana at night. Still, the second sudden change in status in just a few weeks set the seven-year-old Marshanda crying and Adiratna, who was five, skipping around the room.

Kirana made no complaint, but Mia could see she found the

sudden change nearly as overwhelming as her daughters. At her signal, Hannah took the girls away to check that their nursery was as they had left it.

Kirana told Mia the story between bouts of coughing and rests between words to take in more air. The pretty children's nurse had insinuated herself into Jules's bed during his last shore leave. "I was glad, Mia. I would not have ordered it, for even a servant should be free to choose. But if it was what she wanted, I thought it a good thing, since I could no longer meet the needs of his body, and I would not have him risk disease going to the places men visit, or taking up with a society woman who might object to his household."

Mia made no comment, busying herself with making the former mistress comfortable. It took Kirana nearly half an hour to tell her the rest, a phrase or two at a time.

"He is not such a fool as to think the baby Maureen carries is his, for she must be four months gone, and he has had her no more than twice, and that less than two months ago. He was at sea when that baby was made. Yes, and when he went back to sea, his sail had no sooner disappeared from view than she was turning me from my room and keeping my children from me. The Captain will set it right when he comes home, I thought, for the servants would not oppose her, and I had no strength to fight."

Hannah had learned that the butler and his wife, the children's nurse, were gone—left just a few months ago for their beloved India. The only one still remaining of Kirana's original household was the cook, Pranisha. Otherwise, surely Maureen's coup would have failed.

Kirana was no more than skin stretched over bone. She was still the beauty Jules had spoken of seven years ago when he and Mia first met, but turned ethereal as her illness consumed her from within.

"I was wrong to encourage Maureen, but how could I know she would turn against us so? And for what? The Captain would have reversed it all when he returned, if you had not come first."

Kirana squeezed Mia's hand, and Mia squeezed back, smiling, hiding her doubts. Would Maureen have exiled Kirana without

Jules's approval? Surely not. Unless she hoped that Kirana would die before he returned, as she may well have done in that horrible little cell of a room.

She offered Kirana another drink from the fresh jug, and held her friend while she coughed after drinking.

"I am so glad you have come. You will look after my girls; I know that. Jules means well, but he must go where he is sent, and I fear for them while he is away. What would happen to my babies if the Dutch woman from Madagascar has the chance to take my place? She was determined to have him, Mia. Still is, so I am even more grateful that you have come." Kirana stopped talking as her body was racked by another bout of coughing.

"Rest, Kirana," Mia soothed, hiding her rising anger and making a mental note to find out more about the Dutch woman. How many mistresses did Captain Julius Redepenning have? One less than this morning, anyway. The Irish girl had absconded, taking with her some of Kirana's jewellery and money from the safe in the master's bedroom.

"Start as you mean to go on," her sisters and cousin had advised. Mia wondered if Jules had any idea of the wife he'd created by leaving his forlorn child-bride to be raised by his redoubtable female relatives. She left Kirana clean, comfortable, and asleep, watched over by the two little girls and Hannah, and made her way to the kitchen wing.

The walls were whitewashed and the furniture painted, but the quality of workmanship remained as high as in the family and public rooms. Mia stopped and checked the top of a window frame with her finger, and then the back ledge of a wooden seat against one wall. No dust. The kitchen was well kept, despite the neglect of other parts of the house and the revolution that had toppled its mistress in the absence of the master.

The servants were all waiting in the kitchen, watching the door, their faces anxious or impassive according to their natures. She took her seat in the chair set ready for her, following yet another piece of sister-in-law wisdom. *"When seeking to overawe servants who are taller than you, sit while they are standing."*

Hannah had started the impressing, when she conveyed Mia's command to gather here. The servants mostly looked down at their feet as she examined them in silence.

The large brown woman in the wrapped silks of a Hindu would be the cook, Pranisha; the only one remaining of the servants who came with Jules and Kirana from Madras. Pranisha had cared for the two frightened little girls and kept them safe.

The remaining cook's maid would be the one female Mia had not met. Just into adulthood, plump and pretty. Most of the others, all the other women and two of the men, she had encountered as they came in and out of Kirana's room under Hannah's direction.

The three house maids, one young and two middle-aged, had willingly and efficiently prepared the new room, and had all taken a moment to assure Kirana of their support, though with an anxious glance at Mia out of the corner of their eyes.

So, who had been in favour of Kirana's eviction from her place? Japheth, perhaps. The doorman, they called him here. He answered the door, ran messages, and served at table when they had company.

The other two men as well? They worked mostly outdoors, Mia had been told, looking after the household's garden, its carriages and two horses, and any handyman tasks inside and outside of the dwelling. One of them was as black as Japheth, and she had been given his name as Fortune. The other, the only European, was the one servant who had not helped with the move; the one servant who now met her eyes, his mouth stiff with contempt, his eyes filled with scorn. William Dench.

A woman-hater? Maureen's accomplice?

Mia let her gaze fix on each servant in turn, speaking their names out loud. Pranisha the cook and her helper Sunny. Pranisha nodded gravely, with measurement in her calm brown eyes. Sunny's glance was quick and anxious.

The maids, Maria, Lijsbeth and Rosa. Maria turned to Lijsbeth for reassurance, and Rosa managed a fleeting smile.

Japheth, who met her eyes and bowed. Fortune, the black groom, who shot a fearful glance at Dench then looked down again.

Dench exploded as soon as she said his name, as if being

addressed set a match to a smouldering temper. "And who are you?" he demanded. "This idiot," he struck out at Japheth, who ducked so the blow meant for his ears whistled harmlessly over his head, "says you're the Captain's wife. Never heard the Captain had no wife, except that useless yellow bint upstairs."

"Control yourself, Dench," Mia advised, "and keep a civil tongue in your head when you refer to the Captain's friend." She swept her gaze over the assembly again. "I am Mrs Julius Redepenning, the Captain's wife. I have come to care for my friend Kirana in her illness and to look after her children—and I can see that I have arrived just in time. I cannot imagine that the Captain will be pleased to know the condition in which I found his beloved friend, but we will–"

Dench, flushed red, broke in again, taking a step towards her with his fists clenched. "See," he said, addressing the other servants. "She's no more the Captain's wife than I am. What English wife would 'look after' her husband's whore, except the way she 'looked after' Maureen, throwing her out in the street, and her carrying the Captain's baby? What has she got planned for those poor little girls? That's what I want to know."

Mia remained outwardly calm as the other servants exchanged uncertain glances. Would they come to her rescue if the man attacked? She should have brought her little gun downstairs; the one her sister-in-law Ella insisted that she have and learn to use.

"Miz Kirana, she say this Miz Captain Redepenning," one of the maids volunteered.

"Kirana Didimoni write Miz Captain many years," Pranisha observed. "Miz Captain, you write back, yes?"

Mia inclined her head. "For seven years, yes. I did not, by the way, ask Maureen to leave. And I certainly did not throw her out. Nor did I invite her to help herself to the valuables she took with her."

"Lies!" Dench shouted. "Maureen ain't no thief, and she wouldn't have gone without…"

This time, his wild swing was towards Mia, but he stopped it before it struck, and she responded, not measuring her words.

"Without telling you? You are her baby's father, are you not? Kirana said she is too far gone for the child to be the Captain's."

Dench swung around and thumped the wall, a stout blow that must have bruised his knuckles and jarred his arm. The bang continued to echo, until Mia realised that the continuing sound was the front door knocker.

"See who that is, Japheth," she ordered, and they all waited as if frozen out of time while the doorman hurried through the house to do his duty.

"Captain Thrushmore, 'm," he reported, a few minutes later. "He brung the rest of Miz Redepenning's things from the ship. Wants to speak with you, 'm. Fortune, Maria, you come help me with Miz Captain's luggage."

Jason had called to assure himself of her welcome in the household of her husband's mistress. Mia didn't tell him that his arrival had swung a tenuous balance. She would have no further trouble now.

Sure enough, Hannah later reported that each of the servants had assured Hannah they played no part in Kirana's ill-treatment, and were glad that Mrs Captain had come to make things right again. Except for Dench. Dench was not seen again that day, and by the following morning, it was clear that he, too, had gone.

4

As the *Advantage* swept around Lion's Head and into Table Bay, its captain and its youngest cabin boy stood at the deck rails, peering for the first sight of the rooftop aerie that marked their home.

"Do you think Mami will be there?" Dan asked.

Jules rubbed his hand over the boy's hair in an affectionate sweep. "It may be a bit hot for her today, Dan. But we shall see her soon."

He hoped. The *Advantage* had been longer on its mission than expected, and Kirana had been very frail two months ago when he was last home. Still, no point in sharing his worries with his son. They watched in silence for a few more moments, then Jules's first lieutenant called for his attention. "Dan, check that our bags are packed," he told his son. "We're going ashore as soon as we dock."

He patted the report in the inside pocket of his uniform jacket as he mounted the bridge. Lieutenant Myers could deliver it. Jules was going straight home.

Dan was hopping with impatience by the time they could finally leave. His captain should have rebuked him, but his father knew exactly how he felt and let it pass. "Go on, lad," he prompted, shouldering their duffels. He would send someone from the house to fetch the trunk, which had most of what they'd need for their leave ashore, the duffels being largely given over to gifts for his girls.

The boy tore off down the wharf, stopping only briefly to exchange a few words with the guard at the dock gates. Jules followed at a slower pace, but Dan was still in sight, about to turn a corner, when Jules passed the gates, with a wave for the guard and his mind on what they might find at home. Perhaps he should have held Dan back. What if–?

But he had got no further in his mind when he had to swerve to avoid bumping into someone.

"Dench? Good man. Did Kirana send you?" If she was well enough to be on the roof, watching for his ship…

But Dench interrupted that hopeful thought. "I don't work for you no longer, Captain. You want to know why? Ask the woman that calls herself your wife."

"My wife?" Jules blinked, and gave his head a quick shake. Mia was in England with his family, wasn't she?

Dench wasn't finished. "And while you're at it, ask her what happened to Maureen. Thrown out in the street, faster than a blink, and her with your kid in her belly."

"Explain yourself, man!" Jules demanded, reaching for Dench's throat. But the man backed away.

"I don't have to tell you a thing. Go ask your wife. Better hurry. She's been there a week. Who knows what she's done with your yellow whore and your little bastards?" He threw the insults over his shoulder as he took to his heels, but he was safe enough from retribution, at least for the moment. Jules broke into a run, too.

Dear God, let Kirana and the little girls be safe. Dear God, let Dench be a liar as well as a sour bigoted scum sucker. Jules hurried his steps at the thought of Dan arriving to the chaos implied by Dench's words. Surely Mia wouldn't—but he didn't know the girl. Not really. Only what she chose to present in her letters.

He covered the distance to the house in record time, ducking and weaving around people, carts, and other obstacles without really seeing them.

He set up a furious rat-a-tat-tat on the knocker, and brushed past Japheth demanding, "Where is my wife?"

"With Miz Kirana, Captain," the man stuttered, but the room that had been Kirana's since they moved here three years ago—the room that adjoined his own—was devoid of occupants, and nothing of Kirana's remained in it. The clothes on the hangers were Western-style; a vaguely familiar dressing set in the English fashion sat on the table before the mirror; the trunk under the window was one he'd never seen before.

His temper rising with every new revelation, he rounded on poor Japheth, who was standing in the doorway, mouth open. "Where?" he demanded.

With Kirana, so Kirana was still here, and the worst had not happened. But what was that woman thinking, horning in here and turning the mistress of the house out of her own room? Was she staking her territory? Thinking to replace Kirana in his bed? They'd see about that!

Jules followed Japheth up the stairs and along the corridor in the bedroom wing, seething about English wives and their arrogant assumptions. Japheth pointed to the door at the end of the corridor, pressing himself against the wall so Jules could pass. Jules took the handle to fling the door open, then reconsidered the impulse and instead opened it cautiously, hoping to observe before he was seen.

Whatever he had expected, it was not a large clean room, freshly whitewashed and flooded with light. All three windows were open to let the breeze flow through, but someone had fixed canvas awnings outside those on the northern side, to help keep out the glare of the sun. Kirana lay on a sofa, propped on cushions, and the woman he was looking for sat at her feet, reading aloud in a melodious voice.

"Infirmity!" said Elinor, "do you call Colonel Brandon infirm? I can easily suppose that his age may appear much greater to you than to my mother; but you can hardly deceive yourself as to his having the use of his limbs!"

"Did not you hear him complain of the rheumatism? and is not that the commonest infirmity of declining life?"

"My dearest child," said her mother, laughing, "at this rate you must be in

continual terror of MY decay; and it must seem to you a miracle that my life has been extended to the advanced age of forty."

"Mama, you are not doing me justice. I know very well that Colonel Brandon is not old enough to make his friends yet apprehensive of losing him in the course of nature. He may live twenty years longer. But thirty-five has nothing to do with matrimony."

Jules must have made some noise, for both women turned towards him. Kirana straightened, sitting up with a glad cry, and the other woman—it must be Mia, but not by any means the Mia he remembered—leapt from her place to put her arm around Kirana to support her. Just in time, too, for Kirana wilted back against the supporting arm with a sigh of relief and a sideways smile at Mia.

Jules hurried across the room to take Kirana's hands and kiss her cheek. He would not greet Mia with a kiss. His anger was somewhat mollified by the way she treated Kirana, but she still had some explaining to do. He nodded stiffly instead, and received a frosty nod in return. *What has she to be miffed about?*

"I will leave you two to talk," she said, settling Kirana back on the pillows. "Shall I send up tea, Kirana? Or does the Captain prefer something stronger."

"Tea will be fine," Jules said. Did she think him a drunkard? He frowned at a thought. "Did Dan not arrive before me? Where are the girls?"

Kirana, who was still clinging to his hand, answered the questions, gasping for breath between each short sentence. "Perdana is here. Oh Jules, he has grown. You are home before… I am glad." She was stopped by a racking succession of coughs, through which Mia silently supported her, rubbing her back, passing her cloths to cough into, and washing her face with clean water when she was finished.

"Try to let the Captain do the talking, my dear," she advised. "Captain, your son is with your daughters in the kitchen. Hannah is teaching the girls how to make English scones, and I dare say young Perdana is benefitting from the results. He is a fine lad, Captain. You must be proud of him."

As she spoke, she was putting away the book she'd been reading when he entered, straightening the silk sheet that covered Kirana's wasted form, topping up the glass at Kirana's elbow from a jug that stood ready. She looked around, clearly found all to her liking, nodded, and turned to leave the room.

Somehow, Jules had lost all the advantage, and he didn't like it. "I will see you later, Madam," he called after her. "You and I have much to talk about." The maid, Maureen, for one. And for another, moving Kirana so Mia could take her place.

Mia's voice was arid as a desert. "That we do, Captain. That we do."

❦

*D*ear Heavens. The man was gorgeous. In the seven years since Mia had last seen him, she had managed to convince herself her memories had played her false. She had been alone and frightened, when a golden god had wriggled through from the cell next door. He had kept her company in the darkness, comforted her when her father died, fought the smugglers to win her safety, and then married her to save her reputation and give her a home.

Of course, she adored him. She very likely would have developed an infatuation even if she'd met him socially—she had been fourteen, had grown up largely isolated by her father's social position as a poverty-stricken scholar of good family. It was no surprise she fancied herself in love with the first young man she had ever properly talked to.

Handsome is as handsome does, she warned herself as she made her way down to the kitchen. But even in a temper about something, as he clearly was, he was unbelievably handsome. Mia believed she was immune to handsome men. Her brothers-in-law were all good-looking, and Mia had been propositioned at one time or another by most of London's rakes, who clearly believed that a wife who hadn't seen her husband in years must be in need of their attentions. None of them made her breath catch, her heart beat faster, and her insides melt.

Jules did, destroying all her preconceptions. Mia had assumed that, in the renegotiation of their marriage, she and Jules would be equally dispassionate. *So much for that.* Even grumpy; even with most of his attention on another woman, even with all that she'd heard about him to his discredit, she wanted him.

In the kitchen another handsome man, this one only nine, took pride of place in Cook's own seat, being waited on by his two adoring sisters. Marshanda was shuttling between the table and the chair, refilling the plate from which Adiratna was feeding her brother, who was sampling scones topped with different flavours of jam with the judicious air of a connoisseur.

Marshanda saw her first. "Ibu Mia," she announced, then ducked her head. She was not fond of being noticed, whereas her little sister wanted to be the star of every occasion.

Adiratna patted her brother on the cheek as a means to get his attention. "Ibu Mia is Mami's sister, and our elder mother, Mami says."

Perdana narrowed his beautiful eyes, identical to those all three children had inherited from their mother, examining Mia thoughtfully. Then he lifted Adiratna from his knee and stood to bow. "You are the Captain's wife," he announced. "Has the Captain arrived, Ibu Mia?"

Mia nodded. "He is with your mother, children," she told them. "Give him a few minutes, my dears, and I am sure he will be down to find you."

Adiratna was already on her way to the door, but she stopped obediently when Mia said her name. She turned and stamped her foot. "But I want my Papa now," she whined. "He has been gone ever so long. I want to show him the doll that you brought me from London, Ibu Mia."

"And so you shall, darling," Mia reassured her. "But we cannot properly greet Papa without just a little noise, can we? And noise makes Mami so tired."

"Yes, Ada," Marshanda said, her bossy streak overcoming her reticence. "You know you will squeal when Papa gives us presents. You always do."

Adiratna's eyes widened and sparkled. "Presents!" In moments, she was back across the room, tugging on Perdana's hand. "What has Papa brought me, Dan? You know, I know you do."

"Lumps of coal, like the Black Peter we saw on St Nicolas Day," Perdana answered, promptly, "And a switch to beat you with, for you have undoubtedly been a great trouble for Mami and Ibu Mia."

Adiratna sniffed, and poked her nose in the air. "That shows you know nothing, Dan, for Hannah never lets me be a trouble, do you, Hannah?" She smiled at her new nurse, who had been an instant favourite with both girls for her store of stories and the energy and imagination that allowed her to keep them constantly on the move from one interesting activity to another.

"Brothers tease," Hannah told her. "I do not know why they do it, but there it is."

Perdana grinned at her, not in the least perturbed by this set down, but Adiratna wanted the last word. "Papa never beats us, even when we deserve it. So there."

"Do you deserve it?" Jules spoke from the doorway, his tone one of scientific inquiry. Both girls forgot their brother and their dignity to hurl themselves into his waiting arms. Mia exchanged a glance with Hannah, who gave a satisfied nod. The man's clear delight in his children had won that stern arbiter's cautious approval.

Mia, too, found it hard to retain her indignation while watching him listening to their chatter, squatting on the floor with his back against the door jamb, each arm around a daughter on his knee. Adiratna was pouring out two months' worth of news at full speed, and even Marshanda spoke so fast her words were tumbling over themselves.

Adiratna suddenly remembered that Jules had not yet disgorged his gifts. "Where are my…" she broke off, sneaking a glance at Hannah, who had been impressing the little girls with the unexpected information that they were ladies. Marshanda stuck her nose in the air. "Ladies," she informed her sister, "do not ask. Ladies wait to be offered."

Jules frown over her head at Mia. "Who has been telling you that?" he asked.

Adiratna, however, was not to be deflected. "I like presents," she announced. "It makes me very happy when people give me a present. Ibu Mia brought presents for me and Marsha from England. I expect she brought presents for you, too, Dan. I do like presents."

Faced with this flagrant attempt to get around the 'ladies do not ask' rule, the adults struggled to maintain their gravity. Even Jules, who was holding onto whatever grudge had blown in with him, couldn't resist a twinkle. "I happen to have some presents," he commented.

Adiratna, climbing off his knee, stood before him, her hands clasped before her, her wide eyes pleading. "Oh Papa," she begged, then looked back at Hannah again and chewed thoughtfully at her upper lip. Her eyes lit, and she said, "I have been very good, Papa, have I not, Hannah?" Then she added mournfully, "Not as good as Marsha."

"Dan, would you fetch my duffel?" Jules asked his son, shifting slightly to allow the boy to pass.

"Perhaps, you might take your father up to the nursery, young ladies?" Mia suggested. "Hannah could bring you up some scones. I am sure your father would like a scone his daughters have made."

Jules, who had his mouth open—Mia was certain—to repudiate the suggestion, shut it again.

"Oh yes, Papa. Come and see." Marshanda took one of Jules's hands, and Adiratna, not to be left behind, took the other. "Hannah made us some curtains, Papa. And Ibu Mia bought us a table and chairs to do our schoolwork. I can read, Papa. Truly."

"You shall show me, sweetheart," her father said. Over his shoulder, he commanded, "Japheth, fetch our trunks from the *Advantage*. Ask Mr Bourne, and he'll give them to you. Pranisha, I'll have a coffee with that scone." He didn't miss the way both servants turned to Mia, silently seeking her permission, which she gave with a small nod. He narrowed his fine blue eyes, which she met calmly. His lips moved in a silent word before he turned his attention back to the impatient children, and allowed himself to be led away.

She was fairly sure he had said 'Later', and was almost positive he meant it as a threat.

Well. He would find she had a grudge or two of her own.

5

———————

His little wife had grown. Not 'up' exactly. She was still a tiny creature, her head no higher than his chest, but no-one would take her for a schoolgirl now! Was it the modern fashions that gave her curves he'd not seen seven years ago—not a lush endowment but decidedly female?

Annoyed with her though he was, he could not deny that his body responded to hers, as if something primitive within him rejoiced in the link formed by their long-ago wedding and yearned to set seal to his claim. A physical lust. That was all. It could be ignored.

But the change in her was not only physical. She had been an endearing mix of child and adult. Her isolated life as the only child of a reclusive scholar had given her a wisdom and maturity beyond her years and the innocence of a much younger girl. Now she was a woman. Confident and in charge.

Which was extremely irritating, since she had placed herself in charge of his house! As he allowed his two daughters to drag him back upstairs and show him and Dan around their domain, he had to concede she was competent. No. More than competent.

He couldn't complain about the changes in the nursery—new

paint, shelves instead of trunks for books and toys, new furniture—sturdy painted furniture that would withstand much more activity than the rejects from the rest of the house that had been there before.

"Sit in Ibu Mia's chair, Papa," Ada commanded.

Marsha scoffed. "Not Ibu Mia's. Papa is too big. Sit in Hannah's chair, Papa."

"Is Hannah looking after you while she is visiting?" Jules was not above finding out his wife's intentions from his children, if he could.

"Hannah is not visiting. Hannah is our new nurse," Ada explained. She was dragging his duffel bag from where Dan had dropped it by the door.

Marsha offered her morsel of information. "Hannah used to be nurse to our cousin Daisy, but Daisy has a governess now, so Hannah came to be our nurse."

"And to look after Ibu Mia," Ada corrected. "Hannah said Lord Henry said Ibu Mia could not travel all this way on her own. Is Lord Henry our grandfather, Papa? Hannah says he is."

"Yes, sweetheart," Jules confirmed. "Lord Henry is my father, so your grandfather." Father had approved this trip, had he? He had never been happy about Jules's irregular living arrangements, Jules was sure of that, though his letters were devoid of any criticism. Susan, Jules's sister, was more direct in her letters, castigating him for leaving his wife for so long. They probably sent Mia to bring Jules to heel.

But he wouldn't be leashed by her or anyone else.

He pulled the first object from his duffel: a mancala board in carved wood, with stones in bright colours to play the game.

"How pretty!" Ada marvelled. "Look, Marsha. Look at the carvings. What does it do, Papa? Who is it for?"

"This is to share," Jules warned, "and Dan will teach you how to play the game."

Next, he pulled out a skipping rope each. One of the men on the *Advantage* had made the brightly painted wooden handles, sized for small hands, and the ropes fed through a hole in the butt of the handle, so they could be lengthened or shortened to suit the height of the user.

The girls fell on them and wanted to try them out immediately, but settled quickly when he suggested that Hannah would expect them to skip outside, and he had not yet emptied the duffle.

Two of the maids carried in trays with glasses of milk for the children, plates of scones, bowls of jam, and a pot of coffee for Jules. He waved them to the table while he distributed the strings of beads he'd purchased in the market at Toamasina.

"May I serve you a scone, Papa?" Marsha asked.

"I shall pour Papa's coffee," Dan insisted. "I know how he takes it."

Ada's face fell, and Marsha must have noticed, because she gave the prepared plate to her sister. "You shall take this to Papa, because you helped make them, too," she said. Jules's smile must have said how proud he was, for his shy daughter blushed while the bold one climbed on his knee and instructed him on the fine art of scone-eating.

The girls set aside the book he gave each of them for reading later, but when the bundle of silk scarves and the handful of pretty combs for their hair emptied the duffel, they forgot about their milk and scones for the pleasures of dressing one another's hair, and parading the results in front of Dan and Jules.

Jules kept looking to the door, but Mia stayed away. He was disappointed, and annoyed with himself for the emotion. She had charmed his mistress, his daughters, and his servants; and was well on her way to charming his son. She would not find him such an easy conquest. Though, to be fair, most of what he'd had against her had evaporated.

Now he'd had time to calm down, he could not object to Mia moving Kirana from the room next to his own, with only one small window. The top floor at the far end of the wing, with windows on all three sides, was better for convalescing, though he wouldn't have called the room adjoining his over hot. It was, after all, still winter. Though the Cape Town winters were very mild by English standards, Kirana was used to the heat of Ceylon and India.

Still, the difference in temperature and the freshness of the air spoke for itself, and Kirana's praise for Mia was genuine.

The whole house had the Mia touch. The surfaces gleamed. Every corner was scrubbed and clean. The windows sparkled. Since Raquib and Jwala had returned to India, and Kirana's illness left her without the strength to supervise the servants, he'd had to ignore cobwebs and dust in remote corners, because it upset Kirana when he spent the first few days of every leave chasing the servants to do their work.

Even if Mia was overstepping her mark by taking over the house he kept for his mistress—whoever heard of a wife doing such a thing? —he couldn't deny the results were pleasing.

But she had still dismissed a pregnant maid to fend for herself in a port town where men outnumbered women four to one.

And she was still here when she ought to be in England.

⁙

"Should I order dinner served properly?" Mia asked Hannah. She had been sharing the nursery tea with the two children, or taking a tray in Kirana's room. She refused to make extra work for the servants by dining in solitary splendour. "I imagine the captain is used to formal dining, as a rule," she added, thinking back to the ship that had brought her here. Being invited to the captain's table meant dressing in one's best, and displaying company manners.

"Ask the man, Mrs Captain," Hannah advised. Mia had been 'Mrs J.' to Hannah for years, but it hadn't taken her more than a few days to adopt the form of address first coined by the doorman Japheth. "He might want to have his dinner with Mrs Kirana"

"That is true." Mia sighed. "He is not quite what I expected, Hannah." More handsome than she had remembered, but not nearly as charming. Kind and loving to his mistress and children, but abrupt—even borderline rude—to her. And unfaithful. She had no right to cavil at his long relationship with Kirana, but she'd been firmly disabused of her assumption that Kirana was his only lover.

Kirana herself made no complaint about the other women he had bedded, but he was much mistaken if he thought Mia would be as compliant.

She repeated the sigh, more heavily this time. Not that women had a lot of choice. She and Jules were married, whether they liked it or not, and in a marriage, men had all of the legal power and women only as much power as their husbands cared to give them.

"It'll all come out in the wash, Mrs Captain," Hannah soothed. "You need to talk to the captain. Then you'll know how to go on."

But the dinner question became moot, and any discussion would have to wait. A messenger arrived with a note for the captain, who read it and left. "Captain say to tell you he out for dinner, Mrs Captain," Japheth reported.

Annoying man.

6

Jules made his way home in the early hours of the morning, a little drunk and a lot annoyed at a waste of an entire evening.

"Good of you to come out on the first night of your leave, Redepenning," said the admiral when he was finally able to say his goodbyes. Not that his note demanding Jules's presence at his table had offered the choice of refusal.

The evening had comprised interminable discussion of the same points over and over—points on which Jules had given his opinion in his reports from Madagascar and the final one delivered this afternoon. They needed to oust the enemy from the two ports still in French hands, since the enemy used those bases to attack British shipping.

Most of the captains favoured a frontal assault. Jules, Fleming, and a couple of the other captains held the minority view, suggesting the British support the young king of the Merinas, who was in the process of conquering the whole island. The admiral was playing his cards close to his chest, but had dismissed them all with a promise to let them know what he would be recommending to the Admiralty.

No-one had said anything new, and Jules's evening would have been better spent with his daughters and Kirana. Or even having the overdue confrontation with his inconvenient wife.

She had better not be in his bed. If she was, he'd pack her off to her own, as he should have done with Maureen when the little baggage met him there one night, naked between his sheets, after a very similar evening. Instead, tired, frustrated, and lonely, his willpower blunted by alcohol, he had accepted what she had to offer. If she was pregnant with his child, it must have been that night, for the next time—the only other time—he'd worn a pig skin, as he always did with anyone except Kirana. Kirana, who had been too sick to give him the comfort of her body for a long time.

He had been so depressed by the sheer emptiness of copulating with Maureen that he'd sworn off any repeat engagements, though Maureen had not believed he was serious, and he'd left for Mauritius and Madagascar before she could put it to the test.

He'd kept to his resolution, too, much to Gerta van Klief's surprise. The widow had been quite put out when he explained he intended to honour his marriage from this point on.

Which, when Jules came to think about it, he could do while still enjoying the delectable package that might be waiting in his bed. She was, after all, his wife. For a moment, he let himself imagine unwrapping the unexpected gift that was, after all, his. No. They needed to get a few things sorted, first. A ship could only have one captain, and he was it. And he decided who was on his crew and where they went.

His key opened the front door, and he locked and bolted it by the light of the shuttered lamp left waiting for him in the entrance hall. He let himself into his bed chamber. His bed was empty; the sheets crisp and neat over the mattress. He did not feel disappointed. He would not feel disappointed.

But before he could think and put a brake on the action, he crossed the room to the connecting door leading to the one requisitioned by his wife, and turned the handle. It wouldn't budge. She'd locked the door against him!

His indignation expressed itself in a raised fist, ready to pound on the door and demand entrance, until his sense of humour caught up. So much for planning to turn her out of his bed. What a hypocrite he was being, desiring the damnable woman even while he was suspicious of her motives and annoyed about her existence.

He turned towards the bed. He'd be sleeping in it alone, apparently.

He began to strip off. Was his wife a virgin? He'd been thinking of her as a child and the rakes of England had undoubtedly seen her as a woman long before he did. He had no right to expect she would have remained faithful to the man who'd fled England as soon as the knot was tied.

The washstand held a jug of fresh clean water. Lukewarm, but he was late home, and water at all was more than he expected from the ramshackle household his had become. Mia's doing, no doubt.

She wore the locket he'd given her as a wedding present, and next door the dressing table set with which he'd marked her fifteenth birthday took pride of place in front of the mirror. She was his wife. He'd planned, had he not, to try to build a life with her when he was finally posted home to England?

He slipped between the sheets, naked but with a pair of breeches within easy reach as had been his habit since he first had a cabin of his own.

Yes. He should put his offended pride to one side and try to make common ground with Mia.

If, that is, she was sorry for throwing poor Maureen out, and would promise not to do anything like that again.

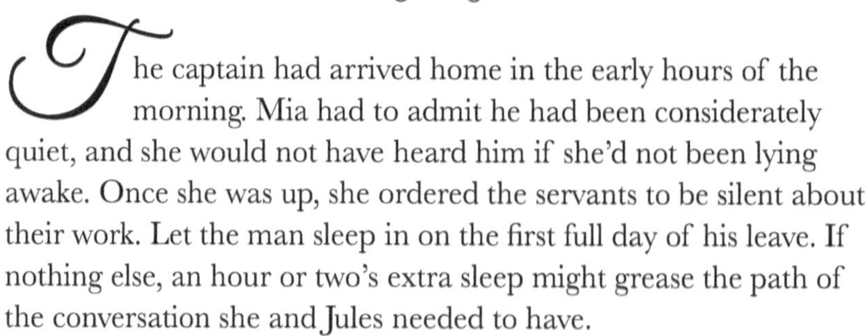

The captain had arrived home in the early hours of the morning. Mia had to admit he had been considerately quiet, and she would not have heard him if she'd not been lying awake. Once she was up, she ordered the servants to be silent about their work. Let the man sleep in on the first full day of his leave. If nothing else, an hour or two's extra sleep might grease the path of the conversation she and Jules needed to have.

She was reserving judgement about their future: unwilling to risk her future on a dream, afraid of wasting the opportunity. Perhaps he had good reasons for all the actions that offended her, as proved to be the case when he went out to dinner on the first night in seven years that he and she were in the same country.

Last night, Adiratna was muttering bitterly about her father's defection and Mia was silently agreeing with her, though trying not to let a hint of her opinion show, when Perdana stopped his sister's complaints. "The captain did not wish to leave us, Ada, but he is an officer in His Majesty's Navy, and when the admiral orders him to come to dinner, it is his duty to obey. You are an officer's daughter. It is your duty not to complain."

Mia avoided letting her mental wince become physical, she hoped; or perhaps not, for Adiratna appealed to her. "But it is unfair, is it not, Ibu Mia? I wanted Papa to stay with us."

"The Royal Navy protects the seas for the King," Mia replied. "That is what your father does, and your Uncle Rick, and the admiral too. Imagine if the ships could not sail because a captain wanted to stay with his little girls, and Napoleon sailed past in his ship with all his soldiers!"

"That would be bad," Perdana agreed. "Our ships are the oak wall that protects Britain and all of its lands, at home and abroad." He was clearly quoting someone else, but his sisters were impressed.

"Yes," Mia agreed. "And the mothers, wives, and children of our brave sailors must let them go, and smile, and never complain at their leaving." She had learned that lesson in her father-in-law's household. He was a general in the Horse Guard, and her brothers-in-law were all naval or army officers. Her sister-in-law was a naval widow; her husband having been killed in the North Sea in a battle against French ships. Men needed to go heart-whole to war, confident their women would provide a safe and welcoming home to which they could return.

Perdana rewarded her sentiment with a smile. "Ibu Mia knows," he told his sisters.

Perdana had his own bedchamber, but was with his sisters again this morning when she went up to the nursery with the maids who were serving breakfast. All three were dressed, and sitting at the table with Hannah. Perdana stood politely when she entered, and held her chair for her as she took the remaining place at the table.

After dismissing the maids, she and Hannah helped the children to serve themselves, and the meal got off to a merry start when Hannah produced a pot of English jam to go on the English crumpets she'd made that very morning, much to the fascination of the Indian cook.

"This was made with the Earl of Chirbury's own blackberries," Mia told the children, as she spooned some of the jam into a dish. "The Earl is your father's cousin, children, and Hannah makes the jam every year."

"Won the prize for that at the Whitsun Fair three years in a row, I did," Hannah told them, and then had to explain the Whitsun Fair, which led to a discussion of the Pet Show, and various animals entered by the children's Chirbury cousins, who had been in Hannah's charge since the birth of Lady Daisy more than eleven years ago.

"We have lots of cousins," Adiratna boasted to Perdana. Stories of the other children in the extended family had been bedtime fodder since Mia and Hannah arrived. "We will meet them when we go to England."

Perdana paused, his hand hovering over another crumpet. "We are going to England?"

"Not yet. Not while Mami is sick," Marshanda explained. "Ibu Mia is staying with us and Mami for as long as Mami needs her.

Perdana frowned, and seemed to shrink a little, fixing his dark eyes on Mia. "I have seen Mami," he said. "She slept well, she says."

She always said that. Every morning, Mia made a visit to Kirana her first priority, and every morning, Kirana claimed she had slept well, though the maid whose turn it was to sleep on a pallet in the room, and check Kirana's wellbeing during the night, always shook her head at Mia's questioning glance.

Perdana must have slipped into his mother's room when Mia went down to the kitchen. His frown deepened as he thought. "She is not getting better, is she, Ibu Mia?"

While Mia was choosing her words, Adiratna answered. "Mami

is going to live with Jesus soon. She told Marsha and me. We are to be very good, and obey Ibu Mia, and Ibu Mia will take us home to be her own girls. I love Ibu Mia, but I wish Mami did not have to go to Heaven."

"Now, Ada, you know Mami hurts and she coughs so bad she bleeds," Marshanda scolded. "Don't you want her to go to Heaven to be well again?"

Adiratna poked out her lips, tears starting into her eyes. "I want her to be well again and here with us," she wailed, and she slid off the chair, her thumb heading towards her mouth before she disappeared under the table.

Mia gathered her onto her lap. "Oh sweetheart," she said. "I wish it could be so. But your Mami is very sick, darling." She hugged the little girl, her own eyes filling with tears. "I love you, too, Adiratna. And Marshanda and Perdana. We shall be a family together, will we not? And we shall always remember your Mami and love her."

Marshanda came for a hug too, and Perdana stood up to walk rapidly around the room, his face set.

"What about another crumpet, Master Dan?" Hannah asked. "What are your plans for the day, Mrs Captain? I thought perhaps Miss Marsha and Miss Ada would like to walk down to the docks to look at their father's ship. Perhaps Master Dan could escort us?"

"The port is not a savoury place for ladies," said Jules from the doorway. How long had he been there, crisply dressed and looking more handsome than any man had a right to? "Two escorts would be better. What do you say, Dan? Shall we show the ladies our ship?"

How much had he heard? His face smiled, but his eyes were sad. "Papa!" The girls shouted, in chorus. Once again, he opened his arms, crouching as they ran for a hug. Yesterday was not just an aberration, then. Mia had been suspicious, assuming Maureen would not have courted his anger by exiling his daughters to the kitchen if she knew he cared about them, but perhaps the girl was just too stupid or too self-absorbed to think that far ahead.

When he stood, he addressed Mia directly. "Mrs Redepenning,

the children's mother would like to see the children when they have finished their breakfast. I have come to fetch them."

Mia softened towards him still further. His first act once dressed must have been to visit his mistress.

Adiratna ran back to the table and scrambled into her chair. "Please, Ibu Mia, may I leave the table?" she asked, as Hannah had been teaching her, and Mia had to suppress a smile.

"You may if you have eaten enough, Adiratna."

Marshanda had followed her younger sister's example in returning to the table, and repeated the request. "Certainly, Marshanda. And, young ladies, that was very nicely done."

"Very nicely indeed," Jules agreed. He offered a hand to each girl. "Come along, Dan. Mrs Redepenning, would a picnic appeal after our visit to the ship? If the kitchen could rustle up a picnic?"

"A picnic would be famous!" Perdana agreed. "Hannah said she made scones, as well as the crumpets." And his voice could be heard as he followed his father and sisters down the corridor, explaining about Hannah's prizewinning jam.

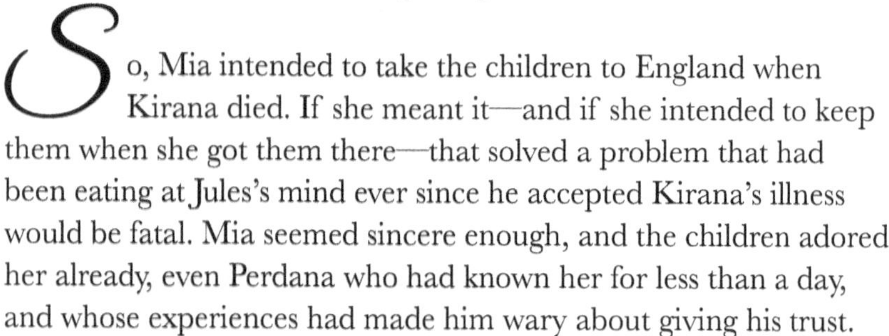

So, Mia intended to take the children to England when Kirana died. If she meant it—and if she intended to keep them when she got them there—that solved a problem that had been eating at Jules's mind ever since he accepted Kirana's illness would be fatal. Mia seemed sincere enough, and the children adored her already, even Perdana who had known her for less than a day, and whose experiences had made him wary about giving his trust.

Kirana had faded more than he'd expected in the two months he'd been away. She fought for every breath, and each time she succumbed to another bout of coughing, he thought she could not possibly survive it. She said only that she felt much better since Mia arrived and moved her from 'that horrid room', and Jules felt guilty for not realising before how hot the room next to his became in the afternoon.

The one useful thing about last night was the presence of the fleet doctor, who had agreed to call this morning to examine Kirana and tell him if anything further could be done. He would arrange for Mia to be with her—both women would like that—and then he would take the children out to give Kirana a quiet house to rest in.

Kirana broke into his thoughts. "Laying plans, Captain?" It had been a joke between them for years. Kirana found it hard to comprehend the restlessness of his mind, which stilled only in that quiet place beyond coitus. Jules admired her gift of sitting at peace with her surroundings, apparently—or so she said—thinking of nothing.

"Plans for you to see the doctor this morning, my love, and afterwards to take Mrs Redepenning and the girls to see the *Advantage*."

Kirana smiled. "Mia and girls will like. But I don't need a—" *doctor, Jules.* He had to finish her last sentence in his head, since she was interrupted by a ruthless spasm of coughing. She reached for the clean cloth that Marsha plucked from the basket of them that stood ready, and covered her mouth as her shoulders shook and shook again.

Dan paled at the sight of his mother's blood reddening the cloth, but neither of the girls showed any reaction, except that Ada lifted the hand she was holding to kiss it, and Marsha stood quietly by to give Kirana another cloth when the first one was too stained to be of use.

The maid who was hovering took the soiled item and put it in a bucket that stood ready, washed her hands carefully and thoroughly at the washstand, throwing the water she'd used into yet another bucket. Another innovation. He would have to ask Mia what that was about.

Another maid appeared in the doorway. "Captain, sir, Mrs Captain say Dr Sturgess here. She bringing him up."

"Perdana, take your sisters back to the nursery," Jules instructed his son. The boy obeyed.

The doctor was a bluff Yorkshire man, one of those typical naval doctors who had begun as a loblolly boy running a ship surgeon's errands, and learned his trade by apprenticeship. Jules's own ship's surgeon had recommended him when Jules had tried to get the Dutch doctor who served the people of Cape Town to visit Kirana a year ago. The man had refused to see "A coloured woman, and an immoral one, at that."

"Dr Sturgess has a gift," the surgeon had said. "If anyone can help your woman, it'll be him." He warned, though that advanced consumption of the lungs was not part of a navy doctor's usual practice. A sailor as sick as Kirana would have been sent ashore long since, and sure enough Sturgess had been able to do little except confirm the disease, and warn it was likely to prove fatal. Jules didn't expect much from today, either. But he had to do what little he could.

Sturgess had a bemused expression on his face as he trailed Mia into the room. Jules hadn't paused to think how her presence might appear to the man, especially when she took station on the other side of Kirana's bed, Kirana's hand in her own. Sturgess's bushy eyebrows near climbed into his hairline, but he said nothing.

"How are we today, Mrs… er."

Kirana, as Jules's acknowledged mistress, had been called Mrs Redepenning since they moved in together in Madras, their previous posting, but Sturgess clearly found it impossible to address her by that name in front of Jules's legal wife. Mia had no such difficulty.

"Mrs Kirana Redepenning does not complain, doctor. She is a little better this week. I arranged to have her moved to this room as the one she was in was hot and stuffy."

"Very good." The doctor was quickly and efficiently examining his patient, feeling under the line of her jaw, tapping various spots on her chest with his ear close to listen to her breathing, waiting patiently whenever another round of coughing interrupted his examination.

"I have been reading about some French fellow who thinks fresh air is the thing," he told Mia. "And he recommends isolation, Mrs Redepenning, so that others in the household do not catch the disease. The children, especially."

"We have been very careful, doctor," Mia said. "We boil the

cloths, and the children must wash their hands carefully before and after they see their mother."

Kirana's stricken eyes sought her lover's. "Keep them away, Jules." She turned her head so she could see her friend. "Mia, keep them out." Coughing interrupted her, and another cloth bloomed with the scarlet evidence of her dying lungs, but she spoke again as soon as the coughing subsided. "You said… keep them safe. You promised."

"Well, now, Mrs Kirana. We don't know for certain how the disease moves from one person to another, except that the things people touch seem to be a problem. What happens to the cloths in the bucket, Mrs Redepenning?"

Mia explained how they boiled the cloths and dried them in the sun, the doctor nodding his approval. "And you make the maid wash after touching the soiled cloths," he noted. "Can you explain why?"

"My sister-in-law insists it makes a difference," Mia told him. "Her father studied with Alexander Gordon, and practiced the cleanliness he was taught. He and his daughter had good results from washing hands and surgical instruments between operations. I hoped it might help to prevent contagion." Jules's brother Alex had married a woman who had travelled with the army learning the trade of surgeon-physician at her father's elbow.

"Precisely! Precisely. I have observed the difference myself. But can I convince these young pups on the other ships?" He shook his head.

He asked a few more questions, then patted Kirana's arm. "You are in good hands, Mrs Kirana. Just depend on Mrs Redepenning, and you will come along right and tight."

Kirana moved her head, a small sign of negation. "Tell Jules I'm dying. He does not believe."

Jules stiffened. He could not show the tears of incipient grief, but it was a struggle to keep the phlegmatic expression expected of His Majesty's naval officers. He knew. He didn't want to accept it, but he knew.

The doctor bowed slightly, acknowledging Kirana's courage and dignity. "Rest, Mrs Kirana. I will speak with the captain."

She relaxed against her pillows and closed her eyes, though Jules didn't think she slept. He followed Mia and the doctor from the room, and one of the little maids—Marie, he thought—scurried into the room and took a seat by the window, pulling some mending from her pocket.

"My study?" Jules suggested. They could speak without fear of an audience in his study.

"Shall I order refreshments," Mia wondered. "Tea, doctor? Or a coffee, perhaps? Or we have a very pleasant local ale."

"Tea, if you would, Mrs Redepenning."

Mia gave the order to Japheth, adding instructions for Jules's preferred coffee. Today, he would rather have brandy or something else to numb the pain, but ten in the morning was a little early to start.

The study was directly under Kirana's sick room, and he'd not been in it at all since he returned home. A quick glance confirmed it was clean and tidy, everything in its place. He seized one of the armchairs by the desk and put it with the pair that faced the fireplace.

Mia took the chair with a large side table, ready to serve the beverages when they arrived. "Please be seated, gentlemen. Doctor Sturgess, what can we expect? What do we need to do?"

"Expect? The patient is correct, Madam. She is dying. I cannot tell you how quickly, but the lungs are severely compromised, and she is very weak. She will find it harder and harder to breath; until at the end the lungs are so consumed her breath will fail her entirely. It could be this week, or next, or a month from now. I do not expect it to be longer, but people surprise me all the time."

He studied Mia with a judicious air. "You call her your friend, Madam. Forgive me, but I don't understand."

None of his business, Jules thought, and was about to say so, but Mia spoke first.

"We have been exchanging letters, Kirana and I, for many years. When she wrote she was dying, and told me her concerns for her children, I knew I had to come. To comfort her in her dying with my presence and with the confidence that her children are safe with me."

"Very Christian of you, Mrs Redepenning." The doctor sounded doubtful. "May I say you hardly look old enough to be married even now?"

Mia's response was dry. "Indeed, and I am not many years older than I look. So, you will understand why my husband and I have not, until now, lived in the same country, let alone the same house. Tell me, doctor, what else can I do for my friend?"

A knock at the door signalled the arrival of the tea and Jules's coffee, and the three of them left the conversation until the maid had retreated from the room and closed the door behind her.

The doctor picked up where they had left off, answering Mia's question. "Keep doing what you are doing. Keep her comfortable. Reassure her that she leaves her children in safe hands. Make sure the air she breaths is as fresh as possible, and if she will eat, make the food nutritious. Milk is good. Eggs. Broth. Food that is easy to digest and full of strength. And…" he trailed off.

Jules straightened. "What else?" Whatever it was, the doctor was uncertain about mentioning it. Jules was not going to let Kirana be bled. She was weak enough as it was. He'd been reading any medical paper he could find about consumption, and bleeding was not useful in the disease.

But Dr Sturgess's next words surprised him. "Excuse me, but may I ask whether Mrs Kirana is a person of faith? Hindi, perhaps, or Moslem? You may be able to find someone of her faith on one of the ships."

"Christian," Mia replied confidently, as Jules hesitated. "As a child, she went to the Dutch Reformed church in Batavia, and later in Ceylon." Mia sighed. "I thought a minister of her own church might be able to give her some spiritual comfort, but he refused to come." She firmly folded her lips over whatever else she thought of saying, but Jules could easily imagine the terms in which the man might have couched his refusal to enter the house of a kept woman of colour who was dying of consumption.

"I will try him again," Jules said to Mia, "and if he still refuses, Dr Sturgess's suggestion has merit. The navy and the army have chaplains who may be more open-minded."

Mia smiled, as if he had given her a present. "Thank you. I am sure that will mean a lot to her."

She turned back to the doctor to ask a few more questions about the danger to the children. The doctor offered comfort. "They have been well fed, get plenty of sleep in their own room and not their mother's, and spend time outside in the fresh air. Keep that up, Mrs Redepenning, and you will have done everything you can."

What did Mia's worried frown mean, and the hasty look she cast at Jules? They really needed to talk!

7

Mia tried to pay attention while Jules and Dan showed her and the girls around the *Advantage*. They were as proud as could be of the ship, speaking of it as 'her', and pointing out all the ways in which she was the best vessel afloat. But Mia was distracted.

For more than a month before she arrived, the girls had worked all day in the hot and stuffy kitchen, and each night slept on the floor in their mother's room, or even in her bed. Pranisha had arranged it, to keep them out of the way of Maureen's spite. Mia wouldn't tell Pranisha about the risks the girls faced as a result, but Jules had a right to know, and she dreaded telling him.

"This can't be interesting for you," Jules said in her ear, making her jump, since she'd no idea he was behind her. "I daresay my brother has shown you around any number of ships in the past seven years."

She collected her thoughts and made an effort. "Not your ship, Captain Redepenning, and that makes all the difference. Besides, is the *Advantage* not a frigate? Quite different from anything Rick has captained. You wrote that she was captured from the French. How does she compare to the British frigates you have sailed?"

Dan was eager to explain, waxing lyrical about the ship's speed and manoeuvrability and her guns while Jules smiled proudly. The girls exclaimed at the size of the cannons on the gun deck, and marvelled when Jules and Dan showed them the mess tables and hammocks that folded away when not in use.

"Where does Perdana sleep?" Mia asked.

"In my cabin. There's a pallet he can pull out in the corner. It is his job to keep the cabin tidy, to run messages for me, and to launder my linens."

Adiratna found that funny. "Dan! You have to do the laundry!"

"I would rather do laundry than wash dishes," Marshanda argued.

"Washing dirty pots is the worst," Adiratna agreed, and Perdana nodded. "I hate washing dirty pots."

The children fell into a discussion about the baked-on grime that was hardest to remove, and Jules pulled Mia to one side, his face thunderous. "When have my daughters cleaned dirty pots?"

"While you were away," Mia explained. "Maureen O'Riley sent them to the kitchen when she took over Kirana's place." She bit at her lower lip, frowning. Now to tell him her fears. But he spoke before she could, his voice cold enough to freeze.

"Took over Kirana's place? Explain yourself, Mrs Redepenning."

"Has no one told you? After you left, Maureen announced she was your new mistress, and was taking over the mistress's room. She had the servants move Kirana to the little storeroom by the kitchen."

"That hole?" Jules took a deep breath and two or three swift paces, back and forth, colour ebbing and flowing in face.

"Quite," Mia agreed, reassured by the strength of his reaction. Clearly, Maureen had not had his authority for the move.

"No wonder she— Kirana told me you'd moved her from a hot stuffy room, and I thought she meant the one you are in now." He took another two swift paces, his struggle to remain outwardly calm clear on his face.

"Papa?" Marshanda left her conversation to run to Mia, putting both arms around her waist and peeping at Jules from that place of safety. "Why is Papa angry, Ibu Mia?"

"Your father is angry you were made to work in the kitchen, and your mother was made to sleep in the storeroom," Mia said.

Jules had himself under control, and his voice dripped ice, though sparks of fire flashed in his blue eyes. "My servants will explain to me how they allowed this to happen—how they helped this to happen."

Marshanda plastered herself closer to Mia, and Adiratna explained. "Dench said you told him you did not want us anymore, or Mami either. I told Marsha he was lying. I don't like Dench."

"You were right, Ada," Jules told her. "He was lying. I don't like him, either."

"Dench hits people if they say he is lying," Marshanda warned. "He hit Japheth when Japheth didn't believe you gave the orders, and he hit Ada when she bit him."

Jules dropped to his knees and took his youngest daughter's face between his hands. "He hit you, sweetheart?"

"Papa will hit him," Perdana promised. "Papa will punch him right through to next Tuesday, won't you, Papa?"

"I will certainly make sure he never lies to my little girls or hits them again," Jules vowed, not taking his attention off Adiratna. "Biting him was a very dangerous thing to do, my darling."

Adiratna stuck out her lip and glowered. "I am not sorry," she insisted. "He was dragging Mami by her arm. It hurt her. I made him stop."

"She was very brave, Papa," Marshanda insisted, her whole body trembling as she stood up for her sister. "Mami tried to walk, but she fell down, and he said a bad word and began to drag her, but when Ada bit him and ran away, he chased after her and Japheth and I had time to help Mami to her new room."

"You were both very brave, then," Jules said. "I am proud of you, and Ibu Mia is proud of you, too." His smile at Mia was strained, and tears stood in his eyes."

"Very proud," Mia agreed. "I do not recommend biting people as a general rule, but difficult situations call for extreme measures.

What happened next, Adiratna? Did you manage to hide from Dench?"

"I ran to Pranisha, and she let me hide in the kitchen," Adiratna explained.

"Yes," Marshanda added, "and she told Dench if he hit one of us again, she would hit him! With the poker."

Jules had Adiratna clutched to one shoulder, and when he held out his other arm, Marshanda ran into it. "You are safe now, my darlings."

"Yes," Adiratna agreed. "Because when you go away again, Ibu Mia will stay. She has promised. She and Hannah make everyone be nice to us."

"Then," Jules said, "we are very lucky that Ibu Mia came." Over the children's heads, Perdana having approached to lay a loving hand on a shoulder of each sister, Jules mouthed a couple of words to Mia, for the first time directing to her the warm look he reserved for his family. "Thank you."

Mia smiled back, but inwardly she quailed. She had still not told him about the girls' increased exposure to their mother's consumption.

⁂

Japheth and Hannah, with Fortune at the reins, met them at the dock gates with the break, a large open carriage capable of taking the entire family along the coast to eat the picnic that was undoubtedly in the covered baskets Jules could see tucked under the seats.

The day was too crisp for one of the beaches. They drove around the bay towards Green Point, where a carriage race was in progress on the informal race track. Beyond that, they found a place to put up the canvas pavilion they'd brought with them.

"Can we see the racing, Ibu Mia?" Ada asked. Already, in less than a fortnight, she turned to his wife rather than him, and no wonder. Mia had saved them from Maureen's vindictiveness and

Dench's bullying, and very possibly kept Kirana alive until he was able to return home.

"What do you think, Captain?" Mia asked him, and he shook off his mood to attend to the question.

"We can take a walk in that direction, but not too close to the crowds or the race track," he decided. "Japheth? Fortune? Can you manage to get the pavilion up? If not, Dan and I will help when we get back."

They strolled towards the race, heading for a spot away from the heaviest concentration of spectators. The crowd gathered where bets were taken and alcohol sold. Jules had gambled on a few races here himself; yes, and drunk more than a few bottles of rot gut to wash down what passed as food sold by the hawkers who circulated in the crowd. It was not a place for his daughters and his lady wife.

The carriage race was over, and a horse race was about to start. Jules stopped them around thirty yards from the track. "You will be able to see from here," he said, "without getting any mud on your pretty dresses."

"Captain!" It was his first lieutenant, approaching with a broad smile and his hand held out. "I thought that was you I saw taking ladies aboard the *Advantage*." He turned his smile on Mia, his eyes full of questions he was too polite to ask, at least in front of his captain.

"Mrs Redepenning," Jules said to her, "this scamp is my first lieutenant, Alloysius Bourne. Bourne, may I make known to you my daughters, Marsha and Ada. Dan, you know, of course."

Bourne was struggling to control his expression. Jules had assumed the story of his English wife arriving to care for his Batavian mistress would have swept through the naval community, but the confusion Bourne was manfully suppressing suggested the introduction came as a surprise.

Mia allowed him to bow over her hand, saying, "I have met your sister, Mr Bourne. When we discovered we both had men serving on the *Advantage*, Mrs Godwit and I struck up a friendship. She speaks fondly of her brother Al."

Bourne's eyes lit up. "Delia has written of you, Mrs Redepenning. I am delighted to make your acquaintance."

Ada squealed as the signal flag went down and the horses sprang into a gallop, thundering towards them. "Excuse me one moment," Mia said to Bourne. She grabbed after the hand Ada had jerked away in her excitement, and pulled the child back against her body, a hand gently restraining each shoulder as the child jiggled with delight, growing more excited as the horses grew closer.

Marsha shrank back against Jules, and he dropped to one knee to wrap her in a comforting arm. "You are quite safe," he reassured her. He had never thought to bring them here, or even take them on an outing in the carriage. He tended to spend his shore leave either at home with Kirana or visiting naval colleagues. He had no idea about their lives when he was away. Did they spend all their time in the house and its courtyard, or did Jwala and Kirana take them out before Kirana's illness took such a toll?

The horses swept past, and Mia let Ada wriggle from under her hands to catch up Marsha's hands and dance her in a circle. "That was wonderful!" she crowed. "Did you like it, Marsha? Which horse do you think is the best? Which one will win? I liked the black one." Dan argued for the chestnut with the white socks, and Marsha tentatively suggested the grey.

The adults' eyes met over the children's heads. "Your trip out must be judged a success, Captain," Bourne commented. "Are you in Cape Town for long, Mrs Redepenning?"

"The length of my stay is uncertain, Mr Bourne." Jules thought Mia would leave it at that. They had not discussed what to say to other people. He had never anticipated introducing his wife to people who had met his mistress, especially in the company of his children. Mia, however, had no hesitation. "I will remain for as long as I am needed to nurse the Captain's friend, the children's mother."

No more than that. She clearly had no intention of explaining, and Bourne was too much of a gentleman to ask questions. She took pity on his confusion, and said, "Perhaps you can help me, Mr Bourne. While I am delighted to be here with my husband, I would not wish to bring the children on my own. Do you know of local places where a woman might safely take children on an outing in the finer weather?" Again, she left the subtext unspoken—a white gentlewoman and her husband's half-breed children.

Another thing Jules hadn't considered. What passed for Society here would look down on the children because of their birth. Places of entertainment for the other classes would very likely be unsafe. He needed to hire a replacement for Dench. Someone reliable. Someone twice the size of Japheth and able to guard his family when he wasn't here.

"Captain?" Mia and Bourne had gone on talking while he was preoccupied, and now Bourne was taking his leave. He nodded towards the pavilion that had risen back near the carriage. "Mrs Redepenning wishes to take the children for their lunch, and I had a bet on Eat My Dust, and want to collect my winnings. Captain, will you walk part of the way with me?"

"Go ahead," Mia said. "We will be quite safe walking a few hundred yards, and will be under your eyes the whole time."

Dan made a wing of his arm, and Mia laid her hand on his elbow and allowed him to escort her away. Lessons in manners, it appeared, were not being confined to the young ladies.

Without looking away from his retreating family, Jules said, "Out with it, Bourne. What did you not want to say in front of Mrs Redepenning?"

"The whole port is buzzing about your domestic situation, Captain Redepenning. Word is that you've taken a white whore before your yellow whore was dead. Not my words, Sir. I'm not the one you need to knock into tomorrow. I thought you should know."

Jules unclenched his fists. This complicated matters. He would hire two replacements for Dench, each bigger than the other. "I dare say people find it hard to believe that any lady could be so kind, so compassionate. My wife is a woman in a million. She intends to adopt the children, and take them home to England with her."

"You are a lucky man, sir. I will certainly tell everyone I know that she is the genuine article, and a friend of my sister. Have you heard when we sail, sir?"

Jules shook his head. "I haven't. I say, Bourne, would you like to come to dinner?"

Bourne's eyes widened fractionally, and he grinned, showing the speed of strategic thinking that made him an asset as a First. "Good idea, Captain. Invite the Navy's and the town's biggest gossips, and let them see Mrs Redepenning for the lady she is."

Jules returned the grin. "I wouldn't have called you the Navy's *biggest* gossip," he teased. "Now, if you would excuse me, Lieutenant, I am off to enjoy lunch with my family."

Hannah had set the picnic up in the shade of the pavilion, and Japheth was cooking *rava dosa* on a skillet over a little fire. Various other dishes waited on a low table—a mix of Indian and English food, and cushions had been spread for them all to sit on.

"We will eat together," Mia told Jules. "There is plenty for all."

The servants filled a plate each and withdrew to one corner of the pavilion, and soon they were all enjoying the spread, the children making a game of teaching Mia the names of food she hadn't tried before.

"Say '*puliyodharai*,' Ibu Mia," Ada instructed, as Mia loaded a piece of *chapati* with the fragrant rice dish.

She repeated the word, and then said it again when Dan corrected her pronunciation. "*Thuvayal*," they told her, as she spooned some of the spicy mixture onto her *dosa*.

"You prefer Indian food," she said to Jules, as he loaded his plate.

"I find it tasty," he agreed, "though sometimes I long for the food of my childhood. Hannah's blackberry jam!" He made a smacking noise with his lips against two fingers and tossed them in the air.

"I think we can persuade Pranisha to come back to England with us," Mia suggested. "She has already hinted she does not wish to leave the children."

"I have finished eating, Ibu Mia," Ada said. "May I please leave the table?"

"It isn't a table, stupid," Dan told her. "May I leave the blanket, Ibu Mia?"

Mia hid a smile, as Hannah interceded. "You may apologise to your sister for calling her stupid, Master Dan. A gentleman never insults a lady, or points out mistakes in ways that hurt others."

Dan flushed, but accepted the correction with surprising grace. "I am sorry I called you stupid, Ada."

Hannah Cottle had a magic way with her.

"You may all get up from the blanket," Mia told the children, "but you must stay close to the pavilion, and within sight. Do not go over to the race track or near other people."

Hannah dug around in the pile of baskets and boxes that had carried the picnic. "How about a game of football?" she asked.

Dan was doubtful. "Just three of us?"

Hannah laughed. "All of us, of course. Come on, Japheth, Fortune. Boys against girls. Mrs Captain? Captain?"

"Could we sit this one out?" Jules asked Mia. "I'd like for us to talk, if you do not mind."

"Of course," Mia said. "Hannah, you and the others go ahead."

The group marked out a couple of goals, using baskets. Dan commiserated with the girls all the while for their coming defeat. In moments, the game was underway. Dan's confidence took a swift knock when Fortune failed to catch the ball Hannah had thrown and Marsha raced in front of him and kicked it to Hannah, who in her turn kicked it between the rocks they had marked as the girl's goal.

He rallied, though, and the next round of play saw him sneaking the ball from under Marsha's nose and kicking his own goal.

"This will do the girls a world of good," Mia decided. "I have not wanted to venture beyond the boundaries of town without an escort, and there is nowhere there they can run and romp like this without censure from the biddies."

"You are determined to turn them into English gentlewomen." Jules tried to keep the censure from his voice. He would allow his unaccountable wife her chance to make her case, but what the hell was she thinking?

"I am determined to make sure they know Society's expectations," Mia corrected. "I know how it feels to be at sea, realising that something you have done has drawn disapprobation, but having no idea what it was or how to correct it. I will not leave them as ill prepared as I was."

What had happened to Mia to fuel the vehemence of her tone? He supposed he understood. The child he'd met in the smuggler's cave had been raised by a reclusive scholar—or had raised herself while ignored by her father.

"I thought my father and Susan would look out for you," he said. They should have. He had trusted them to do so.

"It was not their fault, Captain." Mia smiled, and reached out as if to pat his hand where it rested beside hers on the blanket. If that was her intent, she thought better of it and instead folded it in her lap with its counterpart. "They are part of Society. They grew up knowing all the habits of courtesy your kind take for granted, and all your silly little rituals. It never occurred to them I was ignorant of what to them seemed natural behaviour. They were always there to tell me what I had done wrong, and they tried to predict my next mistake and prevent it—but I made so many!" The last was said with a laugh, but Jules could sense pain beneath it, and his heart ached for the little girl he had abandoned.

"I am sorry," he said. "I had no idea."

"I will not have that happen to Marshanda and Adiratna. Their irregular birth will be barrier enough; though I am confident we can overcome that. But the vultures will be watching for any hint they don't fit in. I am determined they will not find it."

"So, you plan to present my daughters to Society, then? Kirana agrees?" Jules had not thought that far ahead. He'd had a vague idea of settling the girls with reliable caregivers in a cottage somewhere. In England, or—if the war looked as if it might turn against Britain—in Canada or even the United States. In that pipe dream, they had remained the age they were now. He had not thought of them growing up.

No one would know from Mia's calm voice that she was nervous, but her hands in her lap gripped one another so tightly that the knuckles turned white. "I plan to raise your children as my own, Captain. As our own, as the elder brother and sisters of any children we might make together." She flushed scarlet at the last few words and ducked her head to hide inside the brim of her hat.

"I—" Jules began, and had to stop to clear the lump from his throat. How did his ill-thought knight errantry win him a prize like this? "I am more grateful than I can say."

She peeped out from under the bonnet at that, a twinkle in her eyes, her tone dry. "I am not doing it for you, Captain, but for my friend Kirana, and—now I have met them—for the children's own dear sake."

He laughed. What else could he do? She cut him down to size at every turn. "I dare say. But you will permit me to be grateful, anyway."

He sobered, then, and introduced the topic that might destroy the harmony between them. "I need to ask—"

At the same moment, Mia began, "I need to tell you—"

They both stopped, and Jules gave a wave of his hand. "Ladies first."

She approached the topic at such a tangent it took him a while to grasp her point. "Captain, I am so sorry. Pranisha meant it for the best, and we cannot know it will make a difference. I will be watching for any signs, and will give them all the care in the world. Oh, I hope and pray it will not be needed, Captain. I so wish I had come earlier, but…"

"Calm yourself. Whatever it is, we will face it. What is it that Pranisha did, and what signs will you be watching for?" But at some level he had guessed, and his heart chilled.

Mia took a deep breath and composed her thoughts. "When Maureen and Dench sent the girls to the kitchen, Pranisha was afraid of their spite. She kept the girls with her, and at night sent them to sleep with their mother. When the doctor said to keep the children away…" She trailed off.

This time, she did reach for him, undoubtedly seeing his feelings written on his face. He gripped her little hand in his, using it to anchor him while the storm buffeted and he sailed through to a measure of calm.

"We will face it," she said, as he lifted his head skywards and took a deep breath.

The shouts of the ball players—cheers from the girls and a loud groan from Dan—attracted his attention. Another goal, then, with Ada retrieving the ball from among the rocks. He smiled at them, and then at his wife. "We will face it together, and it may never happen," he agreed.

They sat in silence for a few moments, hand in hand, watching the game.

"You had something to ask?" Mia reminded him.

"Yes. Mia, would you take Maureen's baby if she does not want it? I understand why you dismissed her, and I don't blame you, but I feel responsible for the child."

"You do?" Mia sounded surprised. "For Dench's baby? But why?"

"Dench's?" Jules turned fully to face Mia. "Are you sure? I thought…" He trailed off. His only evidence that Maureen was carrying his baby was Dench's claim and his own guilt.

"I am not certain the father is Dench," Mia admitted, with scrupulous honesty, "but Kirana is certain you are not the father. Maureen is at least four months along the way, perhaps five. And Kirana says you had just a few—" she paused to search for a word, "encounters with Maureen and those less than three months ago."

Jules raised his brows, absorbing this new information and letting the pieces settle into a new pattern. "So, she probably knew she was with child when she first inserted herself in my bed. I wish I had told her I didn't want what she offered. I was a fool." An idiot led by the least intelligent part of his body. "It was just before I left for this last voyage. Perhaps eleven weeks ago, at most."

Mia nodded. "The baby is not yours, then, Captain."

"Do you think…? Would you call me Jules? As you did in the cave? When we are in private, that is."

She smiled. "I would like that. And you will call me Mia?"

8

Hannah and Mia sat over a load of mending. Jules was out for the evening, and the children's clothes were in desperate need of some attention. Ada was growing out of everything. Dan had gone through the elbows of his best jacket and all of his shirts were fit for little more than the rag bag. Marsha was slightly less disreputable, but only because she was gentler on her clothes and between growth spurts.

Of course, once Mia could organise access to her funds, she could replace the items they so desperately needed. Jules would know how to go about calling on the account that his father had helped her set up for her travels. "I wonder where we can buy material?" she said. "The children need everything, and new shirts for the captain would not go amiss."

She looked at Hannah, who nodded, but made no comment.

"Shoes, too," Mia added. "There must be somewhere in Cape Town that sells such items."

"I'll ask the maids. They may know the best makers of children's shoes," Hannah offered, "or Japheth." A particular note in Hannah's voice brought Mia's eyes up from the long seam she was sewing.

"Japheth likes you," she suggested. The doorman's eyes followed Hannah whenever she was in a room and he always jumped to be first to help her with a parcel or to fetch something she needed.

Hannah said oppressively, "Just as well for nursery and downstairs to get on." Mia bent back to her work, accepting the dismissal of the topic and was surprised when Hannah went on, "Besides, nothing can come of it. We'll go back to England. He will stay here and find another job. If I wanted a dalliance, I have had my opportunities, saving your presence, Mrs Captain. I am not the sort. I have been… I have known what it is to be used, and what it is to be loved."

Mia nodded without comment. Hannah had been married to a wicked man, though she didn't speak of it, and went by her maiden name. She had nearly married again, and Mia had been present to see her grief when the man she loved died helping to rescue Mia and her friend Kitty from terrible danger. Still, that did not mean Hannah had lost all possibility of future happiness. "What if Japheth came to England," she asked, carefully focusing on her sewing.

Hannah was silent for a moment. "Most folks don't hold with servants marrying," she replied, her own head bent over her work.

Mia fastened off her thread and clipped it, holding the dress up to see that the new flounce was straight. "A senseless attitude, and one that leads to immorality," she proclaimed. "I do not know the captain's thoughts, Hannah, but I have no objection. Japheth seems to be a good man, though I wondered whether he could have done more to help the children and Kirana when Dench and Maureen were so cruel."

Hannah flared to Japheth's defence, which spoke volumes. "He and Pranisha did all they could, Mrs Captain, as you will realise if you think about it. Who would have listened to two servants, and both of them native people, against an Englishman? Perhaps if it had just been that Irish floozy, curse her black heart… Japheth spoke to the guard at the fort, and was driven off, and the same at the harbour."

"I did not realise that," Mia commented. "I wonder if the

Captain knows. He looked for Dench, you know. The man has left Cape Town, and taken Maureen with him."

They worked in silence for a few minutes. Mia reloaded her needle with another colour and started to sew buttons on the shirt that Hannah had just completed, cut down from an old one belonging to Jules. Hannah had poured all her passion and love into other people's children. She had been wet nurse and then nanny to Anne Chirbury's daughter Daisy, and then nanny to Anne's twin sons. Mia was grateful Daisy had graduated to a governess, and Hannah had been prepared to leave the boys to their favourite nursemaids to come to South Africa. Jules's children needed her brand of fierce caring far more than the privileged sons of an earl.

"Should you find a man who captures your heart, Hannah" Mia told the nurse, "I would never ask you to choose between him and the children."

Hannah gave a brief nod of acknowledgement. "This pinafore is not much good, Mrs Captain," she said, spreading the offending item so Mia could see all the patches and darns, "but I think there is enough in this breadth to make a chemise for Miss Ada."

So, the subject was closed. Mia took the hint and said nothing more about Japheth or romance that evening.

***

*J*ules had somehow found the time to organise for the military chaplain from the fort to visit Kirana, and he arrived later that afternoon when Mia was reading to her friend. The chaplain was a middle-aged man, balding and running slightly to fat, but with a kind eye.

Jules presented him to Mia. "Mrs Redepenning, may I make known to you Captain Albrooke, chaplain to the 21st Regiment. He has been kind enough to come to see Kirana."

What was the etiquette for introducing a man of the cloth to a mistress? Mia was certain the question had never been covered in any of her conversations with her mentors. She would have to behave according to her own best instincts, and hope she did not offend the man. "Captain Albrooke, thank you for coming. Please. Take my seat." She rose, putting the book to one side "Kirana, my dear, Jules and I will be close by if you need us. Captain Albrooke, you may be wondering how to address my friend. Mrs Redepenning would be acceptable, or Mrs Kirana, if you prefer."

Jules held the door for Mia, followed after her, and closed it not quite shut behind them. From inside the room they could hear the low hum of the chaplain's voice, punctuated by Kirana's cough.

"Albrooke was a bit non-plussed," Jules told Mia. "More by your presence than by Kirana's, I suspect. Not many wives would be as charitable, Mia."

Mia shrugged, suppressing the movement part way through. Did Jules notice? Possibly not, but anyone raised as a lady would. Every day in a dozen ways she showed she had not absorbed the thousands of tiny rules of Society with her mother's milk. Ladies did not shrug, or slouch, or skip, or shout, or saunter, or stride, or… she couldn't think of another 's' word, but she was sure she could create a list of 'do nots' for every letter of the alphabet.

"Kirana had the prior claim, Jules." Thinking about holding her body straight and still, she failed to guard her tongue. "I have never counted your relationship with *her* as a breach of your vows." She would have caught back the last sentence, with its emphatic stress on the word 'her', but it was too late.

Jules was looking out of the window into the courtyard below, where Hannah was sitting with the two girls, reading them a book. But he heard the emphasis, for his head jerked around and she felt the burn of his blue gaze as he examined the flush that swept her face.

She bit her lip, but the words were said, and they were true.

"But you do count other relationships?" he asked. She was not deceived by the light conversational tone; not when the search beam of those eyes still stripped her soul bare.

"I daresay you think it presumptuous of me." She could offer that much, though she herself did not think it presumptuous. He had acted in honour when he made sure she knew, before they married, that he intended to return to his mistress, and so she accepted that as a codicil to the vows they had exchanged in their hasty wedding. No exception for her, and only one for him.

"Not presumptuous at all." Jules sounded tired all of a sudden, and her indignation evaporated. What a homecoming this had been for the poor man. "You are the one person on earth with the right to comment. And Kirana, perhaps, but she has never complained."

Again, Mia spoke before her brain could censor her tongue. "You might be a better man if she had."

He turned back to the window and his voice was dry as he replied, "You will undoubtedly amend her lapse. You've got yourself a poor bargain, Mia. I told you before I married you that I was not the Sir Galahad type. I'm no saint, either. Don't expect me to be; I'll only disappoint you."

The door to the bedchamber opened. "Mrs Kirana Redepenning will sleep now," Captain Albrooke said. "If I may, I will call again in a few days."

"Of course," Mia agreed. "Kirana will appreciate that."

Jules carried the man off to his study for a drink and Mia set a maid to watching Kirana then went in search of a task, preferably one that involved punching things.

***

*H*er dratted tongue! Mia was fretting about it the next day, as they sat in Kirana's room while she slept. Jules had set up his portable desk on the table under one of the windows, and was attending to correspondence, and Mia was mending a long seam that Adiratna had managed to tear in her pinafore the previous day.

Jules was back to being politely distant, and Mia had no idea how to bridge the gap. She couldn't change how she felt, or lie about it. In his class, marital inconstancy was widely accepted as normal, as long as women were discreet. Men could be as flagrant as they liked and still welcomed in Society. That attitude was not for Mia. To her, a promise, and one, furthermore, made before God, could not be shelved as inconvenient. Still, if she wanted a proper marriage, she might have to accept the kind of philandering her sister-in-law Susan had regally ignored from her own naval captain husband. Mia did not think she could manage it.

Hannah's arrival was a welcome interruption to increasingly miserable thoughts. "I hear tell Mr van der Meir has a new shipment of cotton, Mrs Captain," she said. "Buttons and ribbons too. I'd like to go take a look before the rest of the colony picks it over. Could I leave the girls with the maids? And could I have Fortune to carry my bundles?"

"Excellent," Mia said. "If I come too, Hannah, could we manage the girls? They would enjoy helping to choose the materials for their own dresses."

Jules put his paperwork down on the desk. "You plan new dresses for the girls?"

"And new under things and night rails. I have let Marsha's hems down as far as I can, and Ada has patches and mends on everything she owns."

Jules frowned. Was he upset about the girls' neglected appearance or Mia's plans to amend it? Should she reassure him she had her own money? That said, the income from investing a portion of the generous allowance he had made her since they wed was not precisely her own. In theory, he could claim the lot.

"Why don't we all go?" he suggested. "Three escorts to carry your parcels and ensure your safety. Mrs Redepenning, I have not yet replaced the money stolen from the safe. I suggest we call by the bank and make sure the manager knows you have my authority to draw on anything you might need."

So, they set out for the bank, where Fortune and Hannah stayed under the portico with the children while Jules and Mia went inside. "I do have money," Mia said, as they waited for the manager to be summoned. "You have always given me far more than I needed, and I have quite a bit saved." Would he approve of her investing most of those savings? All investing held some risk, but she researched the opportunities carefully, and took advice from her more experienced relatives in law. She did not put all her eggs in one basket, either; if one venture failed, she had several others to fall back on.

"Good for you," Jules said. "But anything you've managed to put aside is yours, Mia. We are not poor, and I can afford to keep my wife and my children in style. If you spend everything in this account, I have more. Other accounts in England and investments. I should make you familiar with our financial affairs, Mia, in case you have to take over their management."

In case he died, he meant. She shivered. How dreadful if anything happened to this magnificent man.

The manager arrived, full of apologies for the delay. Mia expected Jules to open an account for her own use, instead of which he instructed the manager to make Mia free of the main account, which contained a staggering balance. "My wife has my full confidence," he said, "and you are to regard her wishes as my own."

<hr>

The warehouse was bustling. The rumour must have flown from maid to maid right through the colony, and more than one household had stirred itself to see what was on offer. Jules watched as Mia and Hannah efficiently quartered the room, surveyed the entire selection and narrowed in on bolts of cloth they considered suitable for the girls.

He, Dan, and Fortune trailed behind, ready to lift a bolt at a command, or to carry one up to the table where harried servants were cutting the required lengths. "This one will make shirts for you and Perdana, as well as pinafores for the girls," Mia told him, selecting a fat bolt of crisp white. "We will take it all, Captain." She turned back to his daughter, who was rubbing fabric between two fingers in imitation of her adored Ibu Mia. "Adiratna, that appears to be an excellent quality, and just right for an everyday gown. Do you prefer the mauve flowers or the cerise?"

Ada looked from one dainty floral print to the other, her brow creased, and Jules said, in a whisper in case he was treading on some motherly taboo of which he was not aware, "Why not both?"

Not quiet enough, for Ada spun to turn pleading orbs on Mia, who replied, "If she wishes, but she is having five everyday dresses, Captain, and may prefer more variety in their pattern."

Ada nodded at that but her eyes lit up at another thought, and she signalled to Marsha, who hurried over. "I could get the mauve," Ada said, "and you the cerise." Her sister thought this an excellent idea, and soon Jules was carrying both fabrics to the cutting bench with an order for ten yards of each.

They did the same with the two dresses that Mia decreed each girl would need 'for best', selecting a single pattern and two different colours. After that Mia and Hannah moved on to the trims and fastenings. Male strength no longer needed, Jules sent Fortune back to the house for the buggy, and he and Dan retreated to one corner of the room to stand over their packages.

It was there Gerta van Klief found him. She minced over using her parasol as a walking stick and—ignoring Dan—stood far too close for a married man to feel comfortable. When had Jules developed a preference for small slender ladies, who kept their charms discreetly covered? He was surprised to discover a new inclination for letting his imagination supply what his senses could not provide. He had been celibate for far too long, but Gerta did not set his pulse pounding the way one glance from his wife did.

"Why, Captain," she hummed, the musical tones that had once intrigued him now sounding forced and artificial. "I did not expect to see you here. Are you planning presents, perhaps?"

She tipped her head coyly to one side and smiled sweetly, an expression at odds with her calculating eyes. What had he ever seen in her?

"Mrs van Klief. I was not aware you intended to travel to Cape Town."

She laughed, another practiced and false sound. "That doesn't sound at all welcoming, dear Captain." She walked her fingers up his chest and dropped her voice half an octave. "Let us find somewhere more private to… chat, Captain." Her whole demeanour changed as she half turned to address a glowering Dan. "Boy! Watch your master's packages. Be sure not to lose anything." She dropped her voice to a purr again. "You must count your packages before we leave, dear Captain, so the boy here doesn't sell some of them."

Jules's distaste turned to active dislike. They'd had an off again–on again affair for three years, and the woman still didn't know the first thing about him. Mia's disgust at his fornicating was well deserved.

"Good day, Mrs Van Klief," he said in dismissal, "I am not free for a… chat. My son and I are attending our ladies."

He turned from the spite he could see forming in her eyes, and caught sight of a face he knew. So, his old captain was still in town? He was taking a great deal of interest in Jules's conversation with Gerta, which was at that moment interrupted by Jules's daughters. They converged on him to take a hand each. Hannah and Mia then passed the widow, one on each side, turning to flank the girls.

"Jules, darling, you are here with your family," Gerta crowed with every evidence of delight. "Aren't they charming?" She narrowed her eyes at Mia, elegant in London fashions that made every other lady in the room appear poorly dressed. "You didn't tell me you had an English daughter, Jules. Do introduce us."

Mia's smile managed to be both gracious and feral. "Yes. Do present your acquaintance, dear Captain." In the last two words, she reproduced Gerta's tone and accent precisely, showing she had heard more of the conversation than was comfortable.

"The woman is of no account, Mrs Redepenning," Jules replied. "Have you finished your shopping?"

Gerta flushed scarlet at the snub.

After one swift look of compassion at Gerta, Mia answered Jules. "Not quite, Captain. Our daughters need your arbitration. They both want the same ribbons, and they insist only you can make the decision."

"Please, Papa," Ada begged, and on the other side, Marsha echoed the plea.

"How dare you?" Gerta's loud voice silenced the room, as people craned to see what was going on. "After all we have been to one another? How can you treat me like this, Jules? I have given you…"

Mia interrupted before Jules could blister the infernal woman. "A word of advice, Mrs van Klief. In British society—and the Cape colony has become British—a woman of breeding does not confront her lover in public, and certainly not in front of his wife and children." Her own voice was pitched to reach the avid onlookers. At some level beyond his anger and his embarrassment, he admired her strategy.

"It is a matter of self-protection," she explained, kindly. "However unfair it might be, going public with revelations about irregular relationships always leads to more censure for the woman than for the man." She dropped her voice, but not enough to prevent the audience from hearing every crisp word. "Believe me, I understand why you feel bereaved, but you must have known your lover was a married man, Mrs van Klief. Your arrangement was never going to last."

Was Gerta bereaved? Jules looked at her sharply. It had just been about the physical encounter, had it not? For both of them? Then, for Gerta, there was the value of his gifts, of course. Her husband had left her with little, and the presents of her lovers made up the shortfall between genteel poverty and comfortable living.

But the widow met his eyes, her own bleak.

"Goodbye, Mrs van Klief," he said firmly, unwilling to give her any reason to think he might soften.

She looked from him to Mia and back again. Her shoulder sank, and her gaze dropped. Without another word, she turned and stalked off, beckoning as she went to a coloured maid who hurried to follow. Captain Hackett met her at the door, and she took his arm as they left the building.

What was that about?

Mia regarded Jules with a grave stare. All four females, and Dan, too, were looking at Jules in much the same way.

"She was not very nice," Ada pronounced, firmly.

"Young ladies do not comment on the behaviour of adults," Hannah commented, though it was clear her heart was not in the rebuke.

Jules was pleased to see Fortune at the door. "Shall we take a look at the ribbons?" he asked. "Fortune has brought the buggy, so we can send all our purchases home and walk back, if you wish."

The girls were distracted from the nasty scene, and led him to view their choices. Mia followed behind, but he doubted her thoughts had been so easily diverted. If Gerta had set out to put a rift between him and his wife, he feared she had achieved her objective.

9

Mia sat at her dressing table, clothed in just her night rail, while the maid Maria brushed her hair. Her reflection in the mirror was not reassuring. Even Kirana, wasted by the disease that was killing her, had more curves. Maureen had been bountifully endowed. As for the van Klief woman, it was a wonder she could walk without falling out of her dress and causing a public riot.

The surge of spite shamed her. It was not that woman's fault that she herself was so deficient in feminine assets. She had learned to dress to make the most of what she had. No one any longer mistook her for a child. However, dressed in nothing but a shapeless layer of thin cotton, the truth was plain to see. How could she hope to attract a man like Jules, one who clearly preferred women with large breasts?

She dismissed the maid, and knelt to say her prayers, trying to keep her mind on the familiar words that her tongue knew well enough to shape while her mind ran its well-trodden groove, fretting about her marriage and her husband.

When she had set out from England, she had been confident she could negotiate a business-like arrangement with a man who she was sure could not possibly be as attractive and appealing as she remembered. She had decided she would be a comfortable wife, ignore his affairs and not expect anything beyond his respect in public. She would nurture his children (those he'd had with Kirana and those she would bear him) and to ease the transition, she would have his financial support.

Instead she was confronted by his physical reality. It blew her sideways. His gentleness and affection toward Kirana and the children confounded all her attempts to keep an emotional distance. The trust he reposed in her after the misunderstandings of the first few days left her yearning for the kind of marriage her sisters-in-law, Ella and Mary, enjoyed with Jules's brothers.

I have fallen in love with my husband, she admitted to herself as she slid between the sheets, *and he is a philanderer with a taste for big-breasted women. I can never let him know how I feel.*

It was a long time before she slept, and when she did the nightmare was waiting—the one that had haunted her for years.

In her dream, she was trapped in the dark with the corpse of her father, alone but for the scuttering of rats, knowing that worse was to come. In her dream, the smugglers were coming to fetch her to use her for their own evil purposes. At some level, even in her dream, she remembered that, in reality, she had not been alone. Jules had supported her and saved her. But when the nightmare descended, reality was no comfort as the darkness pressed in on her, the dead weight of her father's cold hand grew stiff in hers, and the smugglers crept closer.

⁕

The sound woke Jules. In the next room, Mia was whimpering. He was out of his bed and halfway across the room before his brain caught up and started to argue with his intentions. He shouldn't invade her bedroom. If she was weeping about the encounter yesterday, she wouldn't want his attention. He stopped to listen. Fear in the sound, as well as sorrow, drove him forward. Something terrifying was in the room with her, but the locked door still stood between them. He'd go around through the reception rooms then.

He had taken two steps out into the entrance hall when he remembered he was naked and turned back to catch up his robe, then hastened his steps to his wife's door, grabbing a carved club from Borneo that lay on a side table in case whatever awaited needed to be subdued.

He found Mia's bedchamber was deserted except for the lady herself, curled in a tight ball on top of crumpled linens, trapped in some nightmare.

He shrugged into his robe before he gathered her onto his lap, his arms around her, soothing her as he would any of his children, murmuring in her ear and stroking her back. She struggled at first but then turned into him, clinging to him with quiet desperation.

"It's all right, Mia. I have you. You're safe," he reassured her, and she gave a deep sigh and relaxed.

He sat back against the pillows, his sleeping wife draped over him, continuing his gentle strokes. The thin cotton of her night rail did nothing to hide the elegance of her shoulder and back, the gentle flair of her hips below the tiny waist. His mind was going where it shouldn't. Time to leave. But when he tried to move her from his arms, she clutched at him. "She is received everywhere," she insisted. "How was I to know he had paid her to lure me into the garden? You believe me, Lord Henry, do you not?" What memory was she reliving? His anger at his father, who had clearly failed to protect Mia, was nothing to his wrath with himself. She was his to defend, and he had abandoned her.

He subsided, giving up the effort to escape, and even in her sleep she sensed his surrender, because she relaxed and wriggled without waking, bending her knee so the buttock nearest him slipped down into the dip between his thighs. Compassion turned to lust with frightening speed. It would be so easy to open the front of his robe, to lift the hem of her night rail, to bring flesh to flesh. He stilled his hands, bit his tongue, and looked up at the ceiling. It would be a long night.

Twice more in the night he tried to leave her, and both times she was hit by another nightmare before he could cross the room to the door. He was reasonably certain that one took her back to the smugglers' cave where he first met her, because she called out for her father, tears streaming down her cheeks. The other was something to do with a baron. "You're dead, baron," she hissed, brave enough to stand up to the monster even as she trembled and her heart pounded so fast, he feared it would burst out of her chest. "Don't let him," she begged, when Jules hurried back to her side. "Don't leave me alone with him. Please, George." Who the hell was George? A lover?

Not his business. The knowledge he was not in a position to complain did not stop the wild surge of jealousy, but it would help him to subdue it, at least where Mia was concerned. He had no such confidence he could keep from throttling the 'he' in the gardens, the anonymous baron, and this George, if he could get his hands on them.

He couldn't blame Mia if she'd succumbed to the sharks that prowled the edges of Society, always on the hunt for fresh blood. He could and would blame them, and he dwelt on their punishment at his hands to take his mind off the warm and fragrant woman in his arms, completely oblivious to the painfully hard male organ on which she lay.

As dawn began to lighten the window, she stirred, and all of a sudden went still and rigid, so he wasn't surprised at the tone in which she demanded, "Captain! What are you doing?" He let her wriggle away until she was crouched at the foot of the bed, vibrating with outrage.

Attack was often the best form of defence. "Do you often have nightmares, Mia? You had four last night. At least one, I think, was about the smugglers' cave and your father."

Most of the tension went out of her shoulders. She picked up a silk shawl that was draped over the end of the bed, and wrapped it around her shoulders to hide her slender form.

"I am sorry," Mia said. "I didn't mean to wake you."

Jules dismissed such nonsense with a wave of his hand. "I am your husband," he pointed out. "How often do these nightmares occur?"

"Not often, now," she assured him. "Just when I am tired or upset."

"As you were after encountering Mrs van Klief." He was right. It *was* his fault.

Mia didn't deny it. "Thank you for coming to my rescue. You cannot have had a comfortable night."

"A very uncomfortable one, given where you were lying," he teased, waving towards his groin. "Would you like to help make it better?"

Even as the words left his mouth, he reassessed his deduction that she had willingly surrendered her virginity to a lover. Her eyes, wide and disbelieving, were fixed on the vicinity of his lower torso, where the tented robe hid the roused beast beneath, without disguising its intent. Two red spots burning on her cheeks were the only colour on a suddenly blanched face.

"I— I—" she croaked.

He took pity. "I was teasing, Mia. I thought… I see I was wrong." He flicked the edge of the sheet up to hide the evidence that Mia's reaction had not changed his rebel body's mind. Too long without a woman. That was his trouble.

Mia frowned, thinking that over, and then her eyes widened. He had forgotten how quick she was. "You mean—you thought I had… that is, you believed I was no longer a—" she dropped her voice to a whisper— "a maid?"

"I have no right to expect you to have retained your virginity," he told her bluntly. "Have you?" If she was a virgin, he would need to slow down. If she had been raped, it could be a long time before she trusted him enough to… She didn't have the demeanour, the fear of men and the unwillingness to trust he'd seen before in women who had been forced, but the nightmare pointed in that direction.

She lifted her chin, proud as a queen. "I have kept to the vows I made at my wedding. I am a virgin."

"I'm flattered, then." Exultant, which he had not expected.

Something primitive inside him roaring its approval; he was the only man who would have her. Nervous, too, for he'd never bedded a virgin. Slow and gentle. That would be the key. For her sake, he could manage slow and gentle.

"No need." She had recovered her poise and the sardonic tone was back. "I did it for me. If I make a promise, I expect to keep it. A middle-class view of morality, I have been told, Captain, by men who would swear their word was their bond. That dictum applies only when the word is given to another gentleman, apparently."

Jules winced at the acidic assessment. "You must despise me."

Mia widened her eyes in surprise. "Not you, Jules. I knew when we married that you had a prior commitment." She blushed again, and wrinkled her brow in momentary thought, then made up her mind to say what she had been holding back.

"I have always known about Kirana, and I thought it only fair that you counted your responsibility to her and your children above a vow to the child I was then. But…" she stopped, closing her lips firmly, and Jules found his eyes riveted on the movement.

This would not do. He couldn't listen to her as he ought when her body was driving him insane.

"Mia, we need to talk. Yesterday, when you spoke of children, I hoped you meant you wanted a future with me. It's what I want, too, but I think we need to face the past first."

His, mostly, and the women he'd dallied with, but hers, too. He had to know what had happened to make her whimper in the night. Who the hell was George?

Mia heaved a sigh, and Jules managed to keep his eyes from dropping to her breasts, rising and falling under the silk wrap. "I do want a future with you, Jules. I— I do not know what that might mean."

"Ask me what you need to know, and I will do the same. Not yet, though. We should get washed and dressed, and see how Kirana is. Then, shall we shut ourselves in the withdrawing room upstairs and be honest with one another?"

Mia nodded. "Let me make sure the children are well and that the household is running smoothly for the day. I shall order us some food and drink, so we can break our fast together." The blushing maiden was hidden, the efficient matron back in control. It was worth remembering that she calmed when given a task to manage.

Jules wriggled to the edge of the bed and swung his legs over, holding the silk ties closed to keep from scandalising his virgin wife. "May I use the door between our bedchambers?" he asked. Ah. His blushing maiden was back again. She followed his eyes to the key in the lock, and her colour deepened.

"Of course."

A knock on the other door had her eyes flying wide with alarm. "That will be Rosa, come with the water for my morning wash," she said, her voice low. "Go, Jules, please."

Jules crossed the room in four swift strides, and had turned the key by the time the handle dipped.

"One moment, Rosa," Mia called, and the handle returned to horizontal.

"Give me thirty minutes," Jules told her, as he opened the door. Ten to deal to his raging lust, before he had to spend more time with his wife while keeping his hands off her, and twenty to wash and dress.

<hr>

*M*ia had coffee served to Kirana's room, hoping it would help soothe her dull headache. She always had one after a bout of nightmares, though today's was relatively mild. Jules had called her back out of the terror, had held her, had stayed with her while she slept.

He'd wanted her. She blushed again at the memory of his clear state of arousal and her reaction to it. She shouldn't build too much upon that, she reminded herself. Men were not known for being discriminating when they'd been without a bed partner for a while.

"Thoughtful today?" Kirana commented, and Mia jerked her mind back from the pictures her wandering imagination had presented, to pay attention to her friend.

Kirana weakened by the day, each breath a struggle, each bout of coughing a racking torture for both the sick women and those who watched. "Much better," she always said, when asked how she felt. Since the doctor's visit, she refused to allow the children further into her room than the doorway, and then only in the evening, to say goodnight, so Mia had already visited the nursery so she could report on their wellbeing.

"Marsha has already covered several sheets with pictures of the dresses she wants made from the cotton we bought yesterday," she told Kirana, "Ada wants a dress for each of her dolls to match every dress we make for her. Dan says that if all the girls can talk about is dresses, he is going back to his bedchamber to read his book." She wondered if they could find another boy of the same age for him to spend time with. The girls had each other, but Perdana was older, and a boy, besides. She would talk to Jules. Perhaps one of the other captains had a family?

Once she had the children back in England, she was confident that the status of the Redepennings and their friends and relatives would ensure the vast bulk of Society would accept her newly acquired children and pretend complete unawareness of their illegitimate origins. Cape Town was smaller and more parochial. It was also a port. She had observed before, in England, that the wickedness that went hand-in-hand with being a port town caused those who wanted to be considered respectable to eschew any hint of scandal and avoid those whose status carried any hint of irregularity.

Jules joined them after a while, distracting her from her thoughts. How did he manage to look so wonderful after such an uncomfortable night? He, too, had looked in on the nursery. "The girls tell me they are spending the day sewing with Hannah and Ibu Mia," he reported. "Lessons first, Hannah says. I have promised Dan that, after he finishes his lessons, I will take him to visit my friend Fletcher, which will get him out of your hair, Mia. Have you really promised to teach him Greek?"

"And Latin," Mia told him. "He is ahead of his age in arithmetic and calculus, but——even if you intend him for a naval career

—he should have a background in classical scholarship that matches that of the other officers."

Jules shook his head, and for a moment she thought he would forbid the lessons. "I have been taking him with me because he is lonely here, without a boy of his own age. Also, the household was under stress enough once Raquib and Jwala left. He is not bound to the navy."

Kirana squeezed Mia's hand, and nodded, a small smile curving her lips. "Good," Mia said, for both of them. "We worry every time you go to sea, especially in war time. He might choose it for himself, of course."

"That's the other thing," Jules commented. "The war will be over by the time he has a chance of climbing up the ranks, and the rungs above him will be crowded with seasoned officers. Still room for people with a passion for it, but he has several years to decide. I would love for him to have the education you propose, and perhaps school once he has caught up with his fellows?"

"Eton?" Mia suggested. "He has cousins at Eton."

"If they get on, that'd be good. My cousin Rede was in the same year as my other cousin, George. Viscount Longford, he was then, and he certainly made sure people knew he was an earl's heir. Tosser. I beg your pardon, ladies."

That opinion of George appeared to be near universal in the family, and Mia could understand it, given what she'd heard about his behaviour. He had died a year after she entered the family, but she remembered him for his kindness when she most needed it. She ignored her husband's lapse into slang. "Rick's and Mary's second boy would be closest in age and their eldest son is at Eton, too. They are both nice boys, Jules. The youngest, and Susan's Michael, are still educated at home."

She had no difficulty interpreting Kirana's hand squeeze. The smile said it all, and Mia leaned closer to kiss the sick woman's cheek. "We will raise them in our family, Kirana. Jules's father has promised, and so have his brothers and his sister. You do not need to fear for them."

"Except for…" Kirana laid a hand on her chest, and even that movement set her coughing again.

Mia held her and handed her the clothes to catch the blood, and Jules was ready with a damp cloth to wash her face when she subsided at last back onto the pillows. "We will watch them, Kirana," he said, solemnly. "I promise. At the first sign of anything wrong with their lungs, they will have the best doctors in the United Kingdom."

Mia took up the theme. "They will be strong. Our sister Ella says those who live in the country, with good food, fresh air, and lots of outdoor exercise, are far less susceptible to the disease and more likely to survive it. We will make sure the girls are strong, Kirana. I promise."

Kirana smiled again and nodded, a slight movement of her head. "Love you," she mouthed, looking from one to the other. She closed her eyes, pushing both of their hands away from her. "Go."

She would sleep a little, perhaps, or drift in that space between waking and sleeping where she spent most of her day. Mia bent to kiss her again, and on the other side Jules did the same.

As they left the bed chamber, Jules took Mia's hand. He said nothing, but his sombre face spoke for him. "Not long," she answered the unspoken question.

"I am back to sea at the end of next week," he said. "If she… If I am not here when it happens… We need to talk about that, too, Mia."

She gave his hand a squeeze. "We will. We will talk about it all."

His smile was sad. "We. I like the sound of that word." He lifted her hand to kiss it, then let it go. "Go and see to whatever needs your attention. I will meet you in the withdrawing room in…?"

"Fifteen minutes," she replied. "Food, fresh coffee, and our questions for one another."

"Fifteen minutes, then."

10

Mia was pouring Jules's coffee when he joined her in the withdrawing room, closing the door behind him. He took a seat and began lifting the lids on the serving dishes to see what was inside.

"Pranisha is a treasure," Mia commented. "She would like to come to England with us, by the way. Japheth, too, though I suspect that is as much for Hannah's sake as for the children's."

That fetched a hard stare from those blue blue eyes. "Japheth and Hannah? Do I need to warn Japheth off, Mia?"

She laughed. "Hannah can do any warning off necessary; I assure you. She shows no signs of wishing to do so, however." Hannah softened when Japheth spoke to her; leaned towards him like a flower to the light. Grief had shadowed her eyes for five years since the death of her betrothed, and Mia was glad to see those shadows lifting.

"You approve of this romance?" Jules did not look at her as he served himself from several of the dishes. His voice was neutral. Was he one of those who thought servants should not be permitted to marry? Or was it that Hannah was English and Japheth a coloured ex-slave? Certainly, Mia's one attempt to attend church with the children here in Cape Town had ended with the pastor asking her not to bring them with her again. She had never gone back. Jules would have to be an awful hypocrite to be of that mind.

"I see nothing against their marriage," Mia said. "Indeed, if servants are happy in their lives, they are more likely to be happy in their work, I think. I will not interfere if Hannah and Japheth wish to marry." She spooned a spicy rice and vegetable mix onto her own plate.

Jules raised an eyebrow. "Romances do not necessarily bring happiness to the lovers," he commented, "and the dramas that result can reverberate through the whole ship. Household, in this instance."

"You only have men on your ships," Mia pointed out.

Jules coloured. "Some men prefer… Have you never heard…? Suffice it to say that I have observed such dramas, lady wife."

Oh. Mia blushed, too. She knew a couple of women who lived together in an intimate friendship, but had not realised that men might do likewise. For a moment, her mind drifted to the mechanics of the act, as she understood them. How did…? She pulled her mind from the direction it had tried to travel.

"You allow it?"

It is not legal, but one can't stop it, so I've always thought it better to ignore it, as long as both parties are willing."

"I have no wish to stop whatever is developing between our servants, and will deal with any dramas that may result, Jules."

He gave one short nod and a slight smile. "I notice you do not object to them being of different races. You know Japheth was born a slave right here in the colony's Slave House? I freed him when I hired him, but that was only three years ago." He was making prodigious inroads into his food.

"Why should I object?" Mia asked. "My own new children are part Batavian and part Dutch, as well as half-English." There. Let him answer that.

He merely smiled, and abandoned the subject of Hannah and Japheth. "I cannot begin to tell you how grateful I am. You've looked after Kirana. You got rid of Dench and Maureen. The way you've accepted the children— I've said it before, but it bears repeating."

She rejected his thanks with a shake of her head. "I did it for Kirana, and for their own sake. They are delightful children, Jules. I love them already." She took another mouthful from her own plate.

Jules put his knife and fork down, side by side on the plate, which he pushed away. He leaned forward. "I know it was not for my sake. I have given you little reason to respect or even like me. I am grateful, nonetheless."

"Is this when our conversation turns awkward?" She took a last mouthful and lined up her own cutlery, avoiding his eyes.

"Shall we deal with the easy items, first?" Jules suggested. "One of the reasons I am grateful is that I have been worried about the children. If anything should happen to me… They have no one else. My will leaves guardianship to my father, and I am sure he would take up the charge. But he does not know them, Mia, and they do not know him."

Mia could at least reassure him on that point. "He is looking forward to meeting them; all the family wants to know your children, Jules. They will arrive in England to a warm welcome, do not doubt that."

"Nonetheless, it eases my mind to know they will be in your care." He stood and gestured to the sofa, and she accepted the hand he offered and allowed him to conduct her there.

He sat beside her, reaching for her hand. "I cannot name a woman as sole guardian; the law will not allow it. However, if you approve, I would like to change my will to give you custody of the children if I die."

The tartness of her response had more to do with his proximity than with the subject matter. "I would prefer you to live, but it is wise to make provision." He was making an effort, and she could meet him part way. "Yes, I approve. While you are making the change, would you consider naming an additional guardian for the children's safety? Your father is not getting younger."

Jules straightened, lifting his far-too-perfect chin in alarm. "He is ill?"

She was quick to reassure him. "Lord Henry is in good health, as are you. I am merely being cautious."

He relaxed again, allowing his spine to bend but not releasing her hand. He was stroking it with his thumb—a disturbing distraction. "One of my brothers, then? Rick or Alex, since they are already family men."

Mia considered tugging her hand away so she could concentrate, but it seemed such a little thing to make a fuss about. He was, after all, her husband. "Why not both?" she suggested. "Rick is often at sea, so Alex and your father can make decisions if he is not available."

Jules said, firmly, "I plan for you to have complete authority in how you raise the children, so they will only be called on to make decisions if you are not available. You may consult whomever you will, of course." The thumb continued to wreak its sensory havoc. Was he aware of what he was doing to her? "Guardianship is for the legal side of it—for protection. I should tell you that it may be needed."

That was alarming enough to attract Mia's full attention. "Surely, if the family accepts the circumstances of the children's birth, they are the only ones who need to know. Others may speculate, but they will not be so ill-bred or foolish to challenge the entire Redepenning family and all our connections to our faces." Susan would eviscerate anyone who tried, and Jules's godmother, the Duchess of Haverford, would scatter their ashes. Metaphorically speaking, of course. In a social sense.

"You have more experience of Society than I," Jules admitted, "and if you say people will accept the children, I must believe you. I have another concern, however." He paused and looked down at their linked hands for a moment before continuing. "You may remember I gave you my reasons for taking Dan to sea with me."

Another pause. He lifted her hand and set it on his thigh before beginning the insidiously pleasant stroking again. "There was another. A man. Captain Jedediah Hackett. He wants Dan. I refused him once. I thought he might come during my absence and try again."

The image that flashed before Mia's mind, Jules's revelation about ship-board romances still in her mind, was of the maid that she and Anne had cared for after the poor child had been imprisoned and abused by a local baron. "Wants him for what?"

Jules patted her captive hand. "Not what you're thinking. Hackett wants to claim Dan as his son."

"His son?" Mia frowned. "But Dan is your son."

Her husband nodded; his eyes sombre. "In my heart, yes. From the moment he was born. I was not present, however, for his conception. I had better tell you the whole sad and sordid tale."

"If you wish," Mia agreed.

He sat back, the hand not occupied with hers flung along the back of the sofa, clearly preparing for a long story. "I told you long ago, I think, that I first met Kirana when the British invaded Ceylon to throw out the Dutch, in 1795."

Mia nodded, and Jules continued.

"Hackett was in the Navy then, and I was an officer under his command. He and I rescued a girl from some rioting soldiers—the daughter of a Dutch merchant and his Batavian mistress. She was fourteen, Mia, just a child. When Hackett said he would take her home to her family, I believed him. After all, he was a married man, and more than old enough to be her father."

Fourteen! Mia had still been fourteen when she was captured by smugglers. They had planned to sell her into a brothel, and one of them had taken pleasure in describing what would happen to her there. She shivered, and Jules squeezed her hand.

"He lied?" she asked.

Jules nodded. "I didn't find out for eight years, until I was once again in Ceylon. The fool who was governor at the time decided to invade the Highlands—the Kingdom of Kandy. The Kandians threw off the invaders and chased them back into British territory. Mine was one of the ships carrying the relief forces needed to protect the colony from the consequences of the governor's stupidity."

"And you met Kirana again," she guessed. That would have

been two years before she met Jules, a second fourteen-year-old in danger but the same knight errant riding to the rescue.

"Her and her children," Jules confirmed, "and in similar circumstances to the last time."

Poor Kirana. "Rioting soldiers?"

"She was living in a house on the coast about half an hour out of Colombo. She told me later that Hackett had, at first, set her up in Colombo itself. But when he left the Navy to become a merchant, his wife travelled out from England to join him. She insisted that she could not live in the same town as his mistress, so he removed Kirana a short distance away. When the Kandian troops invaded, he refused to take her back to Colombo for fear of upsetting his wife."

Jules's voice had risen with his indignation and he was squeezing her hand hard enough to hurt. She could not suppress a squeak and he flinched and loosened his grasp, lifting her hand to kiss it. "I'm sorry. It just… Mia, he left two small children and a heavily pregnant mistress, and scuttled back to Colombo to save his own skin."

Mia had been working sums in her head. "1803. The child she carried was Dan."

Jules nodded. "Yes. He was born a few hours after I arrived. Hackett—I met him in Colombo— told me how relieved he was the Kandians had been stopped. Another couple of miles, he said, and his poor mistress might have been in danger. He left the women in a battle zone, and I knew what troops were capable of after a battle. I told him he should get out there and make sure she was safe. He refused, so I went myself."

"And you saved them," Mia said, without any doubt in her mind. "Where are the other children?" *Two little children, Jules had said, and neither of them here now. Neither of them ever mentioned by Kirana in any of her letters.* "Not dead," she added, but without much hope of being right.

Jules pressed his lips together, as if to prevent the rest of the story from escaping, then sighed and continued. "Before I got there, rioting troops—British troops, Mia—invaded the house. Kirana escaped into the jungle with her children, and hid there, while they looted and trashed. And that's not the worst of it."

He shook his head. "I arrived in time to save Kirana, but too late for the children. The soldiers had found her and dragged her out to make sport of her."

His eyes were staring into nothing, his face as bleak as his voice. "The children—they must have tried to go to their mother and made some sound. The soldiers shot into the bushes. They didn't check first to see that the assassins they feared were only two little children. I wanted to kill them then and there, Mia, but Kirana was prostrate with grief, and she had begun childbirth. I couldn't have them shot down in front of her. I had my men arrest them and lock them in a storeroom that still had an intact door."

He was silent for some time. Mia squeezed his hand, trying to infuse comfort through her touch.

Jules met her eyes, his own flaming with indignation. "You know what Hackett said when I told him what had happened? He asked for his mistress back, cool as you please. I explained she was grieving for the loss of two children, and recovering from the birth of another. He said, and I quote, 'She pays too much attention to those half-bred bastards. It is not a good quality in a mistress.' So, I punched him."

"I'm glad you did," Mia said, fiercely.

That fetched a slight grin. "I only regret they pulled me off before I could kill him."

The grin broadened. "It was at the Admiral's soirée, which was not a good career move. That might have been the end of me if Hackett had still been a naval captain."

He shrugged. "The Board of Inquiry held it was not becoming for a British officer to get into a fight over a loose native woman. Arrogant bastards. But, in the end, I retained my career—if slightly stained. And the gossip was enough to drive Hackett out of Ceylon —not so much for his callous treatment of an innocent girl, but for his cowardice in saving his own skin without lifting a finger to help his mistress and children."

"I'm glad he suffered a little for his actions," Mia told her husband.

He nodded again, in acknowledgement. "So, when he turned up here claiming Dan as his son and demanding that I give him up, I gave him short shrift. Told him and the lawyer he brought with him that there'd be icicles in Hell before I would give him custody of a rabid dog, let alone my son."

Mia approved. "Quite right, too."

"I thought he had left Cape Town, but I saw him recently." Jules looked away, as if seeking counsel from the corner of the room. "He was with Gerta at the warehouse. I suspect he set her up to insult you."

"That is why you were so rude to her! I thought…" Mia did not quite know how to express the disappointment she had felt without disclosing that she had tumbled head over heels back in love with this complicated man. She said, cautiously, "It would be hard to respect a man who could be so rude to someone who had shared intimacies with him, but seeing her with such a man must have made you very angry."

He kissed her hand again, flushing slightly at the implied criticism, but made no comment. His mind was intent on the possible danger to his family. "If he comes back, Mia, I wanted you to be prepared."

She could promise him that. She might be a coward on her own account, but she would face any odds for her family. "If he does, I will deal with him."

"I believe you. I suspect you could deal with anything. You had impressive courage even when we met, Mia, but you have become a formidable woman. I would like to know what has happened to make you so, if you would care to tell me."

Mia had never thought of blue as a warm colour, but his eyes could convince her otherwise. She shifted away, withdrawing her hand from his. He believed her brave, and she must be to capture the future she wanted. "Perhaps, one day. We have other things we must talk about, Jules."

Jules accepted her withdrawal, and put more distance between them by rising to his feet and crossing the room to shift ornaments on the pristine mantelpiece, lining them up in a slightly different configuration. "I think I know the answer to my most important question. You will be a mother to my children. You will protect them, come what may. Do you plan to stay here, in Cape Town?"

Is that what he wanted her to do? No, no second guessing and making decisions she thought would please him. She would speak her mind, and he could then speak his. "I will stay until Kirana… I had thought to take the children home to England. With their mother gone and you away much of the time, they would be better there, I think." His thoughtful nod encouraged her to explain. "Here, they do not have a place to fit. Perhaps when Kirana was well, she had friends with children who could be playmates, but I do not know those connections, and when I take them out in public, I have been roundly snubbed. I can give the cut direct as well as anyone, but I do not wish to subject the children to such hostility."

"You think it will be better for them in England?" Jules didn't wait for her response but answered his own question. "I agree. Even if the sticklers put their noses in the air, the children will have my family. Once Kirana is gone, return to England. I'll talk to the Admiral's Office and ask for you and the children to be given a berth on a homeward bound ship. I'll put in for a posting closer to home and come to see you as soon as I can."

He stared intently at the statuette of a dancing four-armed goddess that he was passing from one hand to another. "That is, if you wish me to. I would like to make our marriage real, Mia."

Jules's uncertainty gave Mia the nerve to open her heart a little further. "That is the third reason I came to Cape Town. Reason one: to look after Kirana. Two: to fetch the children. Three: to see if we could make something of our marriage."

The statuette stopped turning and those blue eyes pierced her. "And your conclusion?"

"I have doubts, Jules," Mia confessed. "I do not want the kind of marriage so common in Society." She took a deep breath. "I thought I could bear it for the sake of children, but that was before I got to know you."

In two quick strides he crossed the room again and knelt at her feet, taking both of her hands in his. "I don't want a Society marriage either, Mia. I want the kind of marriage my mother and father had, the kind Rick and Mary have."

Mia nodded. That was exactly what she wanted. "Yes, and Alex and Ella. Your cousin Rede and his wife, too."

Jules beamed. "There. You see? We Redepenning men make excellent husbands."

"Those who are not rakes," Mia pointed out. George Redepenning had not been marriage material, and by all accounts his father had been a miserable husband.

Jules compressed his lips, then caught her in his gaze again. "I have been thinking about what you said. About our marriage vows. You have kept them, and you had every right to expect me to do the same."

Whatever Mia expected him to say, it wasn't that. "I understood about Kirana."

Jules shook his head. "You should not have had to. I made a promise with every intention of breaking it as soon as I got back to my mistress. I've never thought of myself as dishonourable, but that was not the act of an honourable man."

Mia opened her mouth to reassure him, but Jules interrupted, freeing one hand to hold it up. "No, let me finish." A short bark of a laugh. "I do not often apologise, and I had better get it all out now that I've started, or I might never manage it."

She waited, and he took his own deep breath before continuing. "It never occurred to me that a wife who took in her stride my living with my mistress, would be angry that I was unfaithful with other women. Indeed, I never even thought of myself as married. I remembered the child I left behind. I suppose I knew you had become a woman, but in my mind, you were still a child and so I could not possibly be married at all."

A spurt of irritation at those who thought lack of height equated to immaturity fuelled her response. "This does not sound like an apology."

He shot her something of a grin. "I'm getting there. I haven't had much practice." Amusement fled as he continued. "When I saw your face as we talked to Gerta; when you said, 'Kirana was a codicil to our vows…' Well. I saw myself through your eyes, and I did not much like the view."

Mia responded to his bleak expression. "I am sorry. I did not mean to–"

Again, Jules interrupted. "Precisely the words I should be saying. I'm sorry, Mia. I did not mean to be a cad and a callous idiot. I hope you can find it in your heart to forgive me. I admire you more than I can say, and would like to be a true husband to you."

That was very gratifying, and the sincerity in his eyes went a long way towards melting the barriers she'd erected to protect her heart, but they had to begin with honesty between them. She felt compelled to point out the flaw in his reasoning. "If you did not regard yourself as married, then I am not the only one you owe an apology to."

Jules frowned, bewildered. "But I did not behave as a husband should."

"You still don't understand." Mia would have to explain it to him. "I knew you were not acting as my husband. You were honest before we wed: I knew someone else had first call on your affections. I thought you would be faithful to her."

The source of some of her hurt was her own gullibility. "All these years, I have ignored the stories I've heard about your women. People will gossip, and they exaggerate."

"I am sorry —" Jules said again.

Mia rejected his apology a second time. "It is my fault, not yours. I have often been told I have middle-class sensibilities." She needed him to understand, though she was only just beginning to know the depths of her own error. "I made a fairy tale in my mind. You ignored me, but that was to be expected because you were devoted to your great love, and all the time, you were carrying on with maids and widows. Kirana expected it, and I should have too. That I didn't—I was stupid. I'm sorry to make such a fuss about it, but I *am* middle class, and I don't understand such things."

Jules's brows almost joined in the furrow above his nose. "Mia, what do you want me to say?"

"Nothing." She was still not getting her message across. "This is not about you, Jules. I am the one who ignored anything that didn't fit the picture I created of you. Now that I have met you, I need time to adjust." She patted the hand that still held hers. "If it helps, I mostly like you."

That earned her another quirk of the lips, amusement pointed at himself, she thought. "I mostly like you, too, though I dislike the mirror you hold up to me." He rose to pace again, then turned from the other side of the room to say, "It wasn't—it will lower me still further in your esteem, but I don't want to lie to you. Me and Kirana: it was never the love story you imagined. She had nowhere to go, so I rented a house for her. Kirana was grateful, and I…"

He let his words trail off, but she knew the rest. She was available, and he was a man, which was precisely what Mia feared. Jules might want her now, but what about when she was not available?

She retrieved her hands from his, and he did not try to cling to them. He was still talking about Kirana. "I have become very fond of her; that much is true."

"Yes, I can see that," Mia reassured him. She had thought 'very fond' would be enough. She knew better now she had met her husband again. Could she win Jules's love? If not, what would become of them? He *was* her husband, and she would have to accept whatever he could give her. "You love the children," she added, consoling herself with that thought. He *was* capable of love.

"So, where do we go from here?" Jules asked, his voice carefully controlled. "You said you wanted a future with me." He stood and crossed to the chair opposite her.

Mia responded in the same even tone. "I think it is too early to talk about the future. I will go back to England, and you have duties here."

Jules accepted her decree without argument. "Then let us just agree that we want that future, and will talk about it more another time; perhaps write about it in letters. Shall we instead discuss the practical things? You have access to my bank account both here and in London, and I have made an appointment for you and me to meet with a solicitor to arrange your legal custody of the children. But there is much else to talk about."

"I know," Mia agreed. "For one, I want to know your wishes for Kirana's funeral." She caught his flinch. "I know it is hard, Jules, but if you are at sea, I will need to make decisions for you."

They sat for another hour, discussing the funeral, the disposition of the household in the Cape Colony, and where they might live when they returned to England.

"We have made a lot of progress today," Mia said, as she tidied their cups onto the tray, ready for a maid to fetch to the kitchen. Not just in the decisions they had made, either. They had cleared a lot of what lay between them, and she felt a cautious optimism that Jules wanted the same kind of marriage she did.

He proved that, once again, his thoughts marched with hers when he answered. "To an understanding we can begin to build a marriage on, do you think? I hope so, Mia."

She gave him a smile. "I hope so, too."

11

———

Jules had several calls to make at the harbour. He needed to talk to friends about helping Mia once he was gone, especially if she had trouble with Hackett. He'd consult the fleet office regarding her trip back to England. His own application to the Admiralty for a posting closer to England reposed in a letter in his jacket pocket, which he'd make sure went on the next packet boat.

He took Japheth with him, instructing him to walk at Jules's side rather than a few paces behind; the walk would give Jules an opportunity to find out what Japheth was up to with Hannah Cottle. This kind of conversation was, in his view, the worst part of being a captain and therefore father confessor to the entire ship, and was particularly awkward now. Jules was still smarting from seeing himself through Mia's eyes; yes, and judging himself far more harshly than she did, though no more harshly than he deserved.

He felt less equipped than usual to interrogate another man about his love life. But he was Japheth's employer. Hannah's as well, most would say, since she was his wife's servant and his children's nanny.

Better get it out then. "Japheth, you like Mrs Cottle." A statement, not a question.

III

Japheth opened his eyes so wide that white shone all around them, but he answered sturdily enough. "I never show Miz Cottle no disrespect, Captain, sir."

"I know that," Jules reassured him, adding, "and Mrs Cottle would make short work of you, if you did, and Mrs Captain would sweep up the pieces and do it all again." Employer and servant shared an altogether male exchange of glances that acknowledged the power of their woman.

Jules returned to the point. "You like her," he insisted. "My wife thinks Mrs Cottle likes you, too. If you could, would you court her?"

Japheth shook his head, but soon made it clear that the answer wasn't a 'no'. "Miz– Mrs Cottle, she will go back to England with Mrs Captain and the captain's children. Besides, she is a white lady." The yearning in his eyes told another story.

Jules countered both points. "You could come to England with us, Japheth, and Hannah doesn't mind your differences. What is it to anyone else?"

"Is that what they think in England? Japheth asked. "That my colour don't matter? That it don't matter I was a slave until you freed me?"

Jules couldn't honestly answer in the affirmative. There were bigots everywhere. "I don't care what colour a man is, or what race he is from," he said. "Nor does Mrs Captain."

Japheth glanced sideways but said nothing. They walked in silence for a few minutes before he spoke again. "I was born in the Slave House. I hardly remember my mother, and I never knew who my father was." He held a black hand up in front of Jules's face. "I reckon he must have been a black fellow, but he might just as easy been any other colour. The seamen? They used to buy the woman at the Slave House for an hour or a night. It's hard for a slave to say no. What has a man like me got to offer a lady like Hannah?"

"It is not where a man comes from that counts," Jules told him, "but who he becomes. As to what Hannah deserves, you will need to work that out with her. I know I don't in the least deserve Mrs Captain, but I'm glad to be her husband."

They arrived at the first stop of the afternoon, and the conversation was over, but Jules felt he'd brushed through it fairly well.

⁕

*J*ules's shore leave came to an end, but the *Advantage* was assigned to patrol off the Cape of Good Hope, so Jules was able to sleep at home more often than not.

Lieutenant Bourne and a couple of Jules's other officers had come to dinner after the encounter at the races, and they left singing his wife's praises. At Mia's suggestion, that dinner was followed by others. A couple of times a week, he and Mia hosted officers from the armed forces, Navy and Army, at their table. The admiral came twice, and became a member of the Mia Admiration Society, calling Jules to his office to bark, "I'm supporting your transfer. That lovely young woman should see you more often than once every seven years, Redepenning."

The weather warmed as winter at last surrendered to spring. The Redepenning children, resplendent in their new clothes, went for a walk every day, except when the rain was too heavy. Dan, in particular, fretted at being confined to the house and its small courtyard and garden, but both Jules and Mia were adamant that none of the children leave the grounds without a stout escort. This meant Japheth usually accompanied Hannah when she took the children out, but Mia often went too, and so did Jules, when he had a day in port.

He was making headway with his wife, he thought. He didn't doubt her physical response to him, and if she'd been any other woman, he would have seduced her into his bed by now. His baser self, insisted that if he just once had her under him, writhing with pleasure, her senses overwhelmed, she would be his heart and soul. His baser self was an idiot. If he wanted her heart, he had to be worthy of it. Rushing her before she was ready wasn't a good way to win her respect. He needed to build a solid relationship, not just enjoy a few intimate encounters.

"After the war," he said to her one afternoon, "I'll be needing another job. The navy will be full of half-pay captains, and—even if I could get a ship—I don't want any more long trips away from you and the children."

They had walked as far as the beach, where the children soon began a shrieking game of 'escape the wave' leaving the adults to talk in peace. Mia, pretty in a matching bonnet and coat, smiled warmly. "I don't want you to go far away either. Once you get home, I mean. Have you thought about what you wish to do?"

He had. For years, he had assumed he would die in this war, and had lived for the moment, with a few occasional twinges of conscience about Kirana and the children, easily assuaged by settling money on Kirana and writing a will leaving her and the children as charges to his father. Kirana's illness had destroyed his careless plans, and Mia had awoken in him a desire for something more; a future that included coming home to her and the children.

"All I know is the sea, Mia, but I have more than enough money to purchase a ship, and more than enough relatives to advise me on the best way to set up a coastal shipping service. Yes, and give me cargoes, too. Would that suit you, do you think?"

Mia put her head to one side as she thought. "I should wait to buy a house then Jules. We will not know where to settle until you have had a chance to think about what kind of ship you will buy, and what kinds of cargoes you will carry. I daresay I can rent a house until we decide. In any case, I will go to Longford Court if we are home in time for Christmas. I'd like to spend time with Kitty and if I am reading Ella's latest letter correctly, Susan will be living in the vicinity."

Ella thought that Jules's sister was enamoured of Rede's neighbour and old school-friend, whom Jules remembered from his childhood. "Susan and Gil Rutledge? Susan can't stand him," he protested. "She is the one who began calling him Rock Ledge."

Mia's smile hinted at compassion for the poor dumb male who did not understand the female mind. "He is the only person I know who annoys Susan just by walking into a room. She is cross when he is silent, and even more so when he speaks. He is a sweet man, Jules. I can easily believe her irritation is a cover for deeper feelings."

At that moment, Ada ran from a bigger wave than usual, tripped, fell, and was caught by the water, which washed over and around her before receding. Hannah hurried forward to swing her up and run with her out of the wet zone.

They were prepared for a few drops of water; even wet feet. But Ada was soaked to the skin, and the wind suddenly seemed much icier than it had.

"Run for the buggy, Japheth," Jules commanded, as he and Mia hastened towards the nanny and her burden.

"Bring blankets," Mia added. "Ada is wet through, and Hannah is not much drier."

Ignoring that condition, she wrapped an arm around Hannah's shoulders, and another across Ada's back. Jules left the two women to comfort the wailing child, while he marshalled the other children for the walk back to where they could meet the buggy.

"I can take her," he said, holding out his arms.

Ada clung tighter to Hannah's neck, and the nanny turned slightly, presenting her shoulder, saying, "I am already wet, Sir."

Jules and Mia exchanged a glance full of wry recognition that they ranked lower than Hannah in Ada's world. "As you will," Jules said. "Let me know if she gets too heavy." He shrugged out of his coat. "Here. Help her to strip off and get into this. We don't want her catching cold."

Faster than he would have imagined possible—Japheth must have run like the wind, and Fortune must have galloped the horse on the way back—Jules was loading his three wet charges into the buggy. Ada, in nothing but his coat, sat on Hannah's lap, clinging tightly to Mia's hands. Blankets draped the three, but the sooner they were home and changed the better.

"The rest of us will finish our walk," he said to Mia. "You go and get into dry clothes."

"Walk quickly," Mia told him. "That wind is chilly."

He blew her a kiss. "We'll be fine, won't we Dan and Marsha?"

He turned his attention to the groom. "Get them home, Fortune. Quickly but carefully." The groom tipped his hat in acknowledgement, and the buggy drew away.

Marsha slipped her hand into Jules's. "Will she be all right, Papa?"

Dan rolled his eyes. "It is only a bit of water. She will be home in five minutes."

Jules gave Marsha's hand a light squeeze. "She will be fine, sweetheart. Now. You heard Ibu Mia. Let us walk quickly." He and Japheth made a game of it— run twenty paces; walk twenty paces —counting the paces in all the languages they knew between them. Jules had picked up a little Malay, some Tamil, a bit more Batavian, as well as his native English. Japheth knew Dutch, Malagasy, and English. Dan surprised them with the Gaelic he'd learned from the Scots cook on the *Advantage,* as well as the languages that Jules knew and a little Dutch.

Marsha came out of her shell enough to count in Bengali, which she had picked up somewhere, and then in French, which she said she was learning from Ibu Mia. Since she also knew her numbers in Malay, Tamil, Batavian, English and Dutch, she danced into the house at the end of the work, the victor of the day, her eyes glowing and her cheeks flushed from the exercise, the wind, and the joy of knowing more than her father or brother.

He was proud of her, Jules realised. He'd always been fond of the children, in a distant kind of a way, and certainly regarded them as his to protect. Dan, he knew a little better, especially after having him underfoot on two long voyages, but the girls had been very much their mother's to raise, and—when he was home and Kirana was well—left to the care of their *ayah* so Kirana could give him all her time and attention.

Mia refused to keep them confined to the nursery and schoolroom; she insisted on involving him in their activities and expected him to be interested in them and their lives. He was. Another discredit to him, that he'd taken the children for granted. Another debt to Mia; she had proved they were indispensable to his happiness. One more reason to want a lifetime with her and no other.

ia sat in the courtyard enjoying the spring sunshine. The children were in the schoolroom. Jules—who had been home for two days—had been called down to the fleet office. Kirana was asleep, or perhaps unconscious.

Mia did not know how Kirana kept living. Each breath was a battle, and each day Mia expected her to lose. She denied she felt pain, but groaned with it. She managed to appear cheerful and calm when the children came to the door to say goodnight, but the effort left her with tears of exhaustion running down her cheeks, and she always lapsed into unconsciousness shortly after.

She spoke little; every attempted sentence punctuated by bitter coughing. Mostly, she wanted to hear Mia's plans for the children— for their welcome into Jules's family, for their future in the English gentry. Sometimes, she asked if Mia had taken Jules into her bed yet, and was disappointed when the answer was always no.

Mia came to realise that much of her idealisation of Jules had been absorbed from Kirana's letters. In Kirana's eyes, he was perfect. He had swept in to save her not once but twice. He had given her and her son a home when she had nowhere else to go. He had taken up with other women in casual affairs, but he had always come back to her. His casual affection was more than she expected, and she repaid it by loving him with all her heart.

"Love him," she commanded Mia. "He needs you." Mia had done her best to keep her heart guarded, but his care for the children, his willingness to treat her as a partner, and above all his regard for Kirana had destroyed her resolve.

Whenever his ship docked, he hurried home and Kirana was the first person he asked after. He would greet Mia and the children, and then go to visit Kirana as if the reports he received that she still lived could not be believed until he saw with his own eyes. Every morning he woke in his own house, Kirana's room was his first destination on getting up.

Was there ever an odder situation? A man who won the heart of his virgin wife by caring about his dying mistress?

He was courting Mia, too. He paid her compliments, manufactured opportunities to touch her, brought her flowers and other little gifts. Sometimes, Mia wished he would just demand her physical surrender and be done with it. He wanted her. Mia was not so innocent as to be oblivious to his desire. She could swear, however, that he was sticking to his resolve not to find release with another woman. Presumably, at this point, even a woman as devoid of physical assets as her looked appealing to him.

Mia, on the other hand, had never responded to a man the way she did to Jules. Whenever he was in the house, her whole body hummed with tension. When he pressed her hand or touched a kiss to the corner of her lips or guided her through a doorway with a hand to the small of her back, she tingled. The heat in his eyes made her breasts heavy and her nipples hard and the private places between her legs swollen, warm, and wet.

She waited for him to make the next move; to kiss her, embrace her, bed her, by all that was holy. If only he would push her, she could give in, as was her duty as his wife. Instead, he was showing a gentlemanly restraint that was unutterably frustrating.

"Where would I find Mrs Redepenning, Japheth?"

Jules's voice. He was home. She straightened from her examination of a spire of trumpet-like flowers—one of dozens in various shades of pink that had sprouted to celebrate the spring.

He came out into the courtyard and crossed to her, smiling a greeting, but his brow was furrowed.

"Problems?" she asked.

"I have been ordered back to Madagascar, sailing the day after tomorrow. I'm to take one of the diplomatic fellows to the court of King Radama. With the best will in the world, I can't expect to be less than a month away. Probably longer."

Her face must have fallen, for he took both her hands and said, "I am so sorry."

Mia managed a smile. "You are under orders. We shall manage everything here. You must not worry."

"I have complete faith in you, Mia. It is hard, though, leaving now. I feel guilty about leaving it all on your shoulders. I haven't been up to see her yet. Is there any change?"

Mia shook her head. Unspoken between them was the knowledge that death was almost certain to come before Jules could return.

"I have better news," Jules told her. "I'm to be posted to Portugal—to defend the Portuguese ports and provide escort duties to troop ships, mostly, I gather. When I get back from this mission, I'll be sent north."

"Escort duty? You will be sailing in and out of England?"

"Yes, I hope so. I can't leave the Navy, Mia; not with the war on. But at least I will be able to see my family occasionally."

12

———————

On the final night before the *Advantage* was due to sail, Mia and Jules said their goodnights to Kirana and retreated to the withdrawing room for their usual glass of brandy before separating at Mia's bedroom door.

The children had long since gone to bed. All of the servants had finished their duties for the night and retired to the kitchen wing.

Jules was fretting over details they had discussed a dozen times, and Mia was doing her best to soothe his worry by treating each remark and question as if she heard it for the first time. Only half her mind was on the conversation, for she had resolved to consummate her marriage tonight.

He made his trip to Madagascar sound like a stroll in the park, but she knew the sea was full of French privateers, anxious to take any British prize they could find. This might be their last night together on this earth, and she would not allow her doubts and reservations to keep her from knowing her husband in this most intimate of ways. If he survived the war—how she prayed he would survive! If he came home to her alive, she would deal with whatever came next, but she would not miss this chance. That is, if she could figure out how to make the first move.

"If you let the Admiral's office know, they'll get word to me," Jules instructed. "I will come if I can."

"Of course. If you cannot be here, Jules, I will make sure she is looked after."

"I know you will." He gave her a slight smile over the rim of his brandy glass, but frowned again. "It won't be long, will it?"

Mia sighed. "I do not know. She sleeps most of the time, now. Doctor Sturgess says we are near the end. Hearing her fight for each breath—I cannot wish to keep her here, Jules."

"You are right, of course." Jules swirled his drink making a vortex, and stared into it as if he would find answers to the great questions of life and death in its depths. "I can't help but want it to be over; she is suffering so much… Is that wrong of me?"

Mia's answer was halting. "Ella says the waiting is harder on loved ones than on the person dying, and now I see what she means. Kirana has —I do not know how to say it." She paused, and then described what she had observed. "It is as if she has already moved on, all but her flesh. She comes back to us when she hears the children, and a little for you, but otherwise her mind and her spirit are no longer here."

Jules looked up; his eyes sombre. "You say it very well. You have done that for her, Mia. You have made it possible for her to die at peace. She knows the children are safe with you."

He returned his attention to his glass, but he hadn't finished talking. "I feel the same. I don't want to go tomorrow, but since I have to, it will be easier, having you here."

Another piercing look, remembered anguish blazing from his eyes. "It could have been so different." He put the brandy down to rise and take the two steps needed to drop to his knees at her feet, his hands reaching to frame her face. "I have nightmares, thinking about what I might have come home to, if you had not arrived. I can't imagine how I would feel now, leaving port knowing that I had to depend on hired servants for the safety of my family. I can never thank you enough."

He leaned forward to press a gentle kiss to her forehead, and she put her arms around him, hugging him close. "Ah, Jules. I have only done what I thought right. Besides, I love them. I do not need thanks for looking after the people I love."

He lifted her chin and began kissing the tears from her cheeks. She shifted so that a kiss fell on the corner of her mouth, and he pulled back a little, but only to say, "It was the luckiest night of my life when I was captured by smugglers and locked up with you."

Disappointed that he had stopped, she grumbled, "You didn't think so at the time." This seduction would never happen if she left it all to him. She summoned her courage and put her hands on his face to keep it still before pressing her mouth on his. He'd better take the hint, because she had no idea what she was doing.

His lips froze, and she almost pulled away, and then, thank goodness, they softened on hers and began to move. Was that his tongue, sweeping across the seam of her mouth? Those were certainly his teeth, nibbling at her lower lip until she gasped at the wonderful sensations that reverberated through her whole body, and would have gasped again when his tongue invaded her mouth, except her mouth was full and she could manage nothing more than a strangled moan.

He clearly took that as approval, for he deepened the kiss, pressing her back against her chair, his body firm against hers, his face angled to allow him to invade even deeper. No. Not an invasion, for she had invited him in. His tongue retreated and then returned, retreated and returned, until she took the hint and allowed her own tongue to follow his. Ah. This invasion could be reciprocal, and she could make him moan, too.

She applied herself enthusiastically to mimicking his actions, learning what he taught, sinking deeper and deeper into the sensations he created.

A timeless period later, Jules ended the kiss; not releasing her but drawing back enough to meet her eyes, his own hot. "Sweet Mia, even then I could tell you'd make a rare woman. Brave, clever, caring. I saw all of that. I knew you'd be pretty, too."

She wanted to trust he meant it, but it was a little much to swallow. "How can you say that? I look like a boy!"

Jules's laugh was disbelieving. "Never! A boy?" His hands

rounded her body to run over her breasts, paused briefly to cup
them, brushed over her nipples which had somehow become so
hard that they ached, then skimmed down to her waist. He spread
his thumb and fingers to span her waist on both sides. "I can almost
touch my fingers together. You are perfect."

Did he really think so? "I barely have any curves at all," Mia
protested.

Jules pressed a quick kiss to her mouth, as if to stop her words.
"I beg to differ." He moved his hands, one scooping under her
buttocks and half lifting her from the chair, the other coming up to
once again cup a breast, the thumb rubbing back and forth across
the nipple. "Look. Beautifully curved."

She could barely think as his movement both relieved and inten-
sified the near pain in her nipple. "So small!" she pointed out.
"Gerta–"

Another firm quick kiss. "Does not belong between us. Mia, do
you not know I have been lusting after you since I arrived home?"
Kiss. "Feeling bad about it, too, when at the beginning I thought
you had moved Kirana out of her room and dismissed Maureen. I
felt the lowest of dogs to desire such a woman." Kiss. "But as I
learned the truth and got to know you, admiring you more and
more each day, my desire grew." His hand kept moving, and the
other pulled her closer, until she was plastered to his body, groin to
groin, the hardness behind his falls rubbing close to the place of
sudden, desperate need. Beguiled, she shifted against him.

"Ah, Mia," he groaned, "can't you tell what you do to me?
Sleeping in the room next to me while I lie awake, night after night,
imagining you are in the bed with me and I can, at last, worship you
with my body as I promised so long ago?"

His mouth was on hers again, and his lips, his tongue, his teeth,
his hands, his hard body, all drove her to a place where she no
longer knew where she was and barely who she was. She only knew
that she yearned, hungered, ached—and that Jules could answer
that need.

Then he pulled away, and she reached after him before her
mind registered what he'd already heard—a burst of conversation

as the kitchen door opened and shut again, and then footsteps approaching.

Jules was already back in his seat, his brandy glass in his hand. His hair was ruffled, his neckcloth half untied, but he had shrugged his coat back on as he crossed the room. She caught a glimpse of red swollen lips before he raised the glass to cover them.

She pulled her shawl over a bare breast she didn't remember Jules exposing, and grabbed her own glass, just as Fortune came through the room on his way to check on the door. Heaven alone knew what she looked like.

***

*M*ia wouldn't look at him. Jules had completely messed things up, leaping on her like that. All the ground he'd made up lost in a single lusty moment. She had been so responsive in his arms, and he wanted her so much!

Jules returned Japheth's nod and watched the man check the locks and bolts before passing back through the room.

"G'night sir, ma'am." Japheth kept his eyes turned away from Mia as he spoke. Did that make it worse or better? He wasn't embarrassing her by staring at her red cheeks and rumpled condition, but his very forbearance was clear evidence he knew exactly what they had been doing.

Jules waited until he heard the kitchen door open and close again before he opened his mouth to apologise, but Mia forestalled him, saying, "If we are to continue this, Jules, we had better go through to your bedroom, where we will not be disturbed."

The comment was so far from what he expected that he gaped at her. "Are you sure?"

She pulled the shawl more closely around her body and turned even rosier. "Only if you are."

He was on his knees before her in two seconds flat. "Never doubt that I want you, Mia." He leaned forward and touched nose to nose. "If you are certain that… I was determined to let you set the pace, dear one."

"I am setting the pace, Jules. I am ready, impatient even. I have waited so long."

He rose, and gathered her into his arms. "My bed, then. Let me love you, Mia."

She weighed barely more than Kirana, but that was because she was tiny, not because she was ill. Still, he was terrified of breaking her, or at least of frightening her. He would need to be gentle, and take things slowly.

She was already tearing off his neckcloth, and by the time he reached the bed, she had his shirt and waistcoat unbuttoned and was pushing the waistcoat off his shoulders. He put her down on the edge of the bed and crouched so she could finish the job, which she was swift to do, following that by sliding down his braces and pulling his shirt up. He raised his arms to help her lift it over his head.

She sat back to look at him and her eyes widened. He stood for her examination, and fought the urge to preen as she studied his naked torso with the same serious expression he'd seen when she worked a mathematical problem in the schoolroom with Dan or added a column of figures in the household accounts. She touched one of his tight nipples with a tentative finger. "Is it always like that, or is it like…?" she trailed off.

"Like yours? Yes. Hard tight nipples are a sign of desire, Mia-mine."

She traced some of the scars that decorated his flesh, souvenirs of two-thirds of a lifetime spent fighting for King and country. "One day, you shall tell me about each of these, but for now…" She reached for the buttons of his fall, and he covered her hands with his.

"Soon, dearest, but first, I must amend a mistake I made long ago." Slowly, keeping hold of her hands, he knelt beside the bed. "Long ago, you made your marriage vows to me with every intention of keeping them for a lifetime. Allow me, my Mia, to make mine to you, meaning every word. Tonight shall be our wedding night, and first I must make my promises."

He waited until she nodded, her face solemn. "I, Jules Darius Achilles Redepenning, take you, Euronyme Margaret Redepenning to be my lawful wedded wife, to have and to hold from this day forward, for better for worse, for richer for poorer, in sickness and in health, to love and to cherish, till death do us part according to God's holy law. In the presence of God, I make this vow. I will love you, comfort you, honour you and protect you, and, forsaking all others, be faithful to you as long as we both shall live."

Mia was smiling, glowing almost, as tears slid silently down her cheeks. "I never expected… Oh, Jules, how lovely."

Jules stood and pulled her closer for another long kiss, and this time when she fumbled at his buttons, he did not prevent her. Indeed, he did a bit of his own unbuttoning—unlacing, too—all the time continuing the kiss, until he held his naked wife in his arms and she was pulling him down into the sheets with her, commanding him to hurry up and worship her with his body.

"We have all night, Mia mine," he assured her, capturing her busy exploring hands to ensure that this first time was not cut ignominiously short.

"We can do it more than once, can we not?" she asked, red as a marine's jacket. "Or so I have heard."

"We can," he assured her.

They did it twice, the first rather faster than he intended, and the second sweet and slow. Mia fell asleep in Jules's arms after his second release—her third. Tired as he was, his busy mind kept him awake as he tried to analyse what was different about making love to his wife. He'd been with responsive women before, so that wasn't it. It was making love, not merely indulging a physical urge, but he'd thought himself in love before, so that wasn't it, either. The mixture of respect, pride, protectiveness, and affection was unlike anything he'd felt before.

He'd got this far when he drifted off, to be woken by Mia fighting free of his arms and calling out. "George! Help! Help!"

"Mia mine," he said, urgently, reluctant to embrace her again until she knew it was him. "Mia, wake up. You are safe, dearest. You are with me."

He slipped from under the covers and lit a candle. Climbing back into bed, he held out his arms again. "Mia." She came to him, wrapping her arms around him. "I'm sorry. I'm not used to sleeping with someone."

"You were dreaming," he told her. "You called out a name, again and again. Who was George? Do I need to kill someone, Mia?"

"Not George!" she insisted. "He saved me, Jules. He was not a good man, I know that, but he was good to me."

Jules stroked her hair, thinking about this. "My cousin, George? George Redepenning?"

"Yes. George, Lord Chirbury. I was not… You remember, Jules." She wriggled to snuggle closer, and his male organ responded by inflating slightly. *Not now*, he instructed it, silently.

"I don't have many curves, even now." Mia whispered into his neck. "When you met me, I was as flat as a child."

"I love your curves." Jules protested. "Did I not show you that earlier? They are exactly right, Mia, and when you've finished telling your story, I will show you again."

Her lips moved against his skin as she smiled. "It was my first Season. I was only fifteen, but married, and therefore expected to be in Society," she began. "Your father and Susan—they were so kind. I went out with them; with Susan, mostly, for your father was busy and often away from London. I did not enjoy the same events Susan liked to attend. Balls are boring when you look like a child. No one asks you to dance, and if you have no friends, you have no one to talk to. Later, it was different. I developed something of a figure, and I had my friend Kitty to keep me company. But at first…"

He should have stayed. They might have given him leave if he'd asked, explained the circumstances. Instead, he didn't even try; couldn't wait to abandon her. "I am so sorry, Mia."

"It was not your fault, Jules. You had your duty. I understood." Her easy forgiveness made him feel worse, but his guilt did have the benefit of subduing his lust.

"There was a man," she continued, "an older man. He was kind and I missed my father. He treated me as if I was a daughter, I thought; better, in fact, than my father ever did. I enjoyed his company. He invited me to join him at the kinds of event I liked and

Susan didn't. Musicals, the opera, lectures, art exhibitions—there was nothing untoward. Always, we were in a group, usually with his wife, who was very kind to me, too. She was much younger than her husband, but still many years older than me, and I was flattered by her interest and felt safe with him because she was also my friend."

Even without the evidence of the nightmare, Jules would be getting a bad feeling about this. What was his family thinking? He'd left his innocent child-bride in their care!

"Your cousin George was a friend of his and of his wife," Mia went on. "Especially, or so I found out later, his wife. Susan saw nothing wrong with the outings, and she had other things she wanted to do. She let me go on my own, as long as I was escorted by George, who promised to look after me."

Jules was incredulous. "She trusted George?" George? One of the worst rakes of London?

Mia shifted so she could see his face. "He had no interest in me, Jules. He preferred voluptuous women, and he thought of me as a little girl."

She snuggled in again. "In any case, I went out with them more and more, and I didn't even notice as the groups got smaller. Sometimes it was just me and George, and the baron and his wife.

"Not Baron Carrington!" Jules was horrified. "Why did Susan— I suppose no one told her. Carrington's obscene attraction to children is not the sort of thing one discusses with a lady."

"After it happened, Susan had a word or two to say about putting ladies at risk by not telling them what they needed to know to keep themselves and their sisters safe. Your father was away, or he might have spoken."

He tightened his arms, dreading the rest of the story. The worst hadn't happened—she'd been a virgin until a few hours ago—but she had suffered, or she would not still be having nightmares. "Go on, my love."

Mia went on, her voice as calm as if she was talking about what pattern to use for a dress or when to clean the *stoep*. "One night, I went to dinner at the Carringtons. It was just me and George, that night. We had something planned, but the Baron said it had been cancelled and we would have a quiet evening at home. George and Lady Carrington went off together. That was the first time I realised they were having an affair. I was so sorry for the Baron."

"No need," Jules told her. "He used to encourage her to take up with wealthy young men." His hands moved almost without his volition, stroking her hair and her back, offering what comfort he could while she got out the story that haunted her.

"Yes," she said. "I found that out later, but at the time, he had my sympathy, which was what he wanted, I suppose. He asked me for a hug and the next thing I knew he was on top of me and trying to undress me. He would have succeeded if George had not rushed into the room, dragged him off me, and punched him. Laid him out flat! It was awful, Jules. I was crying, and trying to hold my torn gown together. Lady Carrington was screaming the foulest things at me and George, and Lord Carrington was out cold on the floor."

Jules had never in his life imagined being grateful to Horrid George. "Served the foul old lecher right. George should have killed him."

"George was wonderful," Mia said. "He made Lady Carrington give him a cloak to cover the disrepair of my clothing. He called for his carriage. He gave the servants money to deny I had ever been there. He took me home and sent for Susan. I do not know what I would have done without him."

"I will feel kindlier towards him in future," Jules murmured into her hair.

Mia hadn't finished. "Lord and Lady Carrington tried to spread rumours. Susan and your father stopped them in polite Society. I don't know what George said amongst the scoundrels, but it worked. Later, when I developed what curves I have, and the wild young men began to think a woman with a husband half a world away was in need of their attentions, all of them assumed I was innocent."

"As you were," Jules noted.

"As I was, though not as innocent as I had been. George taught me some moves to dissuade those who would not take 'no' for an answer, and I have had more than one occasion to bless him for that."

Jules murmured apologies into her hair for not being there to protect her, and punctuated them with kisses. Slowly, as she responded to his comforting with passion, their embrace turned into what he had promised earlier. Jules showed her just how much he appreciated her curves.

*ia woke naked in Jules's bed, tucked against his body like a spoon in a drawer, his arm over her body, and his erection hard against her buttocks. She lay for a while, waiting for him to move, but his even breathing showed he was still asleep, and when she wriggled around within the curve of his arms, his eyes were shut.

She examined the strong angles of his face: the square chin, the hard planes of his cheeks, the straight line of his nose. His golden lashes were almost the same colour as his skin, and much longer than they appeared from a distance.

Those lips had kissed her in places she shivered to remember, and it had felt wonderful. His mouth was relaxed in sleep, slightly open. She traced the curve with her finger a fraction of an inch away from touching, then pulled back to drop her eyes to his chest. The same golden hair covered his upper torso, especially thick between the nipples, then arrowed down, the heavier growth becoming a lighter covering that circled around his navel and then narrowed to dive into the curls at the base of his male organ.

The organ itself was not as large as last night, but still hard enough to jut up from the nest of curls. She'd had it inside of her, last night, and her core pulsed again at the memory. She'd held it, too. With that thought, she reached out with both hands, but stopped short of touching him. After all, they had been late getting to sleep, and awake in the night.

"Possibly not a good idea," Jules commented, and she snatched back her hands while shooting him a guilty glance.

"Not that I mind," he hastened to add, "but you must be sore. I was not considerate, Mia, to take you three times on your first night.

I wanted you so much." He chuckled and gestured to his groin, where his erection had increased in size as they talked, arching towards his navel. "I still want you, but…"

She grabbed him firmly in one hand, revelling in his gasp. "No buts. You leave in a matter of hours, Jules, and who knows when we will be together again."

His smile broadened. "I love the way you think. Come here, then, Mia mine, and explore to your heart's content."

⁕

They were up later than usual, and the entire household must have guessed why. Mia told herself not to be embarrassed. They had, after all, done only what married couples were permitted, even encouraged, to do. That didn't prevent her cheeks heating at the pleased glances exchanged between her servants.

Jules was unconcerned, ordering a bath brought to her room, and instructing Maria to add some of the bath salts that Pranisha made for muscular aches. "It has ginger in it, and salts, and I don't know what else, but it is very soothing," he told Mia.

It was, too, but she still sat rather carefully on the hard upright chair set a short distance from Kirana's bed. "How are you this morning, my dear?" she asked.

Kirana, as always, smiled. "Happy," she said. Mia expected her to stop at that one word, as even that was a struggle, but someone had clearly been before Mia with the news, for she continued, a few words at a time with long spaces between. "You and Jules? Together. So glad. Look after him? Love him?"

"I will," Mia assured her. "I do."

Kirana lay back, satisfied, and closed her eyes. Mia thought she had drifted off again, but she lifted her lids part way when Jules entered. He touched Mia's shoulder, and smiled at her, then spoke to Kirana.

"I'm leaving soon, Kirana. I don't know how long I'll be gone this time, but I'll hurry back as soon as I can."

Kirana shook her head, a gentle movement from one side to the other. "Dying, Jules. Go. Be safe, my love."

Jules took a step towards the bed and fell on his knees beside it to take her hand. She tried to pull it away. "No! Sickness!"

"This once," he insisted. "I shall wash afterwards, dear one, but let me take my leave of you. I cannot walk away without telling you how much you have meant to me. Thank you for three beautiful children. Thank you for being my safe harbour these many years."

Kirana's eyes shone with tears that sparkled for a moment then slid down her cheeks. In slow choked phrases she replied, "Thank you. Saved me. My daughters. My sister Mia. Thank you."

She began to cough, and Jules took her in his arms. Mia gave his shoulder a squeeze, and when he turned his face towards her, his own eyes swam with tears. "I will be downstairs," she told him, and left him to part from Kirana in private.

When it was time for Jules to leave, heavy rain prompted him to suggest that Mia and the children say their goodbyes at home. "No point in us all getting wet," he said.

"We have umbrellas and raincoats, and a few splashes won't hurt us," Mia replied. "We would like to come, Captain." She paused and her brow furrowed. "Unless you would prefer not to…"

She was clearly imagining reasons why he might be reluctant to have them farewell him at the harbour. In truth, no one had offered to see Jules off on one of his voyages since his mother stayed at the hotel while his father escorted him as far as the wharf and left him to make his own way to the bum boat to be rowed to his first ship. He'd been grateful—his fourteen-year-old self more afraid of what his peers would say than of brushing his parents aside so he could start his new life. He would have braved any scorn had he known he'd not see his mother again. She had died less than a year later, before he next returned to England.

"I'd like you to come," he told Mia. "I will order Fortune to put the rain covers up on the buggy. "Get your coats," he told his children, but Hannah was a step ahead of him, handing each of them a cape of oiled canvas. Fortune must have had the buggy ready, too, for in minutes it was at the steps, and Fortune and Japheth were manhandling his sea chest onto the luggage rack over the back axle. With Hannah and Dan on the front bench beside Fortune, and the two girls up with Jules and Mia on the back bench, they set off.

Ada sat on his knee, her cheek pressed to his chest, her arms around her waist, and Marsha, perched between him and Mia, clung to the arm he did not have wrapped around his littlest child. Why had he never let them come to see him off before? Kirana had never suggested it, but neither had he.

He leaned forward at the guarded entry, and spoke to the marine on sentry duty. "Captain Redepenning bound for the *Advantage*. My family are coming to see me off." The sentry waved them through, and Fortune threaded the buggy through the busy crowd until they reached the wharf where a boat waited to row the *Advantage's* captain to his little realm.

They could wait another minute or two. He rescued his arm from Marsha and wrapped Ada in an embrace. "Be good for Ibu Mia, Ada, and Papa shall be home as soon as he can." He kissed her wet cheek, and handed her over the seat to Hannah, then turned to Marsha and repeated the hug and the words.

Mia had climbed down while he said goodbye to the girls. He rubbed Dan's hair the wrong way, then hugged his head in a pretence of a wrestle that was really a caress. "Look after your sisters, Dan, and obey Ibu Mia in all things." Dan was blinking hard, and Jules had to swallow before he blew them all kisses, nodded to Hannah, and jumped down to join Mia on the wharf.

"If there's anything…" He trailed off. He'd said it all before, and wouldn't keep her waiting in the rain while he went through it again.

"Go," she advised. "I love them as my own, and you have done everything you can to look after us. We will be waiting for you when you come home to England." She lifted her cheek for his kiss, and he'd given it and turned away—even taken two steps—when all that he felt for the treasure he'd accidentally married overwhelmed him, and he had her in his arms before the thought had properly surfaced in his brain. Was this love? This amalgam of longing and comfort, of desire and peace, of happiness in her presence and a yawning loneliness at the thought of months without her? He crushed her in his arms and kissed her thoroughly.

A loud whistle broke through his focus on his wife, followed by a slap and his bosun's voice. "What are you whistling at? That's the captain's wife, you scurvy scum. Mind your oars."

Jules smiled down into Mia's eyes and she put up a hand to cup his cheek. "You had better go before we scandalise His Majesty's Navy," she said.

He kissed her once more, a peck on the lips, the nose, and the forehead. "I am yours, Mia. Never doubt it. I will be home as soon as I can."

While they had been busy, his sea chest and duffle had been transferred to the boat, and Fortune was climbing back up to his seat. "Go," Jules said. "We won't be sailing for another hour, at least. Probably two."

"We'll watch you from the walk on the roof," Mia promised.

And he could see them there, two hours later, when he trained his telescope in their direction—several tiny figures under a huge umbrella, watching as the *Advantage* slipped out of the harbour.

13

Kirana continued to fade. The doctor came, and the chaplain from the fort visited twice more. Hannah and Mia kept the children busy but close to home, mindful that Kirana might slip away at any time.

A week after Jules left, they were once more in the kitchen, cutting shapes in rolled out gingerbread dough. Mia was telling the children about their Auntie Mary, who had given Mia the recipe, "and she was taught it by a ship's cook when she was a little girl, not much older than you are, Marsha."

Japheth came through from the front of the house. "Mrs Captain? Visitor, ma'am."

"Who is it, Japheth?"

Japheth shook his head. "He wouldn't say, ma'am."

How odd. "I will come."

She washed her hands in a bowl of water that had been set to warm by the hearth for that purpose. She was hardly dressed for company—one of her older dresses, a neat cap to confine her hair, an apron smeared with flour. She could repair the last, and did, untying the strings and draping the apron over a chair. That would have to do. After all, it might be a message about Jules.

The visitor was a man in his fifties, or perhaps sixties, dressed in expensive cloth poorly cut. The buttons of his ostentatiously embroidered waistcoat strained across his portly torso, and his bright blue coat jacket presented an unfortunate contrast to the lime green of his pantaloons. Her London experience alerted her to a would-be macaroni, and one with more money than taste.

He hurried across the room as soon as he saw her, seizing her hands and drawing them to his breast as he cast his gaze to the ceiling. "My dear Mrs Redepenning!" His voice was harsh; the voice of a man who had spent much of his life shouting. Even in this domestic setting, he spoke loud enough to be heard in the far reaches of the kitchen wing. "You have my deepest sympathies, and my utmost respect. When I heard what young Julius has demanded of you… I was shocked. The whole town is shocked. To make his wife live in the same house as his coloured woman and her children? It is an outrage, and cannot at all be what you expected when he sent for you."

Mia withdrew her hands, tugging them out of his and stepping out of reach. "I do not know you, sir."

The stranger bowed. "I beg your pardon. How rude of me not to introduce myself. I was so anxious to let you know that no one blames you for this scandalous situation… I am Captain Jedediah Hackett, Mrs Redepenning," he bowed again, and held out his hand, "and very much at your service."

Mia ignored the proffered appendage. "Indeed."

Hackett smiled, a parody of kindly paternalism. "I had your husband under my command many years ago, and he was arrogant and headstrong even then. You need not pretend with me."

Mia sat to foil his attempt to loom over her. "You will not insult my husband under his own roof, Captain Hackett. I must ask you to leave." She signalled to Japheth, who stood watchful by the wall, and he came to stand at the arm of her chair.

Hackett eyed the fit young man and sneered, but he backed off a little, and changed his expression to a smile, thrusting his face in her direction. "Very admirable, my dear. Your loyalty does you credit, however little that dog Redepe— but no matter." He straightened, and tucked his thumbs into the tabs of his waistcoat. "I have called to lighten your burdens, Mrs Redepenning. It will surprise you, I know, but the children he expects you to live with, the cad? I am willing to take the eldest, and see to his schooling. The boy, Daniel." He dropped his voice. "He will be cared for, I assure you," and then a conspiratorial smile with a dash of laughter, as if what he was about to propose was ridiculous, "if you are concerned."

Mia clenched her hands, itching to drive them into the man's pompous gut. She allowed her voice to take on more aristocratic intonations, but kept it calm, almost bored. "No, Captain Hackett. I will not hand over to you the boy you sired and cruelly abandoned. Your errand is in vain."

Hackett dropped all pretence of civility, taking two paces towards her but drawing back when Japheth took a menacing step forward and Fortune rushed in from the courtyard with the ex-prize-fighter Jules had hired to protect them. Mia caught a glimpse of Pranisha, standing outside the window with her largest soup ladle.

"He is mine," Hackett hissed. "You will give him to me, or I will have the law on to you."

"No, Captain," Mia countered, explaining it to him as if he was a dull-minded child. "He is ours. Mine and my husband's. A base-born child belongs to his mother, and Kirana has given guardian-ship to Captain Redepenning. The papers are signed, and were witnessed by Governor Cradock, who holds a copy. Japheth, escort Captain Hackett to the door, please. If he calls again, I am not at home."

Hackett turned to pleading. "Be reasonable, woman. I plan to make him my heir. I will give him every advantage. Don't stand in his way."

Mia raised both eyebrows, allowing her scorn to fill her voice. "Perdana will have every advantage, Captain Hackett, and he will have a family who love him. If you do not leave of your own accord, I will have you removed."

Swearing and spitting threats, Haddock left the house, escorted by Japheth and Fortune. Mia turned to find Dan watching from the hallway. "Dan, do not leave the house without me or Hannah. That man is dangerous."

"Is it true?" Dan demanded. "Is that man my father?"

"Our captain is your father," Mia assured him, "not that man." He deserved to know the whole story, but Mia did not feel it was her place to tell him. She would keep him close, guard him from Hackett, and wait for Jules to tell Dan about his origins while assuring Dan of Jules's love.

⁕

Kirana died a few days later, slipping away so quietly that the maid sitting with her could not say how long she had been dead. "I checked her, Miz Captain, truly. Gave her some water, then got back to my mending. She didn't make no sound. Next time I check her, she gone."

Everything was ready: the coffin purchased, the grave plot paid for, the chaplain commissioned to conduct the funeral. Japheth and Fortune hurried off with notes to everyone who needed to know: the doctor, the chaplain, the fleet office. The latter would arrange passage for Mia, the children, and the servants on the next packet ship leaving for England.

Her messages sent, Mia helped Pranisha to wash the body and dress it in the gown that Kirana had chosen. Mia herself brushed and pinned the dark hair, coiling it in a simple knot behind each ear.

Then it was time for Hannah to bring the children in to see their mother for the last time. Hannah had protested that the girls, at least, were too young. Mia insisted on asking them what they wanted to do and abiding by their wishes. She had been kept away when her own mother died—sent to a neighbour's house, and told simply that her mother had gone to Heaven. Even now, more than fifteen years later, she still remembered her bewilderment at her mother's disappearance, and the months of anxiously waiting for her to return.

Dressed for the occasion in the black clothes that Hannah and Mia had made ready, the three of them entered the room for the

138

first time since Kirana had banished them to the doorway. Dan led the way, with the two girls following, each clinging to one of Mia's hands.

They stood for a long time, a few feet from the bed, looking at their mother.

"She looks as if she is asleep," Dan whispered after a while.

"She is not coughing," Ada observed.

Marsha let go of Mia's hand and crept closer. She stopped, and glanced back over her shoulder. Mia nodded. She took two more cautious steps then placed her hand on the side of her mother's cheek. "She is cold," she reported.

Ada approached, and Dan lifted her so she could reach for one of the still hands draped across the unmoving chest. She lifted it and let it drop, turning her face into her brother's neck. "Cold," she wailed. "It does not feel like Mami."

Mia retrieved the little girl from her brother, freeing him to take his mother's hand in one of his, while his other arm crept comfortingly around Marsha's shoulders.

"Mami isn't there," Ada sobbed, and Mia struggled to find the words to explain.

"Not anymore," she said. "Mami stayed for as long as she could in a body that couldn't breathe properly. And then, when she couldn't breathe any more, her soul went to Heaven, and left the body behind. Mami is safe and well, but she is gone, Ada."

Marsha nodded. "An angel came to get her. Remember, Ada? She told us that an angel would come to get her when she was too tired to breathe."

Ada cast another glance at the body and wailed, "I want my Mami!" She clutched Mia fiercely, as if she would burrow inside her, and first Dan then Marsha came running to snuggle into the embrace, all of them weeping and taking comfort in one another.

That afternoon, several of the officers Mia had met during her three months in Cape Town called to offer their services, and the next day they and others attended the funeral, even accompanying the body to the cemetery where Jules had arranged a plot; the sins of Kirana's mixed-race origins and her status as a kept woman forgiven by virtue of a rather large donation to the church building fund.

The officers who accepted Mia's invitation to return to the house for refreshments had all met Jules's mistress at various times, and were pleased to find Mia was happy to listen to them reminiscing about the gentle, pretty girl they remembered as being devoted to Jules and her children.

Captain Fleming, the same Fleming whom Mia remembered from her wedding, was one of the last to leave. After drinking rather more brandy than was wise, he told Mia that the whole Navy envied Jules, for the devoted loyalty of two beautiful and charming women. "A Golden Redepenning, ma'am, you see," he confided, mournfully. "Could fall in a sewer and come up with a diamond in his teeth." A couple of his more sober friends escorted him out, and Mia was left alone with her mourning children and a household in chaos as she and the servants scrambled to complete the final packing. They sailed for England in two days.

Japheth, desiring to look after Dan's safety, had asked after Captain Hackett's whereabouts at the docks. He was gratified to learn that, true to type, Captain Hackett, had sailed the day Kirana died.

14

The *Swift* was a schooner brig; so-called because of the
configuration of its sails, Master Dan explained to Hannah. It
was fast and manoeuvrable, apparently. Hannah supposed that
made it ideal for carrying people and messages the length of the
Atlantic. To the usual dangers of wind and weather, the war with
the United States added the risk of American privateers, but they
would rely on speed to remove themselves from trouble.

The Redepenning party was given two small cabins, each with a
share of a skylight and a two-tiered bunk. Japheth and Master Dan
were comfortable enough, but Hannah and Mrs Captain slept with
a child each, and Pranisha spent her nights in the hammock slung in
the narrow walking space between the bunks.

The weather was fair for the first few days, and Hannah was
able to keep the children busy in a corner of the main deck that the
captain had decreed be set aside for Mrs Captain's use. On the
fourth morning out from port, they were having an arithmetic
lesson, using the ship as a source of examples. Neither Pranisha nor
Japheth had joined them, but Hannah figured they were old enough
to keep themselves out of trouble.

"If eight men climbed the mainmast, and three climbed the

foremast, how many would be up in the shrouds?" Mrs Captain asked Miss Ada, who thought for a moment, her lips moving, before she announced, "Eleven."

"As long as none of them fall off," Miss Marsha pointed out. She was certain the sailors were in constant danger of slipping, and watched them obsessively.

"Marsha," Mrs Captain said, ignoring the remark, "if Cookie has four kettles, and each kettle contains nine potatoes, how many potatoes does he have?"

Master Dan, who had been given a page full of problems to calculate, looked up from chewing the end of his pencil, and opened his mouth, but Mrs Captain held up a hand to stop him from providing the answer. She was getting a handle on this mothering business; she needn't speak for the children to obey her, and they loved her dearly. Mind you, they were all subdued at the moment.

Get them back to England and let them run wild with their cousins, and they'd soon begin to show a bit of spirit. Hannah could hardly wait. Miss Ada was going to be a rare handful, and Master Dan already bid fair to rival his uncles for mischief. Hannah had heard many stories about the Redepenning brothers and their cousin as boys, running untamed across the Longford landscape.

Miss Marsha bore watching. She was shy, and frightened of her own shadow, but under that she had spine, and a dry wit that popped out at unexpected moments and seemed to surprise her as much as anybody.

Hannah would have her work cut out for her. She grinned at the thought.

"Miz Captain?" It was Japheth, his cap in his hand. From the anxious crease in his brow and the twinkle in his eye, he'd done something, and wasn't sure how well it would be received. "Captain wants a word, Ma'am."

"What about?" Mrs Captain wondered, but she levered herself out of the canvas chair in the corner, and made her way in the direction Japheth indicated.

"Thirty-six potatoes," Miss Marsha told Hannah, and Hannah nodded, though her mind was still on what Japheth might be up to.

There was one way to find out. "Master Dan, you may set the next problems for your sisters. Addition for Miss Ada and times tables for Miss Marsha. Mr Japheth, step over here, please." In the etiquette of the servants' hall, his position entitled him to the honorific 'Mr'. She should have used his surname, but he did not have one.

The man followed her meekly, and began talking before she had a chance to ask him any questions. "Master Dan is fine with it, and it means you and Miz Captain will be able to get some proper sleep. More space, too, when the bad weather comes, so it will be all good, Hannah."

Hannah narrowed her eyes at him. "What are you talking about, Japheth? What have you done?"

Later that night, as she settled the two little girls into the lower bunk, one at each end, each with their own sheet so they didn't disturb one another in the night, she admired the man's common sense all over again. Of course, Mrs Captain had been anxious about Master Dan sleeping in the midshipmen's cabin, but they'd consented to have his servant come along with him, and Japheth would keep the boy safe. Now, Hannah and Pranisha would share one cabin, and Mrs Captain and the little ladies the other.

Hannah had argued for staying with the girls in case they needed something in the night, but Mrs Captain insisted that Hannah needed her sleep, and to be honest, she was looking forward to a bed, even such a narrow one, that she didn't share with Miss Ada's sharp elbows.

What kind of a life had Japheth had that he was afraid of Mrs Captain's reaction to such a sensible idea for their comfort?

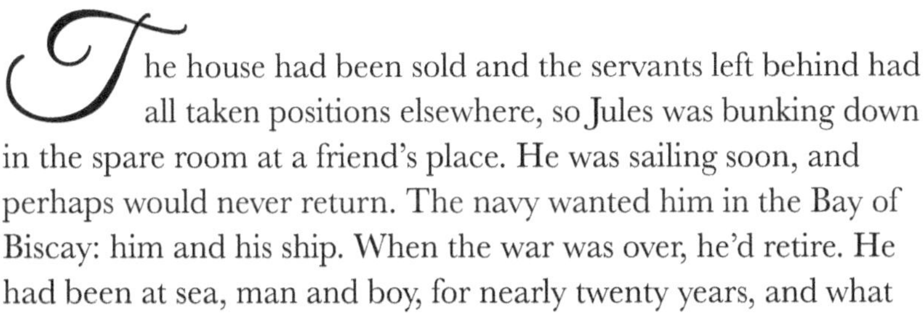

The house had been sold and the servants left behind had all taken positions elsewhere, so Jules was bunking down in the spare room at a friend's place. He was sailing soon, and perhaps would never return. The navy wanted him in the Bay of Biscay: him and his ship. When the war was over, he'd retire. He had been at sea, man and boy, for nearly twenty years, and what he'd said to Mia had been echoing ever since. Once the war was over, the Navy would offer little chance for advancement. They'd have more captains than ships, and he had never been willing to use his family connections to edge out men as well qualified as him and perhaps in greater need.

Besides, he had a family. He wanted to build a home with them, see his children grow, wake to his wife's welcoming smile.

The cemetery was his last stop before he sailed. He stood before Kirana's grave; the flowers someone had left long wilted on the mound of still raw earth. The tombstone he and Mia had planned was not yet in place, but he could see it in his mind's eye. "Here lies Kirana Redepenning, devoted mother and friend. Taken from us far too soon, she will always be in the hearts of Julius, Euronyme, Perdana, Marshanda and Adiratna."

"I will look after them, Kirana," he promised. "They will want for nothing."

*M*ia agreed to bring Japheth because of his budding romance with Hannah, and Pranisha because of her devotion to the two girls, but every day on board she thanked her guardian angel for the decision. Even with one adult for each child and one adult spare, some days she felt outnumbered, especially when Ada evaded her supervision for a moment and had to be rescued from the rigging—again.

Quiet Marsha was Hannah's particular charge and Ada kept Mia on the hop from morning to night. The child had no malice in her, but she would rush to carry out her latest idea without a moment's thought, and could not see why Dan had more freedom than she did.

The ship's captain had warned Mia to keep her female servants and daughters away from certain parts of the ship, and to never let any of them go anywhere alone. "Any man with any sense will leave a captain's females alone," he grumbled, "but give a man long enough at sea, and he loses all reason. They are not gentlemen below decks, ma'am, and you'd do well to remember it. I'll not have that young fire-eater of yours coming after me because you wandered where you shouldn't."

Mia warned Hannah and Pranisha, and Japheth and Dan for good measure, but her family had no trouble. Indeed, the men were polite and friendly, if rather shy. Still, she obeyed the captain's directives, and made sure that her new daughters did so too, though she also rather wished she was at liberty, like Dan, to go beyond the carefully circumscribed parts of the ship allowed them.

As she had discovered on the way to South Africa, sea travel shifted rapidly from boring to thrilling to alarming. Days of skimming over endless waves, seemingly going nowhere, were enlivened by sightings of dolphins or flying fish or even sharks. Twice, their progress was marked by a brief stop at impossibly beautiful islands to deliver and collect mail, and to replenish water and food. Several times, they changed course when a sharp-eyed lookout spotted sails that might possibly be hostile, evading notice or at least out-sailing it on each occasion, much to Dan's and Ada's disappointment. "Our father would have boarded them and taken the ship as a prize," Dan mourned.

Weather was an uneasy ally and frequent enemy. Glorious days might pin them without a breeze under the ruthless sun. Storms might blow them off course or even threaten to sink them. Mia's party spent many uncomfortable hours in their cabins, huddling together in the gloom when no lamp could be safely lit, eating cold food and telling stories. As much as possible, though, they lived their daytime lives on deck, watching ship life go by but never part of it.

Dan, with Japheth as his willing shadow, had managed to inveigle permission from her and the captain to tag along with the midshipmen, aping them as they went about their duties.

Pranisha had talked her way into the freedom of the galley, where she carried on a war of words with Cookie, to the great enjoyment of them both, and from which she emerged with exotic creations that blended Indian and British cooking, and that the crew and officers enjoyed as much as the family.

Hannah and Mia had nothing to do but entertain the girls, and even then, Hannah had the consolation of quiet moments talking to Japheth when both their charges were asleep. Each day, when he came for his lessons, Dan reported on their position, marking it on the map that Mia had purchased before they left Cape Town. Inch by inch, they were creeping closer to England.

The captain relaxed his caution about ship sightings as they reached the waters controlled by the Channel Fleet, and several times they sailed close enough to a British naval vessel to exchange greetings. They were within a few days of England, and then just a single night, and then, as the sun rose over the horizon in one direction, so did the coast in another.

They were almost home. True to its name, Swift had made excellent time.

Their destination was Plymouth Sounds. The Swift would be awaiting further orders, while its dispatches travelled by other means, and the whole ship buzzed with excitement at the thought of being in home waters.

"We will probably go on to Portsmouth, Mrs Redepenning," the captain told her, "and I would welcome you to stay aboard, but I cannot refuse the men their entertainments. It is unlikely to be suitable for a lady, and I have no idea how long until I get my orders."

They had had this conversation before, and Mia's answer had not changed. "Thank you, but we shall disembark. I am anxious to make my way home now that we are so close." Closer than Cape Town, certainly, but still more than two hundred miles, for she planned to go to London first, since that was where she expected to find Jules's father. With the threat of Captain Hackett hanging over Dan, she was anxious to place on record her right to custody of the children, and Brigadier-General Lord Redepenning would be her best ally.

They entered the Sounds late in the afternoon, to the excitement of the children, who ran from one side of the ship to the other pointing out features on the land that soon surrounded them, until Mia and Hannah herded them into one corner. "You must not get in the way of the crew," Hannah scolded. "If you will not be still, you will go to your cabins." The threat subdued them for several minutes before they once again began to point and exclaim.

Dan was fascinated by the beginnings of a massive barrier at the opening to the Sounds, and peppered the sailors with questions as they passed the ships and boats that waited to drop their burdens of rock and return to the land for another load. The work had just started this year, and nothing showed above the water, but the sailors assured them that thousands of tons of rock had been sunk and some of it could be seen when the tide was very low.

Once the ship docked, they were rowed to Plymouth, where they came ashore at last, reeling a little as they adjusted to being on land after the long weeks of a constantly moving deck. Mia led the way to the hotel recommended by the captain, and rented rooms for the whole party. After they were settled in their suite, Mia sat down to write letters to Jules' father and sisters, to announce that they were back in the country, and would be travelling to London.

A pair of footmen brought in the bath Hannah had ordered for her charges, but the much-needed dinner was not forthcoming. With half an ear, Mia heard the maid explain to Hannah that the chef could not provide the nursery supper she wanted. "This hotel prides itself on the finest French cuisine," the maid explained. "Monsieur says it is as much as his reputation is worth to provide a coddled egg and white bread for toasting."

Mia prepared to intervene, but she was not needed. "I will speak to him myself," Hannah said, and commissioned Pranisha to supervise the girls' bath, with Dan to follow under Japheth's eye.

Hannah was not back by the time all three children had been bathed and were in their nightclothes. Mia had great confidence in Hannah's ability to gain what she needed to do her duty by her charges, but clearly something had gone wrong. Mia had one more letter to write, and she'd then be ready for her own supper. *The children must be starving.* "Go down and see what the problem is, Japheth, will you," she asked.

15

The snooty maid who had shown the servants to Mrs Captain's rooms had insisted that servants must use the back stairs, so Hannah went down to the kitchen that way, though she would take the children by the main stairs. They would need to learn early that the best way to cope in English Society was to act as if they belonged. Which they did, since the Captain and Mrs Captain claimed them as Redepennings, which meant certain rights were theirs, through their great-grandfather the earl, their grandfather the baron, and their various lordly uncles.

Hannah, though, was a smuggler's widow from a small sea-side town at the back of beyond, whose only standing came from the family she served. She would use the back stairs.

They came out near the kitchens, and Hannah easily found her way into that cavernous space, where servants scurried to and fro in a frantic dance under the direction of a large figure in white. In the second or two she stood watching, this portly fellow screeched at a boy who had failed to baste the geese on the spit, berated a figure stirring a sauce in a pot, used a long wooden paddle to lightly clip the pate of an apprentice who was moving too slowly for his liking, and ordered more onion into another pot after a single nibble on the end of a spoon that twisted his mouth in distaste.

The chef. Hannah approached him, aware that his eyes tracked her progress as she skirted one hub of activity and cut behind another. She was aware, too, that she bore the signs of her long day. She had tidied her hair under her cap and changed her apron before coming downstairs, but her skirts were still encrusted with salt from where she'd been splashed in transit on the small boat that carried them into Plymouth, and it had not been her best gown when she put it on.

The chef looked down on her, and sneered, summing her up as of no account. "Out of my kitchen!" he demanded, not waiting for her to put her request to him. She knew the sort. Whatever she said, he would not be reasonable. If she tried to be conciliatory, he would see it as weakness.

"No," she answered. "Not until I have food suitable for my mistress's children."

She spoke as loudly as he had, and the whole kitchen hushed.

The chef waved a careless hand towards the prepared food waiting on a table near the doors. "We serve the best of French cuisine," he said. "Your children are *tres chanceaux* to be permitted to taste such *magnifique* dishes."

Hannah shook her head. She didn't know what a *tray chonso* was, but she understood the gist of his claim. "Undoubtedly the finest of its kind," she agreed, "but not right for the first meal on land for children who have been two months at sea, eating navy fare. They would be sick, and their mother would complain to your manager. We can avoid that by serving them the supper that I ordered."

He glared at her. "Toasted bread and gently boiled eggs. Pap."

"Pap is what they need tonight," she insisted, "and warm milk, with perhaps a sprinkling of cinnamon and a sprinkling of finely chopped ginger."

"*Moi*, I have no time for this," the chef announced, and he turned on their interested audience, driving the kitchen servants back to their work with the lash of his tongue and the waving of his paddle. Hannah watched while he ignored her.

When she had had enough, she began to prowl the kitchen, searching until she found a basket of eggs. She put six into a bowl, and picked up a loaf of bread, then looked around for a small kettle she could take up to put by the fire. She would also need a toasting fork and a knife to slice the bread.

"Stop!" the chef roared. Again, the kitchen hushed, as every person in it froze in place—except Hannah, who had just spied the toasting forks, and was picking one up. She ignored the chef as thoroughly as he had been ignoring her, and moved on to a rack of knives. Before she could make her selection, the chef interposed himself between her and the rack, forcing her back a step.

"Woman! What are you doing in my kitchen?" He was puce with indignation, but she caught the bewildered look in his eyes. The avid gaze of his minions reminded her that it did not do to embarrass a king, especially in his own realm. She had already challenged him, though he had given her no choice.

She spoke firmly but politely, in the nearest she could manage to the accent of her ladies. She would not give an inch, but she would not call him a pompous fool, either, however much she thought it. "You are too busy to be bothered by the needs of my nursery, sir, so I shall just fetch what I need for the care of Captain Redepenning's children. If I might have a jug of milk and a few spices, a pat of butter, a knife to cut the bread, and some serving ware—oh, and a tray to carry it all—I shall take myself off. Do not concern yourself, if you cannot spare someone to help me. I've become well used to seeing to my nursery in my lady's travels."

She turned away as if sure of his compliance, and put her burdens on a tray that was lying on the corner of the large table behind them. "This will do nicely," she commented.

The kitchen was silent except for the bubbling in pots and a spit and crackle from the geese slowly roasting over the fire. Hannah's mouth watered. She could murder a mouthful of roast goose.

Perhaps the chef had reconsidered her status in the light of her confidence and her mention of the captain and her lady. Or perhaps he merely hesitated to have a guest's servant removed bodily from the kitchen and realised she would not go without such force. For whatever reason, he capitulated, barking an order for someone called Minnie to "Give this madwoman whatever she wants and get her out of my kitchen."

At last! The poor little dears would be through their baths by now, and their bellies must think their throats had been cut.

With the laden tray, she headed back up the narrow staircase, counting the landings until she reached the floor she needed, where she rested a tray on the block mounted next to the door for that purpose, and opened the way into the main hall. The door had a mechanism to swing it closed, which made exiting with a tray slightly awkward. She backed out, holding the door open with one shoulder, and nearly tossed the tray in the air when she backed into a firm hand, which kneaded her buttocks.

"Hmmmm. A bit skinny, but what's a man to do when the maids won't come to the bell?" The voice was high and nasal. Even slurred with drink, its full-rounded vowels and clipped consonants attested to the aristocratic lineage that gave the thrice-damned tosspot behind her the belief he had license to attack a woman in a public place. He was crowding his body against Hannah so she could not escape without dropping her tray. As he shifted to wrap an arm around her, clutching at her breast, she could feel him grind his hips against her back, but without the hardness she might have expected.

Which didn't mean his physical arousal wouldn't come in the next few seconds as his other hand scrabbled to lift her skirts.

"I'll jus' put this yere tray down, zur, shall I?" she asked. Stress always brought echoes of her Devon girlhood back into her speech, though she'd spent years trying to erase them to do credit to the children in her care.

The nasty man stepped back, though he didn't remove his groping hand. He followed Hannah the few steps down the hall to the nearest table, announcing in lurid detail his obscene plans for her.

Hannah set the tray down and spun to face him, whipping the knife from the tray as she turned. It was serrated for cutting bread, but the sharp point would do some damage, especially pointed up into the man's chest. He was a great beast of a man, fully a foot taller than Hannah, finely dressed but dishevelled, broad in the shoulder and broader in the belly. "I'm taking supper to my lady's children, sir," Hannah told him. "I am not available for what you have in mind, and will thank you to let me be."

The surprise on his face turned to malice and rage, and he shot out a hand hard as iron that grasped hers before she could react, squeezing and twisting to force her to drop the knife.

"You vicious slut," he roared. "I'll teach you…"

The next moment, he was gone, knocked sideways. Japheth had come to her rescue, head-butting him in the side so they both fell to the floor, Japheth on top. In less time than it took for her to adjust to Japheth's sudden appearance, the would-be rapist flung Japheth off and hurled himself after, striking the smaller man with a punishing blow of his fist.

The crack of a gunshot stopped his second punch.

"Step away from my servant, or I shall place my second bullet in your black heart." Mrs Captain stood calmly before the closed door to their suite of rooms, a small pistol in each hand.

Along the hall, doors opened, as the inhabitants of other rooms peeked out to investigate the noise.

The man stood slowly, and Japheth scurried backwards as soon as he could, climbing to his feet, his eye already purpling and swelling.

"Your servant, bitch, shall be hanged for assaulting a belted earl!" the man growled. Hannah cast an alarmed glance at Japheth, whose face was rigid, only his wide eyes showing fear.

The earl took a step towards Mrs Captain, his hands fisted at his side, a great bull of a man with narrowed eyes and lowered head. "Do you know who I am?" he demanded. "I can do as I please, and no one will stop me. I'll tear your boy limb from limb and then I'll have you and your maid."

Mrs Captain lowered the aim of one pistol and raised both eyebrows. "To my knowledge, Lord Wayford, you have not yet supplied your earldom with an heir. Take one more step, and you will no longer have the capacity to do so."

Lord Wayford froze. Hannah was impressed. She knew Mrs

Captain well enough to realise that the calm exterior hid near panic, but no one else could tell from the even, authoritative voice; the untroubled face.

"Your pet boy assaulted me," Lord Wayford complained, though the bombast went out of his face.

"I see no evidence of that," Mrs Captain said. "I did not even observe you striking the blow that colours his eye, though I have no doubt that you did so. However, every person listening to this conversation can attest that you threatened my servants and myself."

All up and down the hall, doors closed, except one, which opened still further. Hannah let out a sigh of relief as she recognised the elegant individual who stepped into the hall, though she doubted he would know her from a bar of soap. He was Lord Chirbury's cousin, and had sometimes visited the family home at Longford Court when Hannah lived there. He was also a courtesy marquis and the heir to a duchy.

"Attempting to rape the maids again, Wayford?" he asked, his languid drawl belying the poise of his athlete's body. "You really are an embarrassment to the peerage."

He bowed to Mrs Captain, who had not relaxed at his appearance, her pistol still pointed at Lord Wayford's groin, wavering only as the drunkard did.

"Mrs Redepenning, I'm pleased to see you back in London. I hope I can tell Her Grace that your mission went without any difficulties? She was most anxious about the children."

"I have them with me, Lord Aldridge," Mrs Captain said. "In fact, until Lord Wayford interrupted my servants in the commission of their duties, they were bringing the children their supper."

The innkeeper hurried along the hall from the main stairs, his face creased with anxiety. He stopped to stare, open-mouthed, at the tableau. He stepped forward, but Lord Aldridge raised a hand to stop whatever he was about to say.

"Wayford, I suggest you apologise to Mrs Redepenning, and take yourself off. We shall hear nothing more about your consequence, or your drunken ramblings about being assaulted. Ah. Lady Wayford." He bowed again to a tall woman dressed in the height of fashion in garments some ten years too young for her, though she'd made skilful use of powder and paint to redress the discrepancy. "Do take your son in hand, my lady. Her Grace my mother would be most distressed to discover that he had attacked one of her goddaughters and that lady's servants."

Lady Wayford offered the briefest curtsey commensurate with good manners, already arguing before she rose. "You must be mistaken, Lord Aldridge. My son does not disport with unwilling gentlewomen."

Unwilling maids were clearly beneath her notice.

Lord Wayford turned to his mother, whining, "That woman pulled a gun on me, Mama. Just because…"

Before he could say another word, Lord Aldridge interrupted again. "I do hope I shall not feel obliged to challenge you, Wayford. I have urgent business in the west, and am expected at my mother's house party for Christmas. But you are close to leaving me with no choice. In the absence of the lady's husband, her brothers, her father (officers of the Crown, Lady Wayford, as you well know, but currently busy with the small matter of a war), and her cousin, it falls to me as cousin-in-law to see all due respect paid to Mrs Redepenning's honour, her person, and her household."

A slight exaggeration—the relatives were all the Captain's not Mrs Captain's, but either the threat or the list worked. Lady Wayford took her son's arm. "Come, Ulric. You do not want to fall afoul of the Redepennings, and you know what the Duchess of Haverford has been saying since that little misunderstanding at her garden party last year."

With a last glare, the monster allowed his mother to lead him away.

Hannah picked up the tray, and Japheth hurried past Mrs Captain to open the door to the suite, where Pranisha and the three children fell back to allow them to enter. Listening at the door, beyond a doubt, which was not gentry-like behaviour, but Hannah couldn't find it in herself to reprimand them.

"Now, my lovelies," she said, "Let's see about some toast and eggs."

Behind her, she heard Lord Aldridge say, "May I meet the children, Mia? My mother really is taking a most personal interest in them, and would be delighted if I make their acquaintance."

Hannah ran a quick eye over her charges and was happy enough with what she saw: they were clean and fresh from their baths, hair still damp, robes on over their nightclothes. It was not the usual thing, but the man was near enough to family. Besides, it was not her place to make the decision, and Mrs Captain was already inviting the marquis in. Good enough. That would keep the children awake and occupied while she and Pranisha made their supper.

She gestured to the Indian cook with her head, and carried the tray into the next room—the bedchamber allotted to Hannah and the two girls. By the time Mrs Captain sent the children through, the eggs and toast had been cooked and were waiting on the table by the window, a mug of hot spiced milk by each place.

Once the children were settled, Hannah came out to find Lord Aldridge had gone, and Mrs Captain had ordered supper for her and the three servants.

Mrs Captain didn't ask her any questions, saying only, "Hannah, Lord Wayford has a very bad reputation. I am sorry you were subjected to his unpleasantness and grateful Japheth was able to help you."

"You should not 'ave put yerself at risk," Hannah said to Japheth, who sat in a chair by the fireside with his head back and a piece of steak on his eye.

His other eye warm, Japheth said, "I would do anything for you, Hannah," he told her, forgetting formal address in the depth of his emotion. "Anything."

⁓ ❦ ⁓

*T*he children woke the next morning filled with a boundless energy after the excitement of the previous day and a good night's sleep. They needed exercise, and—with Aldridge probably already on his way to Cornwall and Lord Wayford who knew where—Mia did not want to leave the servants on their own at the hotel. When she went out to post her letters and to investigate options for removing them all to London, she took the whole party out with her, promising them a walk at Plymouth Hoe when her errands were completed.

The first task was soon accomplished. The inn in which they were staying was not a receiving office for mail, but sent them to the home of the postmistress, Mrs Rivers. Mia handed over a shilling and sixpence, and Mrs Rivers assured her that her letters would be put on the mail coach that left the Kings Arms at 6pm.

None of the travel options were particularly appealing. They could wait, as Lord Aldridge suggested, for him to complete his business and return. He would escort them to London, and his carriages were works of the latest engineering, but he could be gone for as much as ten days. She could hire her own carriage, but could not expect to accomplish the trip in under five days. The mail coach did the trip in less than forty-eight hours, but Mia had no intention of subjecting the children to the rigours of non-stop travel, or other passengers to the children. Several ships were due to leave Plymouth, headed ultimately for London, but those that took passengers all intended stops at ports along the way and would take even longer than the coach.

She was reluctant to call on naval connections, but it might come to that.

"Can we go to see the breakwater now, Ibu Mia?" Dan asked. "It is nearly low tide."

"Two million ton of rock will be needed," he explained to Mia as they walked towards the public park of Plymouth Hoe to a place from which they would be able to see across the Sounds to the construction site. He continued to share the information he had gleaned from the sailors. The breakwater was intended to protect the Sounds from storms sweeping in from the south, allowing safe mooring for many more of the ships that defended Britain against its enemies.

The park's shrubs were a wild scramble, the paths unkempt, and the lawns badly in need of a scythe, but the day was fine—crisp, as was to be expected in December, but sunny, with little breeze. A few other people were also taking the air, but not so many as to require that Mia refuse the children's pleadings to be allowed to run.

She nodded. "Stay where Hannah and I can see you, and be considerate of the other people."

After three months of structuring her routine around sick room duties and eight weeks in the cramped quarters of a naval ship, Mia was pleased to have nothing to do, for the moment, but walk in the fresh air, keeping alert to ensure the children did not need her, but otherwise free to enjoy the fresh air and the view.

The children raced along the path, ignoring the fort to their left, until they reached the slope down to the seashore. When Mia and the servants caught up with them, Dan was eagerly explaining the activity far across the bay. "The back of the ship opens, and the rocks can be dropped straight off into the water," he said. "The little ones with the gantries? They drop gravel to fill up the gaps."

He turned to Mia. "You can see the breakwater, Ibu Mia," he insisted. "Look. Where the waves break. It is because the rocks are all the way up to the surface."

"I cannot see any rocks," Ada complained.

"Look where the waves are white." Dan pointed, his voice rising as he turned back to Mia. "The sea is crashing over the rocks, isn't it, Ibu Mia?"

His earnest explanation had attracted attention from a woman further along the path. She stared at Dan, and then at Mia, before beginning to hurry towards them. In the next moment, Mia knew her. "Mary!"

"Mia! When I heard the young man say your name, I was sure it must be you. When did you get back? How long are you in Plymouth? And these must be Jules's children. Children, I am your Auntie Mary. Welcome to England."

"We arrived yesterday on the *Swift*. Mary, allow me to introduce Marshanda, Adiratna, and Perdana. Children, make your courtesies to your Auntie Mary. I did not expect to see you here in Plymouth, Mary, and without Rick or the boys?"

Mary waved to the foreshore below them, where several children hunted happily among the rocks. "The boys are looking for storm wrack. Why do you not send your three to join them? James! Bring your brothers to meet your cousins!"

Jules's children were shy, but eager to meet the cousins they'd heard so much about, and Rick's boys were friendly and openly curious. A chance remark that Dan had served two voyages with his father cemented their desire to bring this new cousin into their circle, and they cheerfully acquiesced when their mother suggested they took Auntie Mia's children with them to comb the rocks for treasure. Mia sent the servants to watch them.

"I'm delighted to see you, Mary," she said. "What brings you to Plymouth?" Rick's family had a house just out of Portsmouth, and also the use of various family homes around England, but none of those were this far west.

"Rick's ship has been in the Docks," Mary explained, "and we came down to Devon to be with him. Where are you staying? We hired a house but we are leaving tomorrow. Still, you are welcome for tonight."

Mia briefly considered uprooting her family for one night. It might be worth it, to avoid the obnoxious Lord Wayford. "We will be leaving ourselves," she temporised, "as soon as I can find passage to London. I need to deposit some documents with the family lawyer and consult with our father-in-law. He is still in London, I trust?"

"Yes," Mary nodded, "and we are to stay with him until we all go down to Longford Court for Christmas." She took Mia's hands and almost bounced in place, her smile broad as a new thought struck her. "We are sailing with Rick tomorrow, when he goes to London to pick up his orders and the rest of his crew. You must come with us."

Two days. Three at most, unless the weather was most unfair. It was more than tempting. "If you are sure he will not be in trouble with the navy."

Mary laughed at the notion of opposition. "You are his sister-in-law, and the wife of a captain. The ship is not on active duty and will have plenty of room. Of course, you will come."

16

———

The first of a succession of storms blew in after Jules left
Portugal, with orders to find certain British ships on patrol off
France. He carried messages for some, and replacement officers for
others. The Bay of Biscay also held supply ships from England that
required an escort home to protect them from cheeky American
privateers that might venture into the waters the British Navy had
controlled since Trafalgar.

One of his guests was an old shipmate from when he was a
young lieutenant, and—when Jules had a quiet moment or two—
they shared reminiscences of those days. Commander Hart, the
man was now, just appointed and on his way to his ship. Given he'd
been second lieutenant when Jules had been third, and then skipped
to first, Hart might have been bitter, but he was friendly enough. To
become a captain took more than skill and aptitude, though those
were needed. Good luck and connections played into such progres-
sion more than people thought. Perhaps his new appointment as
Commander would break Hart's bad luck and give him an opportunity to make captain.

As one squall succeeded another, Jules continued to quarter the
bay as well as possible in the conditions. On most days, it was too

dangerous to light the fires in the galley, so meals were cold, and so were the men. They struggled with wet canvas and water-heavy lines, lurching from hand-hold to hand-hold as they kept the bow of the ship into the waves, always wet, always tired.

The Bay was known for its storms. They stuck to their mission, but without much hope of carrying it out until the weather cleared. Even a hundred ships of the line would be nothing but a speck on the vast seas of the pocket of ocean bounded by Spain to the South and France to the East. With visibility down to a quarter mile at best and a couple of chains at worst, the chances that the *Advantage* would find the ships she sought seemed slender.

Jules doubled the watches and he and his officers snatched sleep when they could. They and their crew were veterans of the Cape of Good Hope, and they knew how to manage the *Advantage* in this kind of weather, but it was still wet, hard, constant work, with nothing but cold food to fuel their struggles.

Jules had been asleep no more than an hour on the third night from port when someone shook him awake. "Captain, you must come. Quickly."

He was up and into the trousers he kept ready before he was fully awake. Commander Hart? What was a passenger doing disturbing him in the night? "What is it?" he demanded.

"Lieutenant Bourne asked me to fetch you, sir. I saw something off the poop deck. He said I should show you."

Jules frowned, but shrugged into his coat and followed Hart up the ladder and into the blustering rain. It had come on heavy again, and Jules nearly swerved to join the men at the wheel, but Hart beckoned him on up to the poop deck and Jules shrugged and followed.

Hart was leaning over the aft rail, and Jules came up beside him and leant over himself to see what the man was pointing at. At the next moment, he felt an almighty blow to his head, and as he collapsed over the rail, half unconscious, someone grabbed his feet and shoved him upwards.

He flailed, grabbing for the rail, which left him swinging by one hand above the sea, the ship's rudder now directly below his feet and now off to one side and then the other. As he struggled to bring the other hand up, Hart undid his fingers, one by one, saying something in a conversational tone, his words muted by the wind. Still, as Jules plunged towards the waves below, thankfully missing the rudder, he thought he'd put together what the treacherous dog had said. "Compliments of Captain Hackett, you swine."

The sea tried to drag him down, and he stripped off the heavy coat. In just his shirt and trousers, he timed his rise on a wave to lift himself from the water. *There. Those distant lights must be the Advantage receding rapidly into the gloom.* As Jules sank again, going under for a moment, he reflected that at least he need not waste energy on trying to stay in one place in the hopes of being rescued.

After that came an endless time of struggle. He tried not to fight the waves, but to use them. He knew the *Advantage's* heading, so that gave him a direction to the coast. He was being swept for the southeast corner of the Bay, as best as he could guess it; all he had to do was stay afloat, and sooner or later he'd reach land.

What passed for sunlight at least confirmed his general direction, if only because the clouds were a little brighter with the sun behind them. It had passed from horizon to zenith and down to the opposite horizon before the feel of the waves changed. The storm had passed, and the swells, though still huge, were no longer swirling and unpredictable.

He kept himself going with thoughts of the children and Mia, but other notions intruded—the pleasures of simply giving in to the pain and the exhaustion, of letting himself slip under the waves, of not struggling any more.

A distant sound galvanised him. Surely that was waves crashing on land? It had better be a beach, for he had no strength left to battle rocks. He let the swells carry him in the direction of the sound, becoming surer by the second that he was hearing surf.

Even in the dark, he could soon see where the waves were breaking against a darker patch ahead of him, which must be the coast. As a midshipman, he had learned to bodysurf from islanders in the Andaman Sea, and he did his best to remember those long-ago lessons.

He would have to select a wave by feel and pray for sand and not rocks. Lying prone in the water, one hand down by his side, he made his choice, thrusting his other hand forward while spreading his legs and arching his back to drive his centre of gravity down. The wave lifted him and pushed him forward, and he spread his arms to control his position on its face.

For a long moment, he flew towards the beach, and then the wave curled over the top of him and he lost his balance, tumbling along, now upside down, now in front again for long enough to catch a fast breath before being rolled along the ocean floor until the suck signalled the wave was on its way out. Jules managed to get his feet under him and push against the power of the water until it was down to his thigh and then to his knee, and then sucking at his feet. He staggered onward, finally collapsing just above the reach of the waves.

Bruised and battered, every muscle aching, sick to the stomach from the sea water he had unwillingly ingested, Jules wanted nothing more than to lie on the sand. But he was wet to the skin and cold to the bone. He needed to move before he froze, and he also needed to find cover before sunrise, because this was almost certainly a beach in enemy France.

He forced himself to his feet. In the dark, all he could do was set his back to the sea and start walking, feeling for each step, his hands before him to fend off any obstacle before it connected with his face. The rain started again, which at least let him suck in a few drops of fresh water to ease his thirst.

He found a low bank by stumbling over it, stepping up from the sand onto a stiff grass that crunched under his feet. A few yards further on, his hands met leaves. Bushes. He pushed between them, finding they extended for some distance. He stumbled into a hollow in the ground surrounded by the foliage and stayed where he fell, hoping it would be enough to hide him until there was light enough to find better concealment and make a plan.

It was a miserable wait for dawn, but at last the landscape emerged from the darkness. He would stick to the coast, he decided, in the hopes of finding a sail boat he could steal. He could reach

England in anything; even a row boat, given time. He would probably not need to sail all the way; the bay was constantly patrolled by
British ships.

He kept to the cover of bushes as much as he could, running
across any open areas while scanning for other people. In the rain,
they could have been almost upon him before he saw them, but all
the more reason to take pains to stay unobserved.

He also kept an eye out for better shelter; with luck, somewhere
he could find dry clothing, or even something to wrap himself in
while his own clothing dried. This must be the most deserted,
Godforsaken piece of coast in all of France.

Then all of a sudden it wasn't. Out of the mist came a rag tag
army of ruffians, and Jules was surrounded before he could
convince his tired bones of the emergency. Not smugglers again!
Was his and Mia's story to begin and end with smugglers?

Someone shouted at him: a command by the tone. If it was a
question, it was peremptory. *I should have paid attention in French lessons,*
Jules thought. "My regrets, sir," he said. "I do not understand."

A cosh descended, and he sank into blackness.

Some time later, he woke to warmth. He was dry, and cocooned
in blankets. Every bone in his body hurt, and his head felt like hell,
but at least he was no longer cold. He counted that a gain, though a
brief examination of his surroundings added another point to the
minus column. The small room had no windows, and only the one
door—thick, wooden, and undoubtedly locked. It had no furniture;
just the mattress on the floor where he lay. He was naked under the
blanket, and his shirt was nowhere to be seen. Then the door
opened, and suddenly the room was full of soldiers.

⸎

By the time they reached London, Dan was firm friends
with Rick's three sons. Even James, the eldest by two
years, was impressed that Dan had sailed as his father's cabin boy.
Mia and Mary exchanged wry smiles over the stories of his two
voyages, which were heavy on adventure and light on the detail of

the mundane and often dirty tasks assigned to a cabin boy, but they said nothing.

Marsha was far more interested in her new aunt than the activities of the boys, and Ada stayed reluctantly with the ladies, too, after being rescued one time too many from the rigging, and scolded by Rick (who brought her down clinging to his back like a monkey), and then Mia, whose relief expressed itself in anger, and finally Hannah, who had the last word for good measure.

They docked in the London Pool, and left Rick hurrying to the Admiralty while they hired a couple of carriages to carry them and their baggage to their destination.

The townhouse belonging to Lord Redepenning, or Lord Henry as most of Society called him, was London home to all of his children and their families. Lord Henry was not in, but Mia and Mary were greeted as daughters of the house. The children and their nurses took over the children's floor, wholly given to nursery, schoolroom, and bedrooms for the younger members of the household. Pranisha and Japheth were introduced around the servant's hall. "Consider yourself on holiday, Pranisha," Mia said. "And, Japheth, I will need you to escort Hannah and the children if they go out, and to run errands for Hannah, but otherwise you can also have your time to yourself."

Mia then sat down to write a list of things to do before they left for Longford in West Gloucestershire, and Mary joined her in the small parlour to catch up on correspondence while she waited for her husband to return from a visit to the Admiralty.

They were still in the parlour when Lord Henry arrived home, greeting them both with delight and demanding to see his grandchildren. "Let's go up to the nursery," he suggested. "I am longing to see young Dan and the little girls. I feel I know them from your letters, Mia."

Upstairs, they found the children eating nursery tea under the supervision of Hannah and Curlock, who was governess to Mary's sons.

Mary's two younger boys hurled themselves in the direction of their grandfather, pulling themselves up short to imitate James, the eldest, who stood to attention and gave Lord Henry a smart bow. Lord Henry crouched and opened his arms, and they all flew to him, talking over one another in their eagerness to tell him the news of their new cousins, especially that Dan was a right 'un and had sailed with his father.

"I would like to meet Dan," Lord Henry told James. "But first, my boy, you must introduce me to his sisters, for the ladies must always come first."

Mia started to move across to where the three newcomers stood watching the welcome with longing eyes, but Mary put out a hand to stop her. "Let James," she whispered.

James took Marsha by one hand and Ada by the other and led them to Lord Henry. "Grandpapa, may I present Miss Redepenning and Miss Adiratna Redepenning," he said. "Girls…" He caught himself. "Ladies, Brigadier-General Lord Redepenning, our Grandpapa." The girls curtseyed as they had been taught, and Lord Henry bowed, gravely.

"You should call them Marsha and Ada, Grandpapa, like we do," Andrew advised.

"I am very pleased to meet you, Marsha and Ada," Lord Henry told the girls. "I have heard a great deal about you from Ibu Mia's letters." Mia couldn't repress a smile at what her father-in-law called her. He'd picked it up from her letters, of course, but the familiar term helped the girls to relax.

Dan was hopping from leg to leg, bursting to interrupt but constrained by his desire to do the right thing. Lord Henry took pity on him. "And this fine young man must be Perdana Redepenning." He held out a hand as James performed the introduction in proper order.

A few deft questions, with tactful asides to Mary's three boys, and Lord Henry was soon seated, with Ada perched on one knee, the boys crowding around, and even Marsha leaning on the arm of the couch, all engaged in eager conversation.

Mia met Hannah's eyes and they both sighed in satisfaction. Mary raised her eyebrows. "Did you doubt their reception, Mia?"

Mia returned Mary's smile. "Not really. But you have to

concede, Mary, that most families would not be as welcoming as the Redepennings. You know how the *ton* works as well as I." Mary, like Mia, had not been born into Society, though she was closer to the peerage than Mia, since her mother had been the daughter of a viscount who had run away with a humble naval lieutenant of no particular family.

"I would like to have met Lady Henry," Mary commented, and Mia nodded. Lady Henry had been gone nearly twenty years, but the stories her daughters-in-law had heard from her husband, sons, servants, and the least tenant on the estate at which she was *chatelaine* left Mia in no doubt that Lady Henry was responsible for the strong sense of family that had enveloped Mia when Jules first handed her over to his father's care, and that now welcomed the children.

*J*ules was, he figured out after a while, in Gascony. The local militia had taken him up as a spy. He was, after all, not in uniform.

Two men held him while another punched him, and a fourth— the man in charge—shouted at him in words he assumed to be French, or perhaps the local patois.

"Capitaine de la marine anglaise," he kept insisting, which nearly exhausted his French vocabulary.

The puncher and one of the holders changed places, and a fifth man lugged in a brazier. They bared his arm, and applied a hot poker, but that didn't suddenly imbue him with the ability to understand or make himself understood.

After a while, they gave up.

He had been lucky, he concluded, as he lay in a locked room after their attempts to force answers from him. He hadn't fallen into the hands of sadists, and the man in charge of his captors had ordered a stop after Jules was hoarse from screaming and near fainting with the pain.

Someone put salve on his wounds, and returned each day to change it, and he slowly recovered. He managed to convey his name and that he was hungry. He could also remember how to say he saw the king and to ask for the pen of his aunt, but neither seemed likely to be useful in the near future.

They decided to believe him or, more likely, they sent for someone who could make a decision about him. Who knew how long it would take for someone to attend to an Englishman, found naked and alone? He'd been unconscious when he arrived, but he was slowly regaining his strength, helped by the meals brought to him twice a day.

The bruises and scrapes from his landing were all but healed, and most of the injuries from his interrogations. They'd even sent someone to straighten and bind the fingers they'd broken in an effort to improve his understanding.

The lull didn't mean he wouldn't be tortured again, or that he wouldn't be shot as a spy, but in the meantime, he was fed, dressed, and had a roof over his head. Twenty years in His Majesty's Navy had taught him to be grateful for present mercies.

He was warm, at least, and if the food was monotonous— mainly stew, with an emphasis on gravy and vegetables, served with fresh bread—it was at least tasty and plentiful.

Inactivity was the worst. He hated having no one to talk to beyond the prison cat, which somehow managed to find its way into the room where he was kept. He missed his children fiercely, wondering how they were managing in England, but not as much as he wondered how Mia was managing. She was so much more than he expected; more than he deserved. He agonised at being stuck here in a French prison with no way to get to her, to all of them.

He countered boredom by making elaborate plans for his ideal home. Perhaps, if he managed to convince the interrogators who were undoubtedly coming for him that he was an officer in the Navy, he might be treated as a prisoner-of-war. Then, years from now when the war was over, he would be released to go home.

He hoped with a fierce passion that Hart would survive the war to face a court-martial. Meanwhile, he had a house to build.

In a stone-walled room of what was surely the local medieval castle, he lay on his bed, or paced to and fro, or put himself through the limbering exercises he'd learned as a sword-fighter. All the while, in his head, he ignored his surroundings and debated the pros and cons of internal plumbing, a food lift from the kitchen to the dining room, and other domestic facilities.

He planned the layout of the house. Only one bedchamber in the master suite, for he wanted to share a bed with Mia every night for the rest of his life, but space for many children; for grandchildren, too, for that matter. He beguiled his time with pictures of a large tribe of children and grandchildren sailing boats on a pond, playing ball in the garden, building forts in a little wood, fully aware that he was recreating his memories of Longford Court. What of it? No one could have wished for a better childhood.

It would not be the same, with Mia as *chatelaine* rather than Mama. It would be better, and even his father would not think him disloyal for the thought, for it would be their home: his and Mia's. Every night, he went to sleep with memories of Mia in his arms, in two minds about whether such dreams were more likely to keep him sane or drive him mad, but he could no more stop remembering than he could stop breathing.

Whatever the future held, he had his memories and his dreams, and if that was all he would ever have, he had still been blessed beyond what he deserved.

17

Lord Henry accompanied Mia to the meeting with the family lawyer, and his presence may have been a factor in how quickly her business was accomplished. Jules's guardianship and Mia's custody of Kirana's children was now a matter of recorded law, and an attested copy of the will Jules had made in Cape Town reposed in the lawyer's safe.

They'd be leaving for Longford Court once Rick's ship sailed, and meanwhile Mary spent as much time with him as he could spare from his official duties. He and Lord Henry were seldom available during the day, but both made a point of spending time with the children every evening. The children attended to their lessons in the morning, and in the afternoon, Mary and Mia took all six on outings.

Lord Henry's library disgorged a copy of 'The Picture of London', which helped guide their sight-seeing, but the three who had been raised in England already had favourite sites to show their cousins. All of them enjoyed ices at Gunthers. They were awed by the exhibitions at the British Museum. Marsha did not like the sad animals in the Tower of London zoo. Ada was bored by the

Changing of the Guard at St James Palace, but the other children were riveted.

They spent a whole afternoon at Bullock's Museum in Piccadilly, where Mia's children were delighted to show off to Mary's children what they knew about animals of which the latter had never heard, and where the boys would have stayed forever in the Armoury, which was done up like the interior of an ancient castle. Only the threat of missing nursery tea and the promise of a return visit at some future time stopped the grumbles when they were torn away.

They walked several times in nearby Hyde Park, but a sedate perambulation along shingled walks did not much satisfy the children's need for physical activity, so, when several days of fine weather dried the ground, Mary and Mia let them run off some energy chasing balls on the grass.

Dressed warmly, with Japheth as reinforcement to the usual expeditionary troops of the two ladies, Hannah, and the governess, they took over a spare patch of land with balls, hoops, and much riotous activity.

After they came, rosy cheeked and laughing, to drop on the blankets for a bite to eat, Mary proclaimed thirty minutes of quiet strolling while they let their food settle, before they began running around again.

"Stay in sight," she commanded.

The two women returned to the conversation they'd been having before they called the children in for food. Mary was telling Mia about the recent courtship and marriage of Jules's sister Susan, who had wed a man to whom she'd always declared an antipathy, after weeks in his company as they searched together for her kidnapped daughter. Amy had, thankfully, been retrieved at the end of a long chase that took them all the way to Edinburgh, but not before Susan and Gil had acknowledged their love for one another.

"Who is that talking to Dan?" Mia asked, after a while.

Mary looked in the direction Mia was indicating. "I do not know, but she has been watching us every time we've been here this week."

Dan gave a short bow to the stranger and ran off to re-join the other children, who were consulting with the servants about whether their thirty minutes were up.

They came to the mothers for adjudication, which gave Mia the chance to ask, "Who were you talking to, Dan?"

Dan shrugged. "I don't know. Just some lady. She wanted to know when we're coming again."

Mia narrowed her eyes at the woman, who, from what Mia could see, was gathering her shawl and reticule, and preparing to leave. "What did you tell her?"

Dan shrugged more expansively. "I said I didn't think we'd come again soon, because we are going to go and stay with our uncle for Christmas." The other children were already streaming back to their makeshift soccer pitch, and Dan was itching to join them. Mia nodded her permission, and he was gone before she could speak the words.

"Who do you think it is?" Mary asked.

Mia set her chin. "I do not know, but I intend to find out. Stay here, Mary, and keep an eye on them."

The woman was walking away down one of the paths that led out of the park. Mia hurried her steps and came up beside her. Before she could think of the words she needed, the woman spoke.

"You are Mrs Redepenning, are you not?"

Mia answered, coldly, "You appear to know me and my family, ma'am, but I do not know you."

The woman looked to be in her forties; plump, with a discontented face, richly dressed in expensive materials but subdued colours. "You have met my husband, I believe. I am Mrs Hackett. That boy is Captain Hackett's son."

Mia shook her head at that. "Perdana is my son; mine and my husband's. I have already told Captain Hackett that he has no claim on the boy. I have no idea what he means by sending you here…"

Mrs Hackett lifted both eyebrows in surprise. "You do not wish to be rid of the boy? My husband said you were bringing him to England for us, and I thought…"

"No, Mrs Hackett," Mia told her fervently. "That is not the case.

Perdana is ours. We will fight your husband in the courts if necessary, but we will never give him up."

Mrs Hackett shook her head, more in bewilderment than negation. "You do not mind?"

"Mind?"

"That your husband expects you to raise his half-breed bastards." For the first time, some emotion other than confusion crossed the woman's face as her eyes flashed and her voice dropped to a hiss. "That woman… They say you should not speak ill of the dead. But she ensorcelled my husband and yours, tempting them from their duty to their wives. He was infatuated with her—even wanted to keep her in the same town as his real family."

She took a deep breath and recovered her poise. "I was so glad when she left Captain Hackett for your husband. I thought we'd heard the last of her and her brat."

She was mistaken in so many ways. Mia had no idea where to start in untangling her misconceptions. Before she could speak, Mrs Hackett rushed on, determined to have her say.

"The Captain is obsessed with having a son. To have him passing over his daughters—his legitimate children—and planning to leave all to that little yellow bastard; I wish you well of him. I hope your children are not neglected as mine have been."

Mia drew herself up and lifted her chin. "Our son is a joy to us both, Mrs Hackett. I am sorry for your troubles, but they are not mine."

But Mrs Hackett had said what she'd come to say, and left without another word. Mia returned to Hannah. "Collect the children, Hannah. We are going home."

⁂

Mia waited anxiously until Lord Henry had come down from the nursery after romping with the grandchildren and reading them a story. She was about to ask for a private interview when he begged one of her.

Captain Hackett had been to the Admiralty to make a

complaint about Jules, and a friend had sent a message to the Horse Guard, for Lord Henry. "I spoke to him myself, Mia. He seems to have convinced himself that our Perdana is unwanted. I told him Dan is a loved member of our family, and that we all, from the Earl of Chirbury and myself to every one of our family and social connections, will defend him by every means required."

"I hope that will be the last of it." Mia said, after relating her encounter with Mrs Hackett.

"We will be leaving for Longford Court at the end of this week," Lord Henry pointed out. "Between now and then, perhaps you and the children could forego the park. I will make sure you have an escort wherever you go, Mia."

That was easily accomplished. It set in to rain, and their only other outing was to the townhouse—a palace in all but the name— of the Duke of Haverford. Aldridge himself brought the invitation to see his mother, and returned with a carriage the next day to escort Mia and the three children.

Mia knew she had no need to be nervous; the great lady had always been very kind to her, and had promised her support when they'd met before Mia made her journey to Cape Town. None-theless, she hoped Ada would not be too forward, nor Marsha too shy. The support of a duchess could make all the difference to the children as they reached adulthood and needed to make their way in the English world.

She need not have worried. In minutes, the duchess had set the children at ease, and had them chatting about what they'd seen in London, and what they hoped to see on their next visit.

"They are delightful," Her Grace murmured to Mia as they left, their half hour up. "They will do very well, my dear. We shall do all we can to see to that."

⁂

The questioning began again. An army major arrived from Boulogne, with a detail of soldiers to relieve the militia of their current duty. With the major was a man who had some rudimentary English, and between his mangled English and Jules's worse French, they managed some level of communication.

The major would not agree he was an officer and a prisoner of war, but nor was he prepared to shoot Jules out of hand as a spy. He sent for further instructions.

In the meanwhile, Jules was treated well enough, except for the boredom.

He almost welcomed the several times a week when he was taken from his cell to have questions fired at him by various men who came in response to the major's messages—military, some of them. Others were a mystery.

Those who thought he was a spy asked him about troop movements and battle plans, or demanded to know his mission in France. Those who leaned towards thinking him a naval captain were keen to berate him about the treatment of French sailors on the hulks. Jules had heard about the floating prisons from other captains, and found the whole idea appalling. To disable a ship and then stuff it to the gunwales with prisoners? Insufficient space, food, and exercise? Disgusting. No sailor could countenance such misuse.

"The hulks are a disgrace," he agreed to one interrogator, "but what can be done? Napoleon will not exchange prisoners."

The criticism of the Emperor, or perhaps his casual reference to the august personage, fetched him another buffet around the ears and he was returned to his cell.

Once more, he was alone.

***

The day before Rick was due to leave, Lord Henry came home with dreadful news from the Admiralty.

"They could tell me very little; just that Jules fell overboard during a storm and has not been seen since. He is an excellent swimmer, Mia. He has probably come ashore in France. He'll either be hiding and finding his way home, or he'll be imprisoned, which is not the worst. He is an officer. He will be treated well."

Mia could not think; could not even speak, but she heard Rick's comment. "The French have been refusing prisoner exchanges. He could be there until the war ends."

"True," Lord Henry agreed, "but that cannot be much longer. The French were turned back from Russia and are on the run in Spain." He put a hand on Mia's and gave it a squeeze. "He will return, Mia."

Mia nodded. She had to believe that was true, or at least pretend to do so. The children had already lost one parent, and she could not let them think the other was also gone.

The following day, they said farewell to Rick, and then it was time for Lord Henry, Mary, Mia, the six children, and the nurses and servants to leave for Longford in a procession of carriages.

They arrived to an ecstatic welcome from the assembled family, tempered by the absence of three of Lord Henry's four boys. Harry was in the thick of fighting in Spain and Rick was back at sea. As for Jules, the whole family conspired to be cheerful, assuring the children that Jules would be on parole somewhere in France, unable to leave because he had given his word of honour, unable to get word to them, given the war, but free to walk down to the local village for a cup of coffee or a glass of wine.

It was hard, even for Mia, to remain gloomy when the over-flowing nursery floor bubbled with seasonal cheer and simmered with mischief. Between the four families now in residence, and visits from Susan and her sister-in-law, there was a veritable tribe of children, seventeen in all, most aged eleven or under, plus Anne's sister Meg, who was physically an adult but whose mind had never grown up.

Mia's children were absorbed into the tribe as if they had always belonged, and she kept her own simmering worry hidden from them so they could wholeheartedly enjoy their first Longford Christmas. She had plenty to do; enough to keep her composed and cheerful on the surface, even as one horrible imagining after another played out its scenes in the cellars of her mind.

In years to come, she would barely remember the weeks the whole family was together. One of the children would recall those times, and she would struggle for the memory. 'This is the ribbon we bought the first time we helped put up the decorations at Longford,' Marsha might say, pulling it from the box, and Mia would stare at it vaguely.

Each day stretched beyond reason; each restless night was endless. Yet the weeks all blurred together, rushing so fast that they were over before she knew, leaving just a few blurred impressions.

With a moratorium declared on lessons, the young people needed entertainment, and all of the adults were roped into suggesting indoor activities for wet days and outings for fine. Their numbers were often swelled by children from the local village, including the rector's and the squire's children, and the gamekeeper's son, Paul Mogg, who was something of a leader to the mob of Redepenning boys and their friends.

"Paul can be trusted, Mia," Kitty assured her friend, as the boys careened off after Paul one day, into the sodden woods. "He is a sensible lad. The vicar is teaching him his Latin and Geometry, and speaks of seeking a scholarship for him next year, but Luke—that is, Mr Mogg—requires convincing."

"A job for you, Kitty," Mia suggested, prompting a blush. Mia retreated from her teasing. Kitty's admiration of the gamekeeper was a secret to the rest of the family, especially Kitty's older sister, Anne, and Mia had no wish to embarrass her.

"Perhaps Rede can have a word with him," she suggested. Rede was their host, the current Earl of Chirbury. His father had been brother to George's father, the eldest son, and to Lord Henry, the youngest.

Kitty let the subject drop and hurried off to the village to practice with the psalm singers, who were preparing for the Christmas celebration. Paul Mogg had been chosen to sing the carol *This Endris Night* during communion, but his voice had begun breaking, so Kitty was singing it instead.

Mia climbed the stairs to the Long Gallery under the roof, with its barrel-vaulted ceiling, where the girls were playing charades with babies crawling or toddling merrily through the older children's set pieces under the supervision of several nurses, governesses and mothers.

Cook opened her kitchen, or at least a table in the corner of it, for Christmas baking. Auntie Mary taught everyone how to make and ice her famous gingerbread characters. An entire pantry in the huge basement was cleared for the food that would fill the traditional boxes for the tenants and the local poor, but more than enough was collecting in the pantry for the household.

Pranisha was absorbed into the workings of the kitchen, and was clearly talking about her charges, because a hungry tribe of boys soon found that sending Dan to the doorway would bring Cook and half-a-dozen kitchen maids with a basket full of treats for 'Master Julius's poor little orphans.'

On Christmas Eve, the uncles led an expedition to collect greenery for decorating the house, and the aunts set up a competition between the age groups to create the most beautiful swags, the winner to be chosen by Hannah, who had had a hand in raising most of them and might therefore be trusted to be impartial.

Hannah, though, had sought for and received permission to take Japheth to visit her friend Dorcas, sister to John Price, the man she had hoped to marry. The competitors had to be satisfied with a vote by all the adults, and the team made up of the older girls, including Marsha, were declared the winners.

Christmas Day meant a ride to the village church, most of the women and children in one of several carriages, and most of the men on horseback. The Redepenning box was filled to overflowing, and some of its offshoots found places in the rest of the church but Rede insisted that Mia and her three take seats with him, Anne, and their children.

Kitty sat with the psalm singers in the West gallery, of course, and the whole church stilled when she began her solo, those making their way to or from the altar rail for communion moving with exaggerated care so they didn't miss a note.

Afterwards, there were neighbours to greet, and then home to a massive Christmas dinner, all the dishes laid out on the table so that the servants could be dismissed to their own meal.

The family moved up to the Long Gallery to sing carols, play party games, and share stories of Christmases past. 'Do you remember…,' 'Do you remember…' the Redepennings by birth said to one another, and Jules's name came into so many of the stories that, after putting the exhausted children to bed, Mia claimed tiredness herself and retreated to her bedchamber to weep into her pillow.

She put on a cheerful face for the expedition to take boxes to the tenants and the poor of the village. The whole family was set to work, a couple of adults and a handful of children to each carriage full of baskets. One scene penetrated Mia's fog: Marsha and Ada on their knees by a fire, playing with a cottager's half-grown kitten.

That evening, Mia asked Anne if she could put out word for kittens still young enough to move from home to home, but old enough to leave their mother. Anne asked around, and a couple of days later, Rede drove Mia over to Niddleberrow, a small village 30 minutes' drive away, to view a promising out-of-season litter. Two of the wee darlings chosen, they arranged to pick them up in time for Twelfth Night.

The thought of the children's reaction helped Mia to maintain her good cheer for the remaining days of Christmas. She also took heart from the way the children had been absorbed into the Redepenning tribe, even Marsha coming out of her shell to take especial care of sweet Meg, whose adult body held a child's mind.

Twelfth Night was traditionally a party for the whole village and estate, all the public rooms thrown open and full of good cheer, the local gentry mixing easily with tenant farmers, tradespeople, and the lesser sort. They finished the day with a family supper served as a buffet, and Twelfth Night presents for the children.

The kittens were a huge hit, making the urgent search well worth the trouble.

Mia, alone in her room after everyone had gone to bed, reflected on her blessings. She had three wonderful children. She had a family who would be on her side no matter what. She had her memories of Jules. She could wish him back, to build the future of which they'd dreamed, but she could not wish her marriage undone, or any of the steps in it that brought her to this moment.

18

Jules recognised his visitor immediately, though he hadn't seen her since he was a boy. Lady Carrington. He and Alex had made up stories in which the local beauty was the lady in distress, trapped by trolls in a dungeon or a tower, waiting for rescue by the local knights, Jules and Alex at their head. All nonsense, of course. She was her husband's creature and he was monstrous. Dead now, some five years, but before that he'd run a ring smuggling goods and people in and out of England. Not to mention assaulting Jules's wife. Lady Carrington was an accomplice to that foul action, just as she was to the vile man's other schemes.

According to letters from home, she had escaped custody when Lord Carrington was killed. To France, it now appeared. He could easily imagine how she supported herself in a foreign country at war with his own, but what was she doing in his prison cell?

He bowed. "Lady Carrington, to what do I owe the pleasure?"

"Believe me," she purred, her whole presence calculated for seduction, "I intend you to owe me pleasure." Despite himself, he felt a stirring at her overt sensuality.

He could hardly throw her out, with the guard standing at the door to ensure his good manners. "Please," he said, "be seated. I have little to offer you but I can at least give you a chair."

"I will send my servant to fetch wine," she decided. "A better vintage than the swill they serve here. That will be the first pleasure I offer you."

"That will be pleasant", he agreed, cautiously. The lady was a snake and he would be careful not to turn his back.

"We might be able to be of use to one another," she proposed, coming close enough to cup his face with her hand.

Jules felt the hairs rise on the back of his neck. "I have nothing available for your use, my lady."

"Come now, Captain. You are an experienced gentleman. I am an experienced lady. I have arranged for us to be left alone, if you so desire. You have rather a lot I can use." She ran her fingers in a caressing slide around his cheek and he took a pace back, out of reach.

"I must thank you for the compliment, my lady, but decline."

She stepped closer again and put a bold hand on his falls. "Are you certain? I am sure you could be persuaded."

He grabbed her wrist to move her hand away, but the guard growled and waved a rifle at him. "The part of me you hold, Madam, has no sense, but does not rule me. I am not available for your games."

"It seems to me, Captain," she purred, rubbing his stupidest part and smiling at the reaction, "that you are very available. After all, you have no other place to go and nothing to do."

Jules shook his head, and set his mind to thinking of the most horrific images he could. Imagining Lady Carrington as a rotting corpse with worms coming out of her nostrils allowed him to recover his poise enough to say, politely. "It is nothing personal, Baroness. I have a wife. I have promised fidelity to that wife."

"Little Mia will never know," Lady Carrington assured him. "What can it matter?"

"I will know," he pointed out.

Lady Carrington turned from him with a huff of disdain. "You Redepennings are fools. You believe marriage is about love.

Marriage is the most brutal of games and one that nobody wins."
She took a deep breath and faced him, forcing a smile. "Still, that is
not the only reason I came. You will pretend, however, that you are
at least considering my proposition, since that is why I was sent to
visit you. My… hosts… think you will spill your secrets on the
pillow. But you really are a naval captain, are you not? You have no
secrets. I have another proposition for you, one that might be more
to your liking."

Jules inclined his head. "And that is?"

The lady held up her finger and shook it side to side. "Uh, uh,
uh. First, I must be sure that you can be trusted. You will affect to be
tempted by me, Julius Redepenning, or none of this will work."

Several visits followed, during which Jules had to pretend to
respond while not actually allowing himself to be aroused by the
siren's ardent efforts. In some ways, it was easier when he got her
talking about herself. Holding forth on how she felt as a child barely
into her teens married to the monster who was her husband, she
forgot to be seductive. She didn't blame Lord Carrington. That was
somehow more horrifying than the rest, that she regarded his preda-
tory self-interest as the ideal, and castigated herself for failing to live
up to his model. She had helped her step-son to extract and hide his
sisters from the baron, and had later sent her own daughters to the
step-son for their safety. To Jules's horror, she regarded both acts of
charity as sins against her duty to her husband. The woman was
selfish, mean, and sexually voracious, but Jules could not help a
reluctant sympathy when he considered what she'd been through.

At last, Lady Carrington managed to persuade whoever
controlled the guard to remove the man from the room during her
visit. With no witnesses, she came to the point.

"I will have your promise as a gentleman you will not speak of
this to anyone," she insisted.

Jules was suspicious. "As long as staying silent can be done with
honour, my lady."

Lady Carrington heaved a sigh. "You Redepennings." She
tapped him on the chest. She kept looking for excuses to touch him,
and if she were not female, he would have punched her by now.

"Keeping my secret will not dishonour you," she assured him, her voice heavily patient, "quite the contrary. Do I have your promise?"

"Very well," Jules agreed. "I will keep your secret unless it touches my honour."

Lady Carrington nodded. "That will do. I am willing to arrange an escape in return for a favour."

"What kind of a favour?" It must be a big one, and he could not imagine how she would arrange an escape without the help of his guards, so she was either servicing the lot of them (highly probable), or this 'favour' would benefit the French.

"I left England in a hurry," she continued, "so was forced to abandon some items of value."

Jules had heard how she had left England. Held to face charges of kidnapping and murder, as an accessory to her vile husband, she had escaped with the help of Rede's nephew, one of her acolytes. "You wish me to collect them for you," he stated, but she shook her head.

"I wish you to escort me so I can collect them myself. I want you to smuggle me back into England and out again. That is my condition." This must be important to her, because for once she was keeping her hands to herself; leaning forward in her chair, her eyes intent. "You promise me safe passage in and out." She read the uncertainty in his eyes, and guessed the source. "I am not a threat to England." With a passion he could not disbelieve, she added, "I have no further wish to be part of the scheming of men to dominate everyone else. My desires have never been political; I want only to survive."

***

The party dispersed one family at a time: Lord Henry for London and his duties at the Horse Guard, Mary and her children for Portsmouth, Alex and Ella for their horse farm in Leicestershire. Even Rede and Anne left for Anne's estate in Essex, accompanied by Susan and her husband. Soon, only Mia and Kitty remained of the adult Redepennings, and in the nursery and schoolroom, only Mia's three and Meg, who was uncomfortable anywhere but her own home, and seldom travelled.

Mia remained at Lord Henry's advice. "You would be wise to stay away from London until we find out what Hackett is up to," he said.

The children moped for a few days, but Longford Court was a marvellous house for children, with acres of grounds to roam and the whole third floor, including the Long Gallery, available for their entertainment in stormy weather.

"Even his own lawyers have advised Hackett his case cannot succeed," Lord Henry wrote. "The man is stubborn and will not believe it. He thinks Jules's disappearance strengthens his case, but the guardianship status is clear. I doubt that he knows you went to Longford, for he does not move in our circles, but I have sent word around town that the family have all dispersed, to Leicestershire, Essex, and Hampshire. If he does mean mischief, that should keep him busy."

Mia looked up from Lord Henry's letter, at a knock on the door. Hannah came in, with Japheth behind her.

"Mrs Captain? Mr Japheth here has something he needs to tell you."

Japheth crossed the room, his cap in his hand, the accent he had been working to remove thickening his words. "Keep Masta Dan home, Miz Captain. A man? He give money for me to bring Masta Dan to the abandoned cottage, t'other side of estate bridge."

In her agitation, Mia stood, the letter fluttering unnoticed to the ground. "What man? Do you know his name? Did he say what he wants with Dan?"

Japheth was shaking his head. "No, ma'am. Didn' tell me. Jus' give me a crown and said there'd be five more if I brung 'the brat they call Dan Redepenning' to cottage tomorra, between noon and sundown."

"Describe him, Japheth." She had to stay calm. She had to think. Dan was upstairs this minute taking a piano lesson from Kitty, and therefore safe. She let herself sink back into her seat.

Japheth did his best, but could tell her little except that the man was white and burly.

"What did you tell him, Japheth?" she asked.

"Said nothin', ma'am," Japheth assured her. "Jus' took the crown and came and tol' Miz Cottle."

"Good man!" She took a deep breath. "We had better warn the household."

Hannah had not closed the door behind her, and now someone else looked into the room, and advanced when he saw her there. It was Lucas Mogg, the gamekeeper, with his son Paul at his heels.

Mogg inclined his head in respectful greeting. "Mrs Redepenning."

She struggled to remain courteous. A few minutes delay in setting guards and sending people to investigate the cottage would not matter. "Mr Mogg, Paul. Were you looking for Lady Kitty?"

"We were looking for you, ma'am," Mogg told her. "Paul, here, has something you need to know."

At the prompt, Paul came to the front, his face a picture of indecision. "Mrs Redepenning, is Dan in some kind of trouble?"

"What makes you ask that, Paul?" She managed to keep her voice calm. Paul looked as if he would bolt at any moment.

"Go on, Paul," Mogg encouraged. "Tell Mrs Redepenning what you told me."

Paul's next words had Mia back on her feet, her hands trembling with the urge to shake the full story out of the boy. "Only, the men said they came from Dan's father and that Dan would want to see them. They said you would be angry if you knew. I don't want to get Dan into trouble."

Somehow, Mia managed to keep her agitation from strangling her voice. "Paul, Dan is in danger. A man wants to steal him from his family and take him away. I believe he has sent men to kidnap our boy." She met Mogg's eyes as she said, "I have just found out that they tried to pay Japheth to take Dan to the abandoned cottage on the other side of the Nidd—the one near the bridge from the estate."

"That's where they told me to take him!" Paul exclaimed. "Why does the man want him? Is he really Dan's father?"

Mia shook her head. "He believes he is, Paul, but he is wrong. Captain Redepenning is Dan's father, and he loves him dearly, as do I. Captain Hackett has never even met Dan. He came to us in London, and we turned him away." She took another deep breath, the letter fresh in her mind. Kitty trusted Mogg, and so did Rede. The more he knew, the better he could help to protect her son. It was to the gamekeeper she said, "He has been trying to convince the courts that he has a right to our son, just because he knew Dan's mother before Dan was born, but he must realise he will fail. He must be the person behind these approaches."

Mogg nodded. "I told Paul it couldn't be true. Your husband is in France, Lady Kitty told me, and there's no reason he wouldn't walk right up to the front door and be welcomed home."

Mia reached for his hand. "Thank you for coming to me with this."

"We'll watch out for the boy, Mrs Redepenning," Mogg assured her.

"Ibu Mia? Who is Captain Hackett?"

Dan must have finished his lesson, for there he was in the doorway, Kitty behind him. "Will you wait here, please?" Mia asked the other adults in the room. "Kitty, you too. I need a moment with my son, and then we can discuss what we are going to do. Japheth, send a footman for Cole and Bowles, please." The butler and stable master would marshal the house to watch for intruders.

In the next room, she asked Dan what he had heard, and what questions he had. A few minutes discussion reassured him that he was Mia's son and Jules's, and that they did not intend to give him up. "The Duchess of Haverford herself is on our side, Dan, and you know she is a very great lady."

"Yes," Dan said, comforted, "and Uncle Rede is a great man, and so are Uncle Alex and Uncle Gil. Grandpapa, too."

"Exactly," she agreed. "That silly man knows it, too. That is why he is trying to steal you, but we shall stop him, you may be sure of that. Until he is behind bars, though, Dan, you must stay in the house, or go out only with other people. No more running off into the woods on your own or with just Paul. Do you understand?"

The household and ground servants warned, Mia took Paul and Japheth with her to talk to Squire Redmond, the local magistrate, and he promised to alert his constables. "We may be able to catch them at this cottage," he said, but something must have alerted the miscreants, for they did not show up.

Sunday was the first fine day after a week of rain. Meg had a slight cold and remained home with Bethany, her nurse, but the rest of the party welcomed the opportunity to see their neighbours. They lingered in the churchyard after the service, talking to the Squire and the Rector and his wife.

Mia hadn't realised that Dan and Paul had drifted to the lane with the Rector's son, Ben Ashbrook, and a group of village boys until she heard the shouts.

A carriage was travelling too fast down the lane, and those standing in its path scattered even as the coachman battled his horses to slow them. As it approached the boys, the near-side door opened, crashing back against the panel work, and a man leaned out from inside and grabbed for one of the boys.

He had Dan!

But no. He didn't. Dan struggled and pulled back, and Paul threw himself to batter at the man's clutching hand. Ben joined in on the other side, all three of them at risk of being pulled under the wheels as the carriage continued its progress.

Then Lucas Mogg appeared at a run, hurtling into a tackle that took all three boys in his arms, out of the assailant's grasp, and out of danger. The coachman whipped up the horses, and the door swung back and forth twice before the occupant of the carriage secured it from within.

Several of the congregation ran for their horses to follow the carriage, while Mia, Kitty, and the girls hastened out the lychgate and into the lane, where Dan and his rescuers were pulling themselves to their feet, inspecting grazes and congratulating one another on their escape.

"We'll get you home," Mia said, when she'd hugged Dan, careless of the mud that coated him. "Kitty, tell the groom to bring the carriage."

Mrs Ashbrook had already collared her son and was herding him across the churchyard to the rectory. The vicar lingered for a moment as they waited for the Longford Court carriage to arrive. Sir Thomas Redwood, the squire, stood waiting with them. "Those would be the villains you came to see me about."

"I assume so, Sir Thomas," Mia replied. "I hope your men catch them."

However, one of the riders returned to say they had found the carriage abandoned, the driver and the occupant nowhere to be found. "I left the others looking, Squire," he reported, "but they could have gone in any direction. I'm going back with the dogs."

The carriage pulled up, and Mia commanded her children into it, only just quelling the temptation to grab hold of Dan and not let him go. The Moggs turned away, and she stopped them. "You, too, Mr Mogg, Paul. Home, a wash, and clean clothes. Get into the carriage, please, and we'll drop you at your cottage."

Mogg touched the cap he'd picked up from the mud and wiped to something approaching clean on his trousers, which were much the worse for that heroic tackle. "We're too dirty, Mrs Redepenning."

"Samuel," Mia commanded the groom. "spread a horse blanket on the seats, please. There, Mr Mogg. Lady Kitty and I will sit with the girls on this side, the three of you can sit on the other, and Hannah and Japheth can go up top with Samuel."

"We can go up top," Mogg offered.

"You are wet and cold." Hannah's voice was a scold, which indicated how upset she was, for she seldom allowed her emotions to show in her voice. "Do like Mrs Captain says, Mr Mogg."

Mia followed the rest of them into the carriage, feeling cold herself at how close she had come to losing Dan to the abductors. She couldn't break down now. Marsha and Ada, who were clinging to her, one on each side, depended on her to be confident and relaxed. Kitty caught her eye and smiled. "That was exciting," she said cheerfully.

Mogg picked up the thread, congratulating Dan and Paul on their team work, and they responded by admiring Mogg's tackle. Bit by bit, the girls' death grip on Mia's hands loosened as they relaxed. By the time they had detoured past the gamekeeper's cottage and then driven the last quarter of a mile to Longford Court, they were laughing and talking again.

Japheth and Hannah whisked Dan upstairs to be washed and reclothed, and Kitty took the girls to the nursery to see Meg, leaving Mia to wash and change. The incident was over, but it reaffirmed the risk, which would only cease once the squire found the perpetrators.

He didn't, though. The following day he called to tell her that the search had been unsuccessful. "The carriage was an old one, taken from Oak Cottage over at Niddleberrow, which has stood empty for years. The horses were stolen, too. They belonged to Highrood Farm, and had been on winter grazing."

As for strangers, Sir Thomas had constables out asking questions in Longford, Niddleberrow, Chipping Niddwick, and all of the other local villages and hamlets within a fifteen-mile radius. "Some people have been staying in a deserted tower where the Carrington land borders Westinghouse Farm, and we've had tinkers or the like at the old hill fort just north of Springcrest. But both groups seem to have moved on, Mrs Redepenning. If I had to pick, I'd say our miscreants were the tower people. I've told the locals to keep a lookout in case they come back, but without anything further to go on, there is nothing I can do. I think it is all over, though. They must know you will be careful now."

Mia thanked him, but she could not be easy in her mind. "He will keep trying," she said to Kitty. "I know he will." That night, she wrote to Lord Henry, telling him everything that had happened.

"I think it best to remove to another place, in the hopes Captain Hackett will not be able to find us," she wrote. "I have asked Kitty write to her godmother, to see if we might impose on her to take us into her home. I do not mention her name in case, by some remote evil chance, this letter falls into the wrong hands."

Mia had stayed with the Duchess of Haverford before, in her

castle just west of Margate. No one would find them there, and if they did, no one would be able to take Dan out of Haverford Castle.

Now all they had to do was keep Dan safely inside Longford's walls until the duchess replied to Kitty's letter and offered them refuge.

*L*ady Carrington's escape plan was very simple. One day, the young lieutenant in charge of the afternoon guard and another man in a French hussar regiment's uniform entered the cell and commanded him to put on his coat and come with them. Expecting to be conducted to the interrogation room again, Jules was surprised to be escorted downstairs.

They were stopped several times on the way to the main doors, and each time the hussar showed papers and gave an explanation that must have satisfied, because they were allowed to continue.

Outside, Jules took a quick look around at the first sight of the sky he'd had in weeks that hadn't trickled through high windows. He was right about the castle; he was in the courtyard, on a drear and gloomy day. Below in the courtyard, a carriage and two horses waited for them in the drizzle, a driver at the reins and two armed grooms keeping a watchful eye from the top. "Into the coach, Monsieur," the lieutenant commanded, and Jules obeyed as the two French officers swung up onto the horses.

Lady Carrington waited for him in the coach, as did another young man, this one dressed as a civilian. "Surprised, Captain Redepenning?" she asked.

"Lovers of yours?" he responded.

She smirked as the coach rocked into motion. They were stopped again at the gate, and the guard stuck his head in the door but the civilian produced another thick roll of papers, replete with official-looking seals, and they were allowed to go.

"Now what?" Jules asked, as they picked up speed.

"Now, my dear Captain, we go to England," she answered.

Jules acknowledged the other man with an inclination of his

head. "Her ladyship has neglected to introduce us, Monsieur. I am Captain Julius Redepenning."

The man returned Jules's slight bow with an even slighter one of his own, but he said nothing. Lady Carrington laughed. "My friend does not wish to be acquainted, Captain. But never fear. He has served his turn and will leave us when we reach the coast."

The unnamed civilian shut his eyes and pretended to sleep, though his breathing did not shift and his mouth remained closed. After Jules had returned polite monosyllables to several flirtatious remarks from Lady Carrington, they rode in silence for what seemed like hours. In the gloomy light, it was hard to tell the time, but Jules thought it must be late afternoon when they finally stopped and disembarked in a small seaside village.

A scruffy fishing boat was moored to the wooden dock, and half a dozen ruffians lounged either on the wharf or on the deck. The two soldiers immediately flanked Jules as if they thought he might try to escape, and the civilian went along the wharf to consult with one of the ruffians, presumably the captain.

Lady Carrington ordered the driver and grooms to unload her luggage, flirting with the younger of the two grooms while she waited for the civilian to finish his dealings and beckon for them to come. At his nod, she ordered the three servants to carry the bags to the boat for them.

"Our transport awaits," she said to Jules, beckoning for him to be shoved onto the boat ahead of her. He'd have preferred to stay on deck, the breath of ocean air like wine after his long abstinence, but he was not given a choice. Still, he felt the change in the pitch and roll when the vessel met the sea rollers. At least he was once again at sea, and surely, he would have a chance at freedom at some time in the coming days.

19

Mia and Kitty waited impatiently for the duchess to reply, while planning their flight across the country.

"It will be most dangerous while we are on the road," Mia fretted.

Mogg had become part of their discussions. "A strong escort will draw attention, which you will do anyway. Three pretty ladies, a black servant and three exotic-looking children? I think you might need to consider going in disguise, Mrs Redepenning."

"I will consider anything that might improve our chances of safely crossing the country," Mia told him. "What do you suggest?"

In the end, they had a plan, but they'd need help for the first and most important part. Kitty suggested Lord and Lady Avery, friends who lived on the other side of Chipping Niddwick, and Mogg rode over with a message. The Averys came that same afternoon, leaving with packed bags for Mia and Dan.

Now they were ready. As soon as they heard from the duchess, Kitty would go with Mia and her children to return the call to the Averys. The closed carriage would bring Kitty and the two girls back to Longford Court, but Mia and Dan, disguised as servants, would leave Avery Hall the same afternoon, in attendance on Lord Avery.

"Once I hear you are safely at Haverford Castle, Hannah, Bethany and I will follow with Meg and the girls," Kitty assured Mia. "This will work."

Jules hoped the captain of this tub was being well paid. He would not have wanted to cross the channel and the width of the seas south of England in such a vessel in winter weather, with the whole might of the British navy suspicious of every floating bit of flotsam and jetsam that crested a wave.

The cabin to which they confined him had no outlook; no means of egress but the locked door. It was provided with hooks for four hammocks, one above another, barely enough room to stand to one side with head and knees bent to avoid the beams overhead, and not much else. Jules could be grateful he had the place to himself. If all four hammocks were full, every swing and lurch would bounce a sleeper into the one above or down on the one below.

They hit heavy weather immediately, and it got worse as day wore into night and then back to day. Jules could hear how the hours passed—this was no naval ship with its regimented bells to mark the watches, but the demands of the sea meant the crew rested turn and about like any other, and he soon had a feel for the daily routine of the little vessel.

He'd not been told, but he assumed they were heading for the Bristol Channel, the closest sea access to the Carrington lands just west of Jules's childhood home. They'd hug the coast of France and sail north-north-west past Ushant then west until they rounded Land's End, possibly tacking closer to Ireland to give the English Coast a wide berth before cutting in again to head up towards Bristol, pretending to be English fishermen on the way home.

He lay in the hammock and created a dozen plans for escape, each more fantastic than the last, or stood and exercised as well as he could in the limited space. He listened to the noises and tried to imagine what was happening. He ate the food and drank the watered wine delivered to him twice a day by one of the crew, guarded by Lady Carrington's two soldiers.

He didn't see Lady Carrington.

Time crept snail slow, but it passed, until the evening his guards opened the door and ordered him out, using gestures and shoving him when he didn't move quickly enough. Lady Carrington waited with the man he had identified as the fishing boat captain. Before they could speak, he complained, "Do call your dogs off, Lady Carrington. Pushing me around is no way to get my cooperation."

Lady Carrington raised her brows at his tone, but she said something in French to the two soldiers, and they withdrew a few steps, grumbling.

"Captain, the captain has some questions to ask you about the Bristol Channel. We are sailing up as far as the beginning of Severn Firth, and he is unfamiliar with these waters. You know them, I assume?"

Jules nodded, wondering what his duty was in this instance. He could easily run the craft into danger—the Bristol Channel had plenty of hazards, not least massive tidal changes and the corresponding tidal races. He could not guarantee a disaster, and should he, if he could? Surely it was better to get Lady Carrington and her two tame Frenchmen onto land, where he could find help? Or was he talking himself into the coward's way out, putting his own survival ahead of his country?

"You promised your help," Lady Carrington reminded him. "You gave me your word."

That was true, though the promise was coerced. Was he bound by it, when refusing would have brought more torture? He shrugged. For the present, he would cooperate. After all, what harm could one woman and two Frenchmen do?

With Lady Carrington acting as interpreter, he answered the captain's questions. Afterwards, alone again in his tiny cabin, he slipped out of his sleeve the jack knife he had palmed when he passed it. He opened it and tested its blade. Commendably sharp.

His chances of stopping whatever Lady Carrington had in mind had just improved.

⁂

*M*ia was shaken awake. She fought the encroaching hand until she surfaced enough to hear Kitty, her voice sharp with panic. "Mia, you must wake up! Meg is hurt and Dan is gone."

That washed the last of sleep from her mind. She was out of bed, reaching for her robe, and demanding details before Kitty finished her next sentence. "Paul Mogg is here. He was with the other two when they were attacked." *Paul? He was sleeping overnight at the manor. Where were they attacked?*

Mia toed into her slippers. "Where is Meg?"

"At the gamekeeper's cottage. Hannah and Bethany have gone to fetch her, with Japheth and a couple of footmen for safety. Paul said they knocked him unconscious before they took Dan. I've sent to have Samuel woken. They may need the gig to get Meg home."

Downstairs, they heard the whole story. How Dan and Paul had followed Meg when they saw her crossing the forecourt on her way to the woods.

"It was one of the kittens, Mrs Redepenning. She must have taken it down to the woods this afternoon when we went for a walk and forgotten it, for it was still in its basket and crying fit to bust when we got there. The bad men must have heard it, too, for they were before us, and we arrived only just in time to see them hit Lady Meg."

Dan had ordered his friend to stay hidden and run forward to protect Meg. Paul felt guilty about that, and Mia had to reassure the white-faced boy that he'd done the right thing. "If you hadn't stayed out of sight, Paul, you would be lying there with Meg, and none of us would know what had become of any of you."

Paul had gone to his father for help when he couldn't rouse Meg or carry her. Mogg had made sure Meg was safely in the cottage and then instructed Paul to come to the house for help, while he followed the abductors.

"Papa said he would leave marks for the rescuers to follow," Paul said.

A commotion in the hall heralded Hannah's and Bethany's arrival with a very distressed Meg. The nannies were half supporting the girl, who was white and whimpering, tears streaking her muddy cheeks. "She's all right." Hannah spoke straight to Meg's sister. "A bit of a lump on the head. Bethany is going to clean her up and sit with her."

By now, the rest of the household was awake, crowding into the big room at the front of the house and peering through the pierced screen into the entrance hall.

"Where are Marsha and Ada?" Mia asked.

"I told them they must stay in the nursery," Hannah assured her, "and set the nursery maid to watch them. We will take care of them, Mrs Captain. You concentrate on getting our Dan back."

Mia sent Bowles, the stable master, to saddle all the riding horses in the stable: six for the rescue party, and one for Samuel so he could take a message to the Squire. "We're going to follow them," she said to Kitty, as she wrote the note for Samuel to carry. "They have been gone nearly an hour, by what Paul says, and it will take at least another hour for Samuel to reach Sir Thomas, and for him to muster a force and get back here."

Kitty nodded. "And meanwhile, Luke is out there on his own. We don't know how many men they have, and how far they have travelled. You are right, Mia. We must go."

"We will send someone back for Sir Thomas when we know where they are," Mia decided.

Two of the footmen and Japheth would ride with them. Reluctantly, Mia accepted Paul as the sixth rider. He could read the signs left by his father, and she could not afford to miss the trail. She hoped Mogg would forgive her for putting the boy in danger.

"Everyone go and change for the ride. Be as quick as you can, and meet me in the gun room. Cole, go to the gun room now, please, and set out what you think we will need. Plenty of ammunition, remember."

Neither of the footmen had ever held a gun before. She armed them anyway with fowling pieces, hoping the threat would be enough. Japheth refused a gun, but admitted to an illicit skill at throwing knives. With Mia's consent, he left to fetch a set he had seen in a display case in the Great Hall. Kitty and Mia had both learned to shoot under the tutelage of Kitty's brother-in-law, Rede, and Mia's brother-in-law, Alex. They selected guns they were familiar with, and loaded them with practised hands. They knew they could hit targets, both static and moving, with relative ease. Mia had wondered in the past whether she could shoot at another human being, in need. Tonight, she might find out.

"I can shoot," Paul said. "My da taught me. Give me a gun, Mrs Redepenning."

It was a hard decision. Would he be safer with, or without? In the end, Mia let him pick a weapon and the ammunition for it, and watched as he loaded it with expert ease. "You must promise me you will not shoot," she said, "unless I give the command, or it is the only way for you to save yourself."

Hannah came to the door with Japheth, her eyes huge in a tense white face. When he turned away to go out to the waiting horses, she threw herself at him and wrapped her arms around him.

"I have to go, Hannah," he said.

"I know." She buried her face in his shoulder then lifted her chin and shot him a scorching gaze. "Don't get shot. You hear? You come back safe, Japheth."

"I will." He kissed her forehead. "I will, Hannah. I promise I'll come back."

20

———

Beyond the beach, a lane skirted the shore—just two dirt ruts with scrubby grass between them and to either side. Even in the dark, Jules recognised this piece of coast. The Redepenning boys had kept their sailing dinghies not far from here, at Oldbury Pill. Here, Jules had learnt to love and to respect the sea, first crewing for his older brothers and then competing with them in a boat of his own.

They were little more than an hour's hard ride from the Carrington estate, though Lady Carrington had not yet named her destination. Just over an hour's hard ride, too, from the place that had always been home; Longford Court, where his mother had ruled as *chatelaine* throughout his childhood, since the earl and countess of that time had despised the place.

If he could escape, he could leave these three to their own devices and go home, but the hostile glares from Lady Carrington's paramours had become more intent since they disembarked. The two of them had donned greatcoats to hide their uniforms—the enveloping bulk well justified by the chilly night. Jules knew that at least one kept a pistol trained on him at all times. Still, he would watch for an opportunity. Anything could happen in the uncertain light before they reached whatever place Lady Carrington had chosen to hide her wealth.

Though the sky was clear and the moon full, everything was grey on grey, and in the shadows, it was pitch dark.

"We will need transport," he pointed out.

Lady Carrington looked smug. A moment later, a man leading a horse turned a corner further along the lane and four more horses followed behind, all strung together.

"Tha be the 'uns for these 'ere 'orses?" he asked as he approached, looking from one man to another, his eyes a suspicious squint. He ignored Lady Carrington, until she stepped towards him and held out a pouch.

"Your next payment," she told him. "As promised, the third will be ready for you tomorrow night, when we return the horses. We will leave on the high tide, whether you are here or not."

The man touched his cap; a response to her cultured tones. "I be here," he said, his sourness not abated by the purse he weighed thoughtfully in one hand. "See that tha be."

He disappeared back into the gloom, and Lady Carrington ordered the disposition of the horses. Jules was ordered to take position between the two French officers, his horse on leading reins. Lady Carrington led the fifth horse, which had been supplied with a pack saddle and panniers.

"If you take us into a trap, Julius," the baroness said, "Pierre will shoot you without blinking."

"You have my word," Jules told her indignantly. After all, she was not privy to his inner justifications for breaking that word. "However, I cannot show you the way unless you tell me where we are going."

"Iron Acton will do for a start," Lady Carrington said. Iron Acton was five miles from Chipping Niddwick; further confirmation that Lady Carrington's stash was hidden at Carrington Castle, or nearby.

"I take it you want to avoid villages and farm dwellings. Very well. If we head south on this lane," he pointed in the direction he meant, "we will be able to turn inland in about seventy-five yards."

Lady Carrington nodded at his two escorts, and they wheeled their horses to follow his directions. There had never been any doubt about who was in charge.

He kept them to lanes that avoided the villages and towns. Little used except for stock movements and farm carts, they were mostly in poor repair, and recent rain had frozen in every rut and hollow, so that their way was marked by the crackle of breaking ice. Going was slow. From Iron Acton, the baroness directed them towards Highwayman's Hollow, a place just off the Yate to Chipping Niddwick road where, or so local legend had it, highwaymen used to lurk, waiting for a rich prize.

"We shall take a rest," the baroness announced, dismounting. Jules and the two silent Frenchmen followed her example. She beckoned to the three of them. "Come closer so we can talk without me shouting."

Sound did carry in the still night air. Still, Jules thought she was being too cautious. Unless things had changed since he was last here, there wasn't a dwelling anywhere within ten minutes' walk.

Nevertheless, he joined the group, ready to hear their next destination. He did not expect to be seized by Pierre and Victor, one on each side. He struggled, but he was soon bound to a tree and gagged for good measure.

"I know the way from here," the baroness told him. She caressed his cheek, a parody of affection. "I cannot trust you near people who might help you. We will be back, Julius, and you shall see us to the coast as you promised, and then I shall release you as I promised."

Unable to comment, Jules merely glared. Lady Carrington laughed, and leaned towards him, her lips puckered. He twisted his face, so the kiss fell on his ear rather than his lips. She laughed again, and groped at his groin. He kept his face impassive and his mind on the most gruesome aftermath of a ship-to-ship gun battle he could remember. He would not give her the satisfaction of a reaction.

"He is hardly a man at all," she told her French lovers. "Such a disappointment. One expected better of a Redepenning."

Jules raised a sardonic eyebrow. Lady Carrington lifted her nose in the air and walked away to remount her horse. Pierre followed, and so did Victor, but only after a vicious punch to Jules's stomach. "That is for disrespecting madam," he hissed.

Jules had no choice but to keep his response to himself. He gave the baroness precisely the respect she deserved. Probably as well he couldn't speak. Another couple of blows like that, and he'd be in real trouble.

He watched them ride away before testing his bonds. Good. They'd left him enough play to work with, and the jack knife he'd stolen on the ship was still concealed in his sleeve. He sneered. No sailor would have made such a mistake.

<hr>

Despite Mia's reservations about taking a schoolboy into danger, she was glad to have Paul with her. He took them directly to the clearing where Meg had been knocked unconscious, and quickly found a mark on a tree at the mouth of one of the paths into the woods. Bark had been peeled back to make a rough arrow, pointing down the path.

"This way," Paul said, and mounted his horse to lead the rescue party in the direction he'd found.

Twice more, he stopped where paths met, and twice more, peeled bark showed the way.

At last, they came out from under the trees and found themselves on the road that led west from the village of Longford to the nearest market town, Chipping Niddwick.

"Which way now?" one of the footmen asked.

Paul dismounted again to examine each side of the road, but it was Kitty, still up on her horse, who saw two branches tied together in the hedge that bordered the Longford Court estate, the twine binding them so that they pointed west towards the town. "Is this it?" she asked, and Paul confirmed it was.

A few yards further on, where the road verge widened, they found the frost disturbed—the grass beneath showing dark where hooves, boots, and wheels had left prints and scuffs. "It must have been the kidnappers," Paul said, his voice ringing with confidence. "Who else? It wasn't frosty when we went to bed, and the frost hasn't had time to reform where it has been broken. Besides, one set of boot prints is much smaller than the others. This is where they put Dan in a carriage."

Mia could see, in her mind's eye, how Dan had struggled against the much larger men, leaving behind the scuffs as he was dragged to the carriage. "How many kidnappers were there? Can you tell?"

Paul dismounted again, and looked more closely. "Four, I think. Three different size prints, and the two the same size don't have the same sole pattern." He started to point out different prints to prove his case, but Mia interrupted him, conscious of the time that had passed since the abduction.

"I believe you, Paul. Well done."

They rode on, stopping whenever there was a break in the hedge to check for signs, each time being directed to continue down the same road. Just before they reached the outskirts of Chipping Niddwick that changed. This time, the sign was in an oak tree. Three branches had been tied, all pointing down a side lane heading to the right from the road, and, to make the message doubly sure, peeled bark on the trunk, clearly visible in the moonlight that shone through the winter-bare branches, indicated the same direction.

They found themselves in a maze of little country lanes, some barely more than farm tracks. More than once, they had to retrace their steps, looking for a missed sign. Mia fretted impatiently. They wouldn't hurt Dan, would they? Hackett wanted him alive and well. She was not reassured. She'd heard too many tales about hired men who had overstepped their bounds. What if they found the boy too much trouble and decided to cut their losses? What if he continued to fight and they hit him too hard, or gave him too much laudanum?

It was almost an anti-climax when a figure stepped out of the shadows and hissed a greeting.

"Luke!" Kitty greeted him, in almost the same breath as Paul said, "Da!"

"They're here," Luke said. "They seem to have settled in for the night."

"Where is here?" Mia asked, interrupting Kitty who was telling Luke how well Paul had followed the signs Luke had left.

"On Carrington lands, but only just. They are holed up in the old watchtower."

"Denning." Mia addressed one of the footmen. "Ride as quickly as you can without attracting their attention or risking your neck. Let Sir Thomas know where the kidnappers are."

"Mia sent Samuel with a note," Kitty explained. "By now, I expect the squire is up and gathering a troop of constables."

Luke looked up at the mounted footman. "Tell Sir Thomas that I've seen at least six of them. They have one man on guard outside the tower—there's probably at least one more awake inside. Now I have backup, I'm going to try to take out the one I can see, but there'll still be more than we can easily overcome."

"And they have Dan," Mia pointed out.

⁂

*J*ules tried first to work his way out of his bonds without the knife, but the soldiers had managed to tie him securely enough that wriggling didn't move the coils over his wrists and a rope under his arms was looped around a low branch so he couldn't slide down to slither out of the coil or up to climb over it. The knife it would have to be, then. He had almost enough play to wriggle it down from his sleeve, but would need to go slowly so he didn't drop it.

He was not sure how long it took him to get his jack knife safely into his hands, but once he held it, it was the work of a moment to open out the short blade, kept commendably sharp by its former owner. He held the hilt firmly in one hand, sawing at the ropes on the other wrist. *Careful. Careful.* No point in this if he finished up slitting his own wrist.

Bit by cautious bit he frayed the strands, pulling his two wrists apart more and more as one loop of rope after another broke.

Despite his care, his hands bore several shallow cuts before at last he had enough play to wriggle a hand free. Triumphantly, he freed the other; the one with the jack knife. Now he could bring his hands around to the front, untied from the elbow down, and set to work on the rope that bound him to the tree. He had soon cut through that rope, and removed the gag with a sigh of relief.

The gurgle of the nearby stream had been torturing him throughout the half hour of his struggle. In a few strides, he was prone on the frosty bank, scooping the chilly water up in one hand. It felt like heaven as it slid over his dry tongue and down his throat, though he would have preferred something hot.

Right. Where were they going? Jules was not the world's greatest tracker, but he should be able to find evidence of the passage of five horses down a frosty country lane. Already wishing for solid boots instead of soft boat shoes that allowed the cold to penetrate to the bone, he set off in the direction they had headed.

*L*uke shrugged off Mia's apology for making use of Paul. "He's a good tracker," the proud father said. He fixed the boy with a stern glare. "And he can follow instructions to keep himself out of danger," he added.

"Tell your men to tie their horses down here where they can't be seen from the tower or the lane, Mrs Redepenning, then follow me. Quiet now." He led them all to a hollow screened by shrubs and trees. "We can talk here as long as we keep it low. The tower is above us, about a hundred yards away. Paul, now you know where we are, go back and sit by the horses. I need you to bring the squire's men when they arrive."

Paul opened his mouth and then closed it again, and trudged off, his shoulders slumped.

"You can see the tower from just up here," Luke invited, and Mia and Kitty followed his example, crawling up the hill through the bushes.

The tower sat on a small rise, surrounded by open ground for dozens of yards.

The outside guard sat by a brazier a few feet from the door to the tower, keeping a suspicious eye on the surroundings, and every now and again hoisting himself to his feet and circling the tower before sitting down again.

After the guard had repeated the pattern a dozen times, Luke beckoned, and slid down into the hollow where the others waited.

"I can come in from the other side while he's sitting, then take him out as he does his next circuit," Luke said. "I want one of you in the bushes where we've just been, watching the door, and one around by me ready to shoot the guard if I miss my chance. Who is the best shot? Mrs Redepenning or Lady Catherine?"

At the thought of shooting someone, perhaps killing them, Mia's stomach lurched, but she firmed her lips. Dan needed her to be strong. "I am," she affirmed.

"You on my side, then," Luke suggested. "Kitty, your job is to warn us if he changes his routine in any way."

The plan worked like a charm. The guard was easily subdued and Japheth helped Luke drag him off down to their hollow, where he quickly disclosed all he knew at the point of Luke's knife.

"Ent nothin' to me," he declared. "Oim in it for the blunt. Not worth getting stuck over."

He confirmed what they already knew; that five other men were inside with Dan, and that a swell would be coming to get him. "'e en't hurt," the rogue assured them. "We was told to treat him good."

They left him bound and gagged, set the other footman to guard him, and went back to the tower to see what else they could find out. Mia followed Luke across the open space to the window. It was as well she did, because it was more than an arm's-length above his head, and he could not find purchase on the stones to climb up.

Standing on his shoulders, though, Mia could just peep in through the grimy panes. She had a good view of the room. Dan sat at a rough table with four men, and beyond him, another man stirred a pot that stood on a trivet by the roaring fire. She pressed her face closer to the window, trying to see details through the dirt. The five at the table were playing cards; indeed, from what she could see, Dan was teaching them a game, probably one he had learned from the sailors of the *Advantage*. Left there much longer, her little scoundrel would undoubtedly fleece the lot of them.

At that moment, the churring of a nightjar had her straightening. Again. A third time. It was the agreed signal. Someone was coming.

"Quick, Mrs Redepenning." Luke was urging her down, his hands firm on her calves as he knelt. She leapt from his shoulders. "Quick," he said again. He led the way slightly around the tower to put it between them and the carriage they could now hear approaching.

This side of the hill was less even, full of bumps and hollows. Mia followed Luke as quickly as she could. He had just entered the trees, and she was less than a dozen paces behind him, when she caught her foot and came down flat on the hillside.

For a moment she could only lie there, winded. Voices from the other side of the tower had her pulling her knees under her to get up, but she froze again as they grew closer.

"I'm telling you, Captain, we didn't hear anything."

She recognised Hackett's voice. "And I tell you to find him. You!" His voice retreated. "Get the boy. I'm not waiting to be ambushed."

"Hey!" The man closest to her shouted after Hackett. "Not so fast. We haven't been paid."

"I don't have time for this. Follow me, and you'll get your money."

Now. While they were arguing. Mia crept towards the tree line, keeping low.

She would have made it, if riders had not appeared at that moment, coming up the hill through the trees on a path that approached the tower from the side. One of them turned his horse and in a few quick strides was in front of her. The moonlight glinted off the barrel of his gun.

"Stand up very slowly," said a cultured English voice; a woman's voice, and one she had heard before, though she could not, for the moment, place it. The other riders had joined the first.

Hackett and his men came down the hill towards them. Any thought that the two parties were aligned faded in the light of the weaponry each pointed at the other. Perhaps Mia could use this to her advantage.

"Madam," she said, "please, I beg you, help me. Those men have kidnapped my son."

The woman nudged her horse closer and bent to look into Mia's face. It was Lady Carrington! What was that wicked woman doing here? She had fled England long ago; indeed, most of the Redepenning family thought she must be dead. The lady raised both eyebrows.

"Euronyme Redepenning. How interesting. Fancy running into you, here of all places." She looked up the hill at the approaching ruffians. "Do come closer," she invited. "I may have captured someone of interest to you, and I am willing to trade."

21

———

Jules trudged down one country lane after another. At the first fork in the road he found a pile of still warm horse manure to indicate his way. Broken ice on a large puddle led him down a side lane, and crushed vegetation where a gate into a field had been pulled open across the frosted ground told him when to turn off.

Tracks in the frost led across the field to another corner.

They were not heading directly for the castle where Lady Cunningham had once lived, and where her stepson now dwelled with his family, but more towards the eastern side. Could they be going to the old dungeons under the ruins on the Brooke farm, where the dead baron had once kept his human stock prior to shipment?

No. They had turned again, into the lane that led between Brooke land and the Cunningham estate. They must be an hour ahead of him by now. Wherever they were headed, he was more than likely to arrive after they had completed the lady's errand and moved on.

Jules stopped at the corner where a little farm track led down the hill towards the Nidd river. As the crow flies, he was two and a half miles from home. Even with the river to ford, and a few bends on the way, he could be home at Longford Court in an hour. Or he could go the other way and in thirty minutes, he could knock up his old friend, Gil Rutledge, and be settled in front of a warm fire with a hot drink, or maybe a brandy.

He was sorely tempted. He could report the presence in England of Lady Carrington and her two Frenchmen. He could leave someone else to hunt for them, find out where Mia and the children were, and go to his family. He looked east towards Longford, south towards Rutledge Manor, and sighed heavily.

Lady Carrington's party had gone south west. Duty called. As he forced his frozen feet in that direction, a flicker of light attracted his attention. There. On higher ground to the west, inside the Carrington estate.

Was that the old ruined tower? He narrowed his eyes. Of course. It looked totally abandoned, but Jules had reason to know that the ground floor was habitable, and had been used as recently as twenty years ago. He and Alex, during the period of their obsession with Lady Carrington, had spent several uncomfortable nights outside of it, watching to make sure that no one disturbed their goddess, who was trysting within.

It was a likely place for her to have hidden whatever valuable items she had managed to steal from her husband. The estate wall was too high to climb at this point, but unless things had changed in his time away, he would soon come to the gap he and Alex had used.

Duty first. Then, a warm fire and brandy.

Once inside the tower, Mia ignored the two hostile parties and hurried to Dan. He leapt up from the table, wrapping his arms around her. "Ibu Mia!"

"Dan! Are you all right? Let me look at you."

"Very affecting," Lady Carrington said. "He cannot be yours. You had no child five years ago, and seven years ago your woman's courses had not started. He is nine or ten by my guess. He must belong to Jules."

Captain Hackett took an indignant step forward, stopping when one of Lady Carrington's companions brought up his gun. "He belongs to me," he spluttered. "My son. Redepenning stole him from me."

"Lies!" Dan took his own step forward, his fists clenched at his sides. "Captain Redepenning is my father, and Ibu Mia is my mother."

Captain Hackett snarled, "Mind your tongue, boy. Didn't your mother teach you any manners?"

Lady Carrington once again took control of the conversation. "We have not been introduced," she said to Captain Hackett. "I am Lady Carrington. The dowager Lady Carrington now, I suppose." She shuddered. "And you are?"

"Hackett. Captain Hackett." He waved at his men. He had presumably left his driver with his carriage further down the hill, and the two men he brought with him were outside guarding the door, but he still had the five who had already been in the tower. "You are outnumbered, my lady."

Lady Carrington raised a delicate eyebrow. "You, sir, are outgunned."

Mia looked around the room. Lady Carrington and her two men had taken station near the door. Captain Hackett had joined his five men near the table. Six to three, but only Hackett and Lady Carrington's two men had guns.

"However," Lady Carrington continued, "I am willing to negotiate. What will it take for you to agree to leave?"

"I only want my heir. You can keep Redepenning's bitch of a wife."

Lady Carrington gave Mia a slight smile. "What on earth would I do with Jules's wife?"

Mia ignored the provocation of her husband's personal name, and spoke directly to Lady Carrington. "He lies, Lydia. Jules is Dan's legal guardian. Captain Hackett has no right to him."

Hackett turned purple at her accusations. "Redepenning is the liar. Kirani was my whore first, and I got the boy on her before Redepenning stole her."

"How fascinating," Lady Cunningham commented. "You mean to raise the son of your husband's mistress, Euronyme? You always did have a soft heart."

Hackett slashed at the air with his hand. "She can have Redepenning's girls. It is nothing to me. But the boy is mine."

"The boy does not agree," Lady Carrington said to Hackett.

"The boy has been lied to," Hackett insisted again.

Dan narrowed his eyes, and followed Mia's example in speaking to Lady Carrington, ignoring Captain Hackett. "My Ibu Mia told me of this man. He made my Mami lie with him. He made babies in her, and then, when the soldiers came, he ran away to save his own skin, and left Mami to the soldiers. I had two sisters, and the soldiers killed them. They would have killed Mami, and me inside her, if Papa had not come in time to save us. I will not have that man as my father. He is a coward. He betrayed Mami, and now he betrays his wife."

Hackett had been trying to speak over him, calling him a fool. "I am a wealthy man. Did she tell you that? As my heir, you'll have a place in Society, the best of educations, money to burn. I'll train you in my business, and one day it will all be yours." He turned away from the scorn on Dan's face and appealed to Lady Carrington. "Anyone would think I plan to hurt the boy. He is my only son, I tell you. He will have every advantage. Let me take him, Lady Carrington, and I will leave you in peace."

"You put me in a difficult position, Captain Hackett," Lady Carrington purred. "Not only would you have me ignore the law, which—if we are to believe dear Euronyme, and she has always been drearily honest— has decided in favour of her husband; you would also have me ignore the wishes of the little boy."

"Bah," Hackett spat. "The child does not know his own best interests. I am his father. It is for me to decide."

Lady Carrington held up a finger. "You interrupted, Captain. I have a third point. Now. What was it? Ah, yes." As she spoke, her eyes slid to Mia, and her thin-lipped smile broadened. "Dear Jules has become a friend of mine just recently. A very, very close friend. If I am to betray my friend, am I not to have some kind of a reward?"

Hackett sneered. "You mean he is your lover."

Lady Carrington shrugged. "What will you pay me to take care of Redepenning's wife and let you leave with the boy?"

t was them all right. Jules recognised the horses. From this distance he could not clearly see the two guards who restlessly circled the tower, one in each direction, over and over again. He'd bet the brandy he'd been fantasising about, though, that they weren't Lady Carrington's Frenchmen. Too short, for one thing. Too wide for another.

So, she had English reinforcements. He needed reinforcements of his own, if he was to take them on with any chance of success. He weighed up the distance between this tower and any likely allies. He needed someone who knew him well—that went without saying. Someone who would order the horses put to without needing to be convinced he was genuine. Someone with the manpower—yes and the fire power too—to box Lady Carrington in, along with any men she had with her, and force them to surrender.

His best bet was the magistrate in Chipping Niddwick. He began to work his way around the fringe of the woods. He could use the path on the other side to cut across Carrington lands and come out on the outskirts of the town in a matter of ten minutes.

Focused on his plans, he almost missed the crackle of frost, which was his only warning as a cosh descended on his head. He had time to swerve so it fell on his shoulder, before a voice hissed and an urgent whisper, "No, Masta Luke! It's the Captain."

He knew that voice. "Japheth?" His servant emerged from the bushes, grasped his hand, and began shaking it vigorously, with a broad grin spreading around a tumble of words. "Captain! We thought you was drowned! Have you been to the house? Did they send you?"

"Clearly a Redepenning," said the man who had coshed him. Jules's whole arm felt numb from the blow. "I take it you're Captain Julius Redepenning. Sorry about the cosh. We thought you must be with Hackett." He held out a hand. "I am Mogg, Chirbury's gamekeeper."

Jules released Japheth's hand so he could shake Mogg's. "Hackett is here? I was following a French spy. Wait. Is Dan safe?"

Mogg's eyes widened at the words 'French spy', but he didn't ask questions. "Best come with us," he said. "We need to tell the others what has happened, and we might as well tell it once."

Jules followed Mogg along a path through the woods that led to a hollow where they were out of sight from both the carriageway and the tower. Japheth had melted away into the trees, but he appeared again from the other side of the hollow followed by three other figures, one a tall man, the other two with the slenderness of growing boys.

Not much of an army.

One of the slender figures addressed Mogg. "Luke? Where is Mia?"

A woman's voice! What the hell was Mogg thinking? And Mia? "My wife is here? What's going on?"

"Jules? You're Mia's Jules?" The woman took two steps closer and held out her hand. "I am her friend Kitty, Rede's sister-in-law. Whatever are you doing here?"

Jules let her shake his hand, despite the impulse to ignore such courtesies. "More to the point, what is my wife doing here? And where is she?"

Mogg explained in a few terse words. "Hackett's men took Dan. I trailed them here, and Mrs Redepenning followed, with Lady Catherine, my son Paul, Japheth, and two of Chirbury's footman. This is Frost," he indicated the tall man, "and Denning has gone for the Squire."

Mogg brushed his hand over his head in a gesture of frustration. "The men have been holding Dan here, waiting for Hackett, who arrived not long before you did. Mrs Redepenning and I were out in the open. She would have been all right, but the Carrington female arrived, rounded her up, and delivered her to Hackett. They are all in the tower now, and the new guards are a lot more alert than the old one."

He pressed his lips together, his eyebrows meeting over his eyes. "But, Redepenning, before I trust you, I need to know how you got here. Last we heard; you'd fallen overboard off the coast of France."

Jules suppressed the surge of irritation. He could see the man's point. "Fair enough. I was washed up in France and imprisoned. Lady Carrington has some kind of deal going with the French, or she's cheating them, too, which I think more likely. They sent her to collect a fortune she says she concealed from her husband—in the tower, I'm guessing, since this is where she came. Her bargain with me was to guide her here at night since I knew the countryside, in return for my freedom, but I fully expect the plan was to have her two tame Frenchman shoot me once I got them back to Severn Firth. She trusts me about as much as I trust her."

Mogg nodded. "Only a fool would trust that twisted hellcat. You got away, clearly." He didn't sound convinced.

"Several miles back," Jules agreed, "in Highwayman's Hollow, she had them tie me to a tree, gagged, but they didn't know I had this." He flicked out the jack knife.

Mogg scowled at it. "How do I know you're not part of Lady Carrington's treasure hunt? She is known to have a taste for pretty boys."

Jules shook his head. How did one convince a suspicious stranger? "I'm hardly a boy. I'd like to stop whatever she's up to," he added. "If it is good for her and for France it can't be good for England. But my first concern is Mia and Dan."

Mogg frowned, but must have decided to shelve any further reservations. "Lady Carrington has two men. Hackett has five inside with him and two outside, and a coachman and guard for each of the two coaches down by the road."

"Weapons?" Jules asked. "The French contingent have guns— flintlock pistols. At least a pair each. The men have their swords, as well, of course."

"We don't know about Hackett and his men," Mogg said. "We

haven't seen any guns. No swords, but I daresay they carry knives. Your spies might be outnumbered, but I'm guessing they have the edge on both weaponry and the skill to use it."

Kitty shook her head. "Lydia won't make a fight of it. She'll find a way to charm or negotiate." She was right, and that gave Jules an idea.

"Lady Carrington will want to get rid of Hackett, and the fastest way will be to give him what he came for. How would it be if we took over Hackett's coach and delivered him and his men to the Squire, leaving someone to watch Lady Carrington so she doesn't get away? He won't hurt Dan. The risk will be to Mia."

Mogg considered the plan. "It could work. They don't have outriders. Just two coaches. If we put a driver and guard on Hackett's coach, there's a good chance the other one will follow."

"I'll be guard. Japheth can drive. Chances are, Hackett'll leave in the coach he arrived in."

"Frost, can you shoot?" Mogg asked. The tall footman shook his head but admitted, "I know enough to point it and pull the trigger, Mr Mogg."

"We'll conceal Frost up on top to give you extra firepower," Moggs suggested, "just in case they have weapons we don't know about." Jules agreed, pleased with the addition to the plan.

"That leaves me and Lady Catherine to watch Lady Carrington, with Paul," Mogg said. "Right, then. Let's go and steal a coach."

22

———————

"Don't do this," Mia begged Lydia. "The man is a monster. Dan belongs with those who love him."

"Love?" Hackett snorted. "I'll make a rich man of him. Love, indeed!"

"Lydia?" Mia pleaded.

Lydia smiled, coldly. "If you won't keep quiet, Euronyme, I will have you gagged. Console yourself with the thought that two little girls will be burden enough for a widow. Oh. Did I not mention that I met dear Jules in France? Such a shame, and you still a virgin, I suppose. You were always such a prude, Euronyme. Does it console you to know your husband was worth waiting for? Such a good lover. You must be sad you will never find out."

Hackett interrupted. "Redepenning was a tomcat. Good riddance, I say. We'll be taking the boy, then."

Lydia pointed her gun at his chest. "Not so fast. There is the small matter of my payment."

Hackett glared, but pulled a pouch from his coat pocket—a heavy one, by the way it weighed in his hand. "This is all I have on me. It will have to do."

Lydia peered inside, tipped a couple of coins onto her hand, and nodded. "Go ahead, then."

Dan evaded Hackett's hand to wrap both arms around Mia's waist. She hugged him back. Two of Hackett's bullies grabbed his shoulders. "Let me speak with him," she said. "Dan, you must go with them. Be brave, and remember that we love you. We will come for you. Trust us."

Dan released his grip, stepping back from her. "She says Papa is dead." Tears stood in his eyes. He blinked as if reluctant to let them fall.

"Don't trust anything she says," Mia said. "Your Papa is a brave and clever man. He will come home, Dan; he promised."

She followed Dan with her eyes as he left, one of Hackett's bullies before and another after. Before the last of Hackett's men had cleared the room, Lydia spoke in French to her own two henchmen, telling them to tie Mia to a chair. "I will need you to help me retrieve the treasure I promise to the Emperor," she told them.

Mia kept her face impassive. If they thought she did not understand French, she might learn something that would help her to escape.

*L*ounging by the horses' heads, a scarf up to his ears, a hat pulled down as far as it would go, Jules watched his son being escorted into the clearing. He seemed unharmed, but where was Mia?

Hackett was arguing with another man, who was indignant that Hackett had given away the payment promised to the kidnappers.

"I tell you," Hackett insisted, "I have more back in Chippenham. Get me there safely and I'll pay you a fifty percent bonus on the money promised."

The man grumbled some more, but gave the order for the horses to be hitched to the other coach, and for Jules and Japheth, huddled in the coats and hats of the men they had replaced, to be ready to roll as soon as both coaches were loaded.

Japheth leapt to obey, and Jules followed, doing his best not to watch his son climbing into the carriage Jules would be driving. At least something was going right. He would have to trust Lucas Mogg and Kitty to protect Mia till he could return.

It took long minutes, but at last the other carriage was ready to go. Jules made sure that his carriage led the way, though Hackett's destination fell neatly into Jules's plot. The road over the Cotswolds to Chippenham passed through Longford. What he would do if they did not meet up with the rescuers before they reach Longford, he had no idea. Surely, the Squire and his men must be on their way by now?

The moon was near setting by the time they left the farm lane to turn into the road he knew so well from his childhood. Five miles, now, more or less, in which to encounter those riding to the rescue. Farms lay on both side of the road, the farmhouses set too far back to be of any assistance. Jules smiled reassuringly at Japheth, who grinned back and pumped a fist in the air. Frost stayed flat on the roof so he couldn't be seen by the driver of the trailing coach.

Jules could hear nothing from the carriage. Even the leader of the kidnapping gang had fallen silent. There. That copse of oaks marked the corner of the Allin farm, part of the Chirbury estate. They were halfway to Longford village. In another few minutes, they would pass the main gate to Longford Court. Jules wondered about the chances of attracting attention at the gate lodge. Perhaps he could let Japheth off to rouse the house?

No. With the other coach travelling close behind, it would not work.

As they began to pass the grey stone wall that divided the road from the Chirbury parkland, he saw lights not far ahead, coming over a rise and then disappearing again as both the carriages and the approaching horsemen dropped into the dips on either side of the gate.

"Be ready," he whispered to Japheth.

The on comers must have seen the carriage lamps, because, as Jules slowed the horses near the gates, he could see the road for another mile, and it was empty. He halted the horses, forcing the carriage behind to stop. Someone thumped on the inside of the roof, and Hackett shouted, "What is the hold up, man?"

An answer became unnecessary, as the road suddenly swarmed with armed men, some running to the heads of the horses, others surrounding the carriages with guns trained on both doors and roof.

Jules raised his hands as ordered, but called out, "Sir Thomas?! Well met, Sir."

The Squire came closer, peering up. "Who's that?"

"Julius Redepenning. My servant Japheth is with me, and my son Dan is inside the carriage with his kidnappers."

"How did you…" the Squire began. "Never mind. Take off your hat, and put your face near the lantern. Slowly now. No sudden moves."

Jules obeyed, shaking his chin loose of the muffling scarf.

The Squire nodded, and several of the men with him muttered agreement. "You're a Redepenning right enough," the Squire acknowledged. "What about my apples, young Julius?"

Jules gave an exaggerated sigh. "The best in the world, Sir Henry. I've not tasted better in the East or South Africa or anywhere else I've been. Not since the last one I stole from your orchard when I was thirteen. It was well worth the birching."

"It's all right," the Squire said to his men, and those with guns pointed at Jules, Frost and Japheth turned them elsewhere.

Inside the carriage, Hackett and his men were arguing.

"Tell them we will slit the boy's throat if they don't let us go," said the leader of the kidnappers.

"Never!" Hackett shouted him down. "Leave the boy alone."

Sir Thomas went to yank open the door, and Jules dropped to the ground on the far side to open the other door. He peered into the coach just in time to see Hackett, with a roar, throw himself between Dan and the two men who were grabbing for him. Gunfire. At least two guns went off as Dan slithered out the other side.

"Halt!" Jules yelled, frantic to see who had been shot. A body hurtled towards him, and he managed to get off a shot before it hit him, forcing him to the ground. He struggled out from underneath it, just as the other men descended from the carriage in a rush, trampling over him and the body in their haste to escape.

Jules ignored the struggle between the Squire's men and the would-be escapees. "Dan," he roared in a voice trained to be heard over storms. "Here, Papa!" The reply came from the other side of the carriage, and Jules began to limp that way, doing a physical inventory as he went. He must have banged his knee as he fell, but he was otherwise fine.

"Papa!" Dan barrelled into him. "That bad lady said you were dead. Ibu Mia promised she was lying."

Sir Thomas smiled and held out a hand, which Jules shook without letting go of his son. "I have no idea how you did it, young Julius," the Squire said, "but I'm pleased to see you."

Around them, Hackett's men were being disarmed and crowded into a group against the wall. "There's a dead man round the other side," reported the Squire's lieutenant.

"I couldn't see him clearly," Jules said. "but I'm pretty sure it's Hackett."

"It were an accident!" shouted one of the prisoners. "He got between me and the boy, and tried to take my gun. His went off, and so did mine. It were an accident."

A groan from the top of the carriage interrupted. "Japheth?" Dan called out. "Japheth, is that you?"

A quick check confirmed that one of the shots from inside the carriage had found a home in Japheth's leg. "Longford Court is closest," the Squire said. "We'll take him and the prisoners back there and send for the doctor."

"I must ask for a horse and some of your men," Jules told him. "Lady Carrington and two French spies have my wife, and I'm going back to get her." A hand pressed just above his knee came away wet, but in the dark no one had noticed. As soon as he was mounted, he tied his neckerchief around the spot. Nothing was going to stop him from going to rescue his wife.

The objects Lydia had come to retrieve were hidden under some floorboards in the shadow of the staircase that rose to an upper floor that no longer existed. At her direction, the Frenchmen levered up the boards. With a *moue* of distaste Lydia lowered herself to the ground, let a lamp down into the hollow, and crowed her delight.

"Ah. Good. It is still here."

She had the men empty the space. They grumbled about dirt and insects, but they obeyed. It was a motley collection of wooden crates; the kind used for household supplies. Lydia broke open a couple, and her cat-with-the-cream expression deepened as she pulled out some of the contents. A condiment set in gold. A velvet pouch containing a tiara resplendent in rubies and diamonds, which Lydia placed on her head, laughing. A bowl, carefully packed in wood shavings, with the eggshell appearance and rich blue dyes of a genuine Chinese artefact.

"These will buy many guns," one Frenchman said to the other.

"Where do we meet Murat's contact?" The other Frenchman asked Lady Carrington.

Mia, having seen Lydia gloating over her treasure trove, suspected that Murat and his contact had no place in the lady's plans.

The baroness gave the tiara another loving caress and then put it back in its bag. "You do not know the area, so you would not know the place if I told you. You will see soon enough," she said. "Pierre, you finish emptying the hole. Victor, fetch the pack from the horse. We have one more cache to empty before we ride for the rendezvous. Don't worry, Euronyme, dear. I plan to take you with us. You will be useful persuasion for… Well. Never mind."

Victor obeyed Lydia's instruction, putting on his heavy greatcoat and leaving the tower. Pierre continued bringing crates one at the time from the hole and Lydia went on looking in one and then another. After a while, she said, "What can be keeping that fool?" but as she turned towards the door, it opened and the imposing figure in the greatcoat slammed the pack she had sent him for down on the table.

"Be careful," Lydia said sharply, reaching for a couple of pouches that had been pushed to the edge. He stepped to the side as if to avoid her just as Pierre strode forward from his position by the stairs. In a move so fast Mia did not see it coming; the newcomer struck Pierre, and stood over his body, the cosh that felled the Frenchman swinging from one hand.

"What are you–" Lydia stopped. "You're not Victor."

"Hello, Lydia," said the gamekeeper, shaking off the hat that hid his face.

"Lucas!" Lydia took a step towards him, her hand held out in supplication. "You must help me. I have been a prisoner of the French and they are forcing me…"

Kitty interrupted. "Stay right where you are, Baroness." She was standing in the doorway, and she held a gun; Victor's, Mia rather thought.

"You! Lady Kitty." Lydia sneered. "Or should I call you, Lady Stocke?"

Kitty handed the gun to Luke and came to untie Mia. "If you do not speak," she said, "you will not need to call me anything at all, and we will not need to listen to your lies. Just take a seat and we will wait for my cousin Jules to return with the Squire and his men.

"Jules?" Mia said. "Jules is here?"

"He's my…" Lydia began.

"He told us all about you, Lydia," Kitty told her calmly. "You have lost. Retain your dignity and accept it."

Luke finished tying Pierre up and came to look at the things on the table. "Quite a haul," he commented. "No wonder you thought it worth returning for. How much did you offer to Napoleon? The lot, I am guessing."

"Only until she betrayed Napoleon, too," Mia commented. She did not phrase it as a question.

Kitty, who was closest to the door, raised her head. "I hear someone coming." She opened the door cautiously, and then shouted. "Jules! We have her. She is unhurt."

Moments later, Jules entered, striding straight to Mia as if no one else was in the room, and she was in his arms. "I have Dan safe," he told her as he took her in his arms. "It is over, Mia. Thank God. Thank God."

23

Mia wanted nothing more than to stay in Jules's arms, but far too soon he lifted his head, smiled down into her eyes and relaxed a little so she was no longer clamped to his chest.

"Touching." Lydia's cold sarcasm intruded on their privacy. "You really ought to tell your little wife about us, Jules, darling."

Kitty told her to be silent, and Jules snarled, but Mia smiled at the unhappy woman, and if she allowed her tone to be smug, who could blame her. "Really, Lydia. You are such a liar."

Jules kissed Mia's forehead, and she gave him a smile, hoping that her trust shone in her eyes. She had no idea how Jules had appeared so suddenly, but she would not allow her own insecurities to overwhelm her faith in him, and she would not question him in front of others. She would let him explain when he had the chance.

Now was not the time. The two Frenchmen had already been taken out and tied onto their horses, and Mogg was now directing the squire's men to do the same with Lydia.

"We'll leave a guard here at the tower," he said, "and give these three to the squire. I take it the others are in custody?"

Mia and Jules followed the gamekeeper and Kitty out to Paul, waiting with the horses. Jules answered Mogg's question. "Hackett is dead, but the squire has all his men."

Mia needed only one more piece of information to be going on with. "Dan is unhurt?" she asked.

"Yes," Jules assured her, "and safely home at Longford Court." He lifted her to her saddle, clinging for a moment before letting her go. He brought his own horse alongside, and they rode in silence down the dirt track and onto the high road.

Back at Longford Court, the squire was waiting. He turned away from ordering the prisoners sent to the village to join those already in custody. "I have some questions, Redepenning."

"Of course," Jules began, not letting go of the saddle he'd grasped when he dismounted and almost fell.

Mia narrowed her eyes. "Tomorrow, Sir Thomas," she said. "Julius Redepenning, where are you hurt, and why on earth did you not say?"

Jules waved dismissively, but she noticed he still held on with one hand. "It's just a scratch," he assured her. "My leg. Hurt it when we stopped Hackett.

"You rode all the way to the tower and back on a wounded leg?" she grumbled. She marshalled two footmen. Behind her, she could hear Kitty and Mogg saying farewell to the squire, and reassuring the household. She was concerned only with Jules.

They half carried her husband into the entry hall, where the village doctor was just putting on his coat.

"Japheth?" Jules asked.

The doctor eyed Jules up and down as he answered. "I've taken out the bullet. No reason why he shouldn't recover. He's a stout fellow. I see I have another patient, however. What is it? Your leg? Another bullet?"

Jules shook his head. "My knee, I think. But there's blood."

Mia looked. Nothing showed against the dark of his trousers, but in the brighter light of the entry hall's lamps Jules's face was drawn and white.

"I'd best examine you then," suggested the doctor.

"Bring the Captain to my chamber, and fetch hot water and a wash cloth," Mia ordered the footmen.

Jules had a slash in his lower thigh and a badly strained knee swollen to twice its size. "The man who fell on me must have had a knife," he commented. "I've had worse."

It was nearly dawn by the time the wound was stitched and dressed, the knee bound, the doctor sent on his way, and the last of the household chased off to bed. Jules wrote a full report for the Admiralty before he would allow his wife to hustle him off to bed, and sent it on the same mail coach that took the message telling Lord Henry what had happened. Jules didn't seem to be disposed to sleep, and Mia was happy just lying on the bed, tucked against his good side.

"Thank you for my rescue," she said to him.

He kissed her hair. "I think Kitty and Moggs were well on the way to managing without me," he told her.

She shook her head. "Kitty said taking over the coach was your idea. You saved Dan, and then you rode miles on a damaged leg and appeared out of nowhere to save me."

"To think," Jules mused, "I was within a hair's breadth of giving up the chase, and finding my way to a warm house and a brandy."

"How did you come home to us, my love? The last I heard; you had been lost overboard. Lydia had some tarradiddle, but…"

He touched her chin, guiding her to lift her face towards him. Those deep blue eyes were grave. "You know she lied, do you not? You said you did. I am not, and never have been her lover."

Mia had been hiding the last lingering vestiges of doubt, but that statement washed them away. Jules had never lied to her. "I thought she was lying. You made me a promise, Jules."

His lips curved in a smile and he pressed another kiss to her forehead.

"I'll tell you my story, and you tell me yours," he proposed.

After a while they slept, and it wasn't until afternoon that the squire came back and they were able to take stock of their losses and gains. Japheth was laid up, of course. The doctor was confident he'd make a full recovery as long as he avoided infection. He would if Hannah had anything to do with it. After fainting when he was carried through the door (an incident of which she was heartily ashamed) she had taken over his care with a ferocity that repelled any suggestion a single woman should not be caring for a single man.

"We are to be married," she told Mia, "and evil is to those who evil think."

As for the rest of what Paul called 'the side of the angels', they sported a few bruises and scrapes, but nothing more.

The other side had fared less well. Hackett, as they'd thought, was dead. One of his men had a broken arm, sustained in the struggle, and another had fallen on his own knife, embedded it in his gut, and was not expected to live. The rest, along with Lydia and her French officers, were straining the lockup facilities in the village while Sir Thomas waited for word from London about their disposal.

"This is beyond my usual experience," he told Mia and Jules. "French spies, kidnappers, baronesses wanted for murder and extortion. I will let Henry deal with it."

Lord Henry, walking stiffly after a full day in a mail coach, arrived at dusk on the second day after the kidnapping, bringing with him a quiet civilian from the Home Office and orders for Jules from the Admiralty.

"There is some question about how you came to fall overboard, and about how you got back to England," Lord Henry said. Jules raised his eyebrows, but did not allow himself to express any worry.

He was given one week to recover from his injuries, and two days had already passed. At the end of that time, he was to proceed to London, and in less than two weeks, he was to present himself to the Admiralty to answer such questions.

Within a few days, Hackett's hired men had all been bound over for the Bristol assizes and the Home Office had carried Lady Carrington and her Frenchmen off. Jules and Mia left the children in Longford with Hannah and, as requested, travelled to London in a comfortable Chirbury coach, there to wait on the convenience of the Lords of the Admiralty. Jules was to face an enquiry into his reasons for leaving his command in war time.

"You have acted throughout in accordance with your duty," Mia said on the morning he was summoned. She brushed imaginary fluff from the uniform jacket that had arrived pristine from the tailor's the day before. "They will ask a few questions and then commend you, Jules." She straightened his already perfect epaulets, and smoothed back his tidy hair.

He trapped her busy hands and bent to kiss her. "I expect so," he said. "I will come and tell you all about it as soon as I can. Don't worry, my love."

"I am not at all worried," she proclaimed, forcing herself to smile as he hurried down the steps and into the waiting carriage. She waved as if she had no care in the world, then took herself through to the parlour to pace the floor.

She could not settle to anything. Presumably they had spoken to Hale and the officers from Jules's ship. She knew, because Lord Henry had heard, that they'd interviewed Lady Carrington. What had they been told? The clock on the mantle must be broken; its minute hand crept as slowly as an hour hand, and the hour hand did not move at all.

The housekeeper came to see if she wanted tea, and she was now feeling awash as she had had three cups just to pass the time.

But still the minute hand crept.

Finally, she heard voices in the hall, and hurried out to be clasped in her husband's arms and swung around. "I have a frigate!" he exulted, "Fifth rate, forty-four guns. The *Retribution*. She's in the Pool, and I'm to take up my post almost immediately."

"Immediately?" Mia faltered, but managed to smile. "It's good news, then."

"She is still being supplied, my love," he assured her. "You will have me underfoot for a couple of days yet." He bent to kiss her, disregarding the interested audience of servants, and she ignored them too. "It is only till the war ends," he promised. "Then our lives together can really start."

"You must do your duty, Jules," she agreed. She stretched and he bent to meet her in another kiss.

"You're home," Lord Henry said from the doorway, his voice rich with amusement.

"Yes, and Jules has been given a frigate," Mia told him.

"Apparently, Jules's first lieutenant clapped Hale in custody when he went overboard." Lord Henry shook his head. "Your naval masters played that one close to their chest, Jules. The man was complaining below decks about what a monster you were. So, when he was the only witness to your fall, Bourne was suspicious."

Jules nodded. "Good to know. They did tell me that Lady Carrington confirmed my version of my escape from France, so all's well that ends well."

Lord Henry pursed his lips and hesitated for a moment, then said, "The French were behind the whole escape, as you suspected, Jules. Lady Carrington had promised them her ill-gotten gains, to be used by French agents here to pay their informers and other expenses. She claims she never intended to go through with it, and I think—in that at least—she was honest."

"Hence the two French officers, sent to make sure she handed over the treasure once she retrieved it," Mia speculated.

"Hardly efficient of the French to send two men she could easily seduce," Jules commented. "What is their fate? Prisoner-of-war? They were wearing their uniforms, after all."

Lord Henry nodded. "Yes. They'll be here for the rest of the war, no doubt. Lady Carrington is imprisoned, too, but has brokered her information about the French organisation here in England to avoid the hangman. The Home Office is making arrests as we speak, and rubbing its collective hands in glee." He abandoned the question of Lady Carrington's fate. "This is a promotion for you, my son. We should have a celebratory dinner."

Jules looked at Mia and then his father, and shook his head. "If you don't mind, Papa, Mia and I have two or maybe three more nights before I sail."

Lord Henry nodded, amusement rich in his voice. "Well what are you waiting for, then? I'll send that celebratory dinner upstairs."

EPILOGUE

COAST OF DORSET, 1827

The house stood on a hill above the bay, exactly as Jules had imagined it when mouldering in a French prison fifteen years ago.

Jules and Mia saw the land in 1814. It was the same day that they'd signed the contract to purchase the small coastal shipping business that became the foundation of J. Redepenning & Sons. They'd grown the fleet from three to ten, and diversified into passengers as well as freight, with ferries to Bournemouth and Portsmouth to the east, and Torquay and Plymouth to the west.

They paid the previous owner more than he asked, because he'd lost all three of his heirs: two sons and a nephew that he'd counted on to come home from the war and take over the operation. What were a few more hundred pounds in comparison to such a sacrifice to the naval defence of England?

Then they bought the estate of Five Oaks, named for the trees that now shared the knoll with their house. They both agreed immediately it would be perfect, though it was only the second estate they'd seen. It was an easy row from the harbour to an elevated site for the house, and had woods to supply timber and endless entertainment for the children, plenty of space for pleasure and kitchen gardens, a small farm—currently abandoned, but easy to put back in operation. They'd signed the deal and never regretted it.

As soon as Jules's sails had been sighted coming through the heads today, someone in the house would have been on watch for his cutter to cross from the port. He could see the cluster of figures hurrying down to the wharf to greet him. Not Mia, he hoped. She was too close to her time to be risking the steep path.

On this trip, Jules had been away for a fortnight, and he'd missed his beloved wife every moment. There she was! Even at this distance, he knew his Mia, Dan at one elbow and Marsha at the other. Their other children clustered around, waving vigorously in welcome. Jack was doing his best to escape off the side of the wharf, but Hal scooped him up and returned him to Ada.

His cutter was coming into the wharf right tidily, and now Marsha realised who his passenger was and had eyes for no one else. As for young Fortnum, he nearly missed his step and started his stay at Five Oaks with a thorough soaking. Just as well the wedding was less than a fortnight away, for Jules would get no sleep until his darling girl was safely hitched to the man who could bring that look into her eyes.

A quick salute to his wife's cheek. He'd make his proper greeting later, and she expected him to pay attention to the children before all else. Daughters first. Ada, bless her, was not too dignified at twenty to hug her Papa, and happy for Jack to share the embrace and to allow the little boy to transfer himself to his father's arm. Sukie abandoned the dignity of her fourteen years to greet him enthusiastically, and little Ellie, his eight-year-old and youngest daughter, latched onto his waist as if she would never let go.

Jules kept half an eye on Marsha the whole time. Fortnum, under the eye of his beloved's parents, had dared no more than a kiss to the hand and an intense exchange of glances, and now Marsha freed herself from her betrothed to come and greet her father. Jules kissed her cheek and whispered, "How do you like my surprise, sweetheart? I met him in Southampton, champing to reach your side, and offered to bring him with me. His parents are following by coach."

The Earl and Countess of Stanthorpe could find no good reason for refusing to recognise their fourth son's marriage to the acknowledged daughter of a Redepenning, relative of a number of peers and protégée of a duchess, but they were not in a hurry to arrive at the wedding, either. No need to say that. Marsha would not have to live with them, at least. Fortnum was an accomplished engineer, and well on the way to making a name for himself in designing passenger railways.

Jack was still on Jules's arm when Hal offered his hand for a solemn shake—at twelve, he thought himself too old to be embraced. Dan, at twenty-four, was now mature enough to hug again.

"All is well here, Papa," he said, as he gripped Jules's shoulder in a firm clasp. "The girls are mad with wedding plans, of course." He grinned. "Hal and I have been doing a lot of riding and rowing."

Jules offered Mia his arm, and led her up the path amid a happy chattering crowd, all trying to tell him of their past fortnight and their plans for the next, none waiting for the others. Jules wondered how Fortnum was coping. He had the slightly bemused look that often struck visitors from the more formal world that Jules and Mia refused to honour in their own private kingdom.

"He will enjoy it, I think," Mia murmured, with her usual uncanny ability to sense his thoughts. "He is not nearly as stuffy as the rest of his family. We will have to warn the children to put on their company manners when his parents arrive."

Jules supposed it was necessary, but he rather hoped they wouldn't stay for long. Again, Mia tracked his thinking, and she was laughing when she said, "You, too, Julius Redepenning. Company manners."

"Yes, ma'am," he conceded. "How are you keeping, my love? You look like you're about to give birth to an elephant. Are you sure of your dates?"

She gave him a playful tap with her free hand. "You pay the sweetest compliments, husband."

"You know I find you irresistible when you are carrying my

child, dearest one. The bigger the better, except I wish I could bear part of the burden for you."

The children had moved ahead, giving them a modicum of privacy. They had Marsha and Dan to thank for that, no doubt.

"You may give birth with my blessing," Mia said, "and as to what you think of this swollen body, you may show me later."

"Where are the Cottles?" Jules asked. Japheth, who had only a forename, had adopted his wife's surname on their marriage. Usually, their three children ran with the Redepenning pack, the seven younger children eating, playing, and learning together.

"Daisy arrived today, and I gave Hannah and Japheth the day off to spend time with her," Mia explained.

They came over the lip of the cliff and onto the plateau before the house. It was an elegant two storeys, plus basement and attics, built of Cyprus Freestone, a local limestone in a rich cream. The windows placed symmetrically across the face changed in size at each storey: largest on the entry floor, slightly smaller on the floor above, and smallest of all in the dormers to the attics.

The walk now took them through formal gardens and up wide steps to a terrace, where the nursemaid and governess who worked under Hannah's authority waited to carry the younger children back to their lessons.

"Mama," Marsha said, "after Gerard has had the opportunity to tidy up, may I show him the garden?"

"You may," Mia told her, and Jules added, sternly, "your sister Ada will accompany you for propriety's sake."

"Perhaps a spot of tea first," Dan suggested. "I shall order refreshments to the summer parlour. After that, I'm afraid, I'll have to get back to work."

Escape to his office rather than watch Marsha and Gerard Fortnum make cows' eyes at one another all afternoon, Dan meant. Jules grinned. He didn't have to stick around for that exhibition either. He was patriarch of this family, and by George he intended to use the authority that vested in him.

"You will excuse me, Fortnum, if I leave my children to entertain you. My wife is in need of rest, and I am a little tired myself, after all this travel. My age, you know."

His children, the cheeky trio, cast their eyes skyward at the blatant falsehood, but Fortnum took Jules's words at face value and stammered some earnest thanks for the welcome and his hopes that Mrs Redepenning would rest well.

"I'll make certain of it," Jules said, ruthlessly aware that his lovely wife was blushing and he was scandalising his children.

He managed to content himself with merely holding Mia's hand until they reached their bedchamber and closed the door between them and the rest of the world, and then he trapped her against the wall for a feverish kiss.

"You are a wicked man, Julius Redepenning," Mia scolded, but she was undressing him as fast as he was undressing her.

"Yes, but I am your wicked man, love of my life," he replied between kisses. "On that I make you my solemn promise."

HE END

ABOUT JUDE KNIGHT

Jude has been trying to be a novelist since she was fourteen. She was a good enough reader to see that the first two attempts (one when she was fourteen and one in her early twenties) weren't good enough to publish. Then along came life. A seriously ill child who required years of therapy; a rising mortgage that led to a full-time job; her own chronic illness… the writing took a back seat.

As the years passed, the fear grew. She'd waited so long. If she never finished any of the dozens of novels she started, no one would ever judge them.

Jude's mother believed in her, and on the way home from that great lady's funeral, Jude realised she'd left it too late for her Mum to ever hold a print copy of one of her books. So she replaced the fear of finishing with the fear of not finishing, by telling everyone she knew that she was writing a novel.

In the five years from publishing her first fiction book in 2014, Jude published seven novels, thirteen novellas, a heap of shorter stories, and more novellas in group anthologies. She plans to keep going till she runs out of years.

Jude writes historical fiction with a large helping of romance, a splash of Regency, and a twist of suspense.

She then tries to figure out how to slot it into a genre category.

She's mad keen on history, enjoys what happens to people in the crucible of a passionate relationship, and loves to use a good mystery and some real danger as mechanisms to torture her characters.

In her other identity as Judy Knighton, she is a plain language consultant specialising in contracts, insurance policies, and financial disclosure statements. Fiction is more fun.

Website and blog: http://judeknightauthor.com/
Book blurbs and links: http://judeknightauthor.com/books/

Do you like news before anyone else, plus discounts, and free stuff?

Sign up to Jude's newsletter. The main newsletter goes out once every two months, and includes news about coming books, discounts, contests, and events. Every newsletter also has news abut books from Jude's author friends, and a free story that Jude writes just for newsletter subscribers.

In between newsletters, if Jude has something exciting to share she occasionally sends a one-topic email.

Free book as a thank you

As a thank you for subscribing to Jude's newsletter, you can expect a series of three emails, the first offering a free copy of one of Jude's books, and the next two with links to other free stories. So why not subscribe today?

Subscribe to newsletter: http://judeknightauthor.com/newsletter/

facebook.com/JudeKnightAuthor

twitter.com/JudeKnightBooks

bookbub.com/authors/jude-knight

ALSO BY JUDE KNIGHT

Regency books

The Golden Redepennings series

True love is rare and elusive, but they won't settle for less

Candle's Christmas Chair (A novella in The Golden Redepennings series)

Candle and Min are separated by social standing and malicious lies. He has until Christmas to convince her to give their love another chance.

Gingerbread Bride (A novella in *The Golden Redepennings* series)

Mary runs from an unwanted marriage and finds adventure, danger and Rick, her girlhood hero, coming once more to her rescue.

Farewell to Kindness (Book 1 in *The Golden Redepennings* series)

Love is not always convenient. Anne and Rede have different goals, but when their enemies join forces, so must they.

A Raging Madness (Book 2 in *The Golden Redepennings* series)

Their marriage is a fiction. Their enemies are all too real. Uncovering the truth will need all the trust Ella and Alex can find.

The Realm of Silence (Book 3 in *The Golden Redepennings* series)

Gill has a list. Rescue Susan's daughter, destroy her dragons, defeat his demons, return to his lonely life. How hard can it be?

Unkept Promises (Book 4 in *The Golden Redepennings* series — published July 2019)

Mia hopes to negotiate a comfortable marriage. Jules wants his wife to go home to England, where she belongs. Love confounds them both.

A Baron for Becky

Becky was a fallen woman. How could the men who loved her help set her back on her feet?

Revealed in Mist

As spy and enquiry agent, Prue and David worked to uncover secrets, while hiding a few of their own.

A Suitable Husband

Marcel knows that a chef from the slums, however talented, is no fit mate for the cousin of a duke, however distant. But Cedrica can dream.

Lord Calne's Christmas Ruby

Lalamani is a wealthy merchant's heiress with an aversion to fortune hunters. Philip is an impoverished earl with a twisted hand. Combating a villainous rector to save her aunt, they find that their differences count for nothing.

House of Thorns

Bear's rose thief bride comes with a scandal that threatens to tear them apart.

*Paradise Regained (*novella in the Bluestocking Belles collection *Follow Your Star Home)*

In discovering the mysteries of the East, James has built a new life. Will unveiling the secrets in his wife's heart destroy it?

*The Beast Next Door (*novella in the Bluestocking Belles collection *Valentines from Bath)*

In all the assemblies and parties, no-one Charis met could ever match Eric, the beast next door.

Lunch-length reads: story collections

Hand-Turned Tales and Lost in the Tale

A double handful of short stories and novellas, free from most retailers. Try the range of Jude's imagination one bite at a time, in a lunch-length read.

If Mistletoe Could Tell Tales

A repackaging of six published Christmas stories: four novellas and two novelettes. Because nothing enhances the magic of Christmas like the magic of love.

Hearts in the Land of Ferns

Five stories all set in New Zealand: two historical and three contemporary suspense. *All That Glisters* has been published in *Hand-Turned Tales*. The other four have all been published in multi-author collections, but never before in a collection of Jude Knight stories.

Victorian books

Never Kiss a Toad (with Mariana Gabrielle)

Caught together in her father's bed, Sally and Toad are wrenched apart, to endure years of separation. But neither distance nor malice can destroy true love.

God Help Ye, Merry Gentleman (with Mariana Gabrielle)

A Christmas collection: two purpose-written short pieces in the world of *Never Kiss a Toad*, showing Sally's and Toad's childhood and youth. Plus some other published pieces from blogs, newsletters, and books set in the same world.

Forged in Fire (novella in the Bluestocking Belles collection Never Too Late)

Burned in their youth, neither Tad nor Lottie expected to feel the fires of love. Until the inferno of a volcanic eruption sears away the lies of the past and frees them to forge a new future.

Post-apocalyptic fiction

A Midwinter's Tale (novella in the Speakeasy Scribes collection Resist and Rejoice)

Verity Marchand is an orphan of time, her family tavern under the ice that grips Boston. When Verity's dreams lead her into a nightmare, she'll need a miracle—or the family cat—to save her.

Contemporary

A Family Christmas (novella in the Authors of Main Street collection *Christmas Babies on Main Street*)

Kirilee is on the run, in disguise, out of touch, and eating for two. Trevor is heading home for Christmas, after three years undercover, investigating a global criminal organisation. In the heart of a storm, two people from different worlds question what divides and what unites them.

Abbie's Wish (novella in the Authors of Main Street collection *Christmas Wishes on Main Street*)

Abbie's Christmas wish draws three men to her mother. One of them is a monster.

Beached (novella in the Authors of Main Street collection *Summer Romance on Main Street*)

The truth will wash away her coastal paradise

www.ingramcontent.com/pod-product-compliance
Lightning Source LLC
Chambersburg PA
CBHW021651110726
47902CB00007B/1910